A SIGN OF THE TIMES

It's 1959, and Boots Adams and his wife Polly are helping to celebrate the retirement of barman Joe at their favourite Camberwell pub when they witness a sudden and vicious attack on Joe by a knife-wielding young thug. Is this a sign of the times? While Gemma is courted by one of the young men who works for her father, her twin brother James finds himself affected by his girlfriend's intriguing family secrets – and just who is the mysterious girl who arrives from Finland to study at Gemma's college?

A SIGN OF THE TIMES

by

Mary Jane Staples

Magna Large Print Books
Long Preston, North Yorkshire,
BD23 4ND, England.

British Library Cataloguing in Publication Data.

Staples, Mary Jane
    A sign of the times.

    A catalogue record of this book is
    available from the British Library

    ISBN   0-7505-2625-4
    ISBN   978-0-7505-2625-8

First published in Great Britain in 2006 by Bantam Press

Published in Large Print 2006 by arrangement with
Transworld Publishers Ltd.

Magna Large Print is an imprint of Library Magna Books Ltd.

Printed and bound in Great Britain by
T.J. (International) Ltd., Cornwall, PL28 8RW

THE ADAMS FAMILY

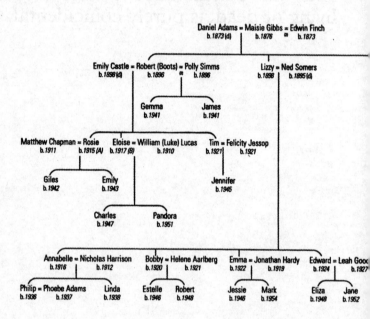

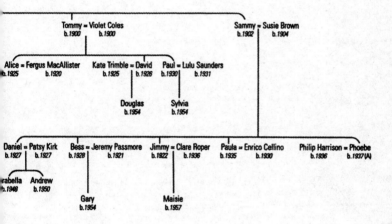

Tommy = Violet Coles
b.1900   b.1900

Sammy = Susie Brown
b.1902   b.1904

Alice = Fergus MacAllister
b.1925   b.1920

Kate Trimble = David
b.1925   b.1926

Paul = Lulu Saunders
b.1930   b.1931

Douglas
b.1954

Sylvia
b.1954

Daniel = Patsy Kirk
b.1927   b.1927

Bess = Jeremy Passmore
b.1928   b.1921

Jimmy = Clare Roper
b.1922   b.1936

Paula = Enrico Cellino
b.1935   b.1930

Philip Harrison = Phoebe
b.1936   b.1937(A)

rabella   Andrew
b.1948   b.1950

Gary
b.1954

Maisie
b.1957

(A) – adopted   (B) – by Cecile Lacoste   b. – born   (d) – deceased

Prologue

Russia, 1906.

The Yakanov estate in the Crimea was huge. It was impossible to take in the extent of its boundaries, unless one was able to perch on the topmost dome of the magnificent family church. The present owner, Prince Mikhail, had inherited the estate from his father, who had inherited it from his father. Inheritance on these lines went back to the time of Catherine the Great, when Vasily Yakanov, an officer and a member of her bodyguard, caught her roving eye.

He became one of her many lovers, and must have especially pleased her, for she conferred a princedom on him as well as a great tract of land in the Crimea and a palace in St Petersburg. Since then successive Yakanovs had become an imperious breed, proud and haughty, in the grand manner of Russia's autocratic nobility.

On an autumn day in 1906, Prince Mikhail was riding in search of his steward, a faithful and invaluable servant, but lately inclined to be elusive. Prince Mikhail knew why. The steward's fifteen-year-old son, a kitchen hand, had been shown to be something of a pilferer and even insolent. That insolence had reached out to touch Prince Mikhail's eight-year-old daughter, whom he had addressed without permission. Such audacity was unheard of in a being whose status was akin to that of a serf. And all serfs were required to doff their hats, bow their heads and look at their feet whenever a nobleman or any of his family passed by.

The punishment for such pilfering and insolence, a flogging, was laid down, and Prince Mikhail was intent on making sure it was carried out.

He found his elusive steward summarizing the contents of the main grain-storage barn, and spoke sternly to him. The steward dared to protest.

'Excellency, I am to order and witness the flogging of my own son, a boy impetuous and unthinking in his ways but by no means a serious law-breaker?'

'Other servants tell me otherwise. So does my daughter's chaperone.'

'Excellency, hear me. Other servants exaggerate what they tell you, and as to what was said by your daughter's chaperone, the truth is that in an unthinking moment, the boy made an impulsive comment on your daughter's enchantment. "Ah, how fair you are, my lady," was what he said in his impetuosity. I beg you, therefore, to allow me to lecture him on his foolishness and to spare him this excessive punishment.' The flogging would amount to forty lashes, each one inflicted by the appointed wielder of the knout. 'Excellency, I beg.'

'There are laws appertaining to wrong-doing by servants,' said Prince Mikhail. 'These laws must be and will be obeyed. See to your son's deserved punishment.'

'Excellency–'

'See to it, and report to me when it is done,' said Prince Mikhail, and rode away, back to his palace, where he found his wife, and his son and daughter, waiting for him. They were all to enjoy lunch on the grand balcony overlooking the cliffs and the warm, shimmering sea.

It occurred to the prince, when lunch was long over, that his steward had not yet reported to him. However, at that moment the steward's assistant arrived at the palace and begged, in tones of extreme agitation, to be allowed to see His Highness in private.

'In private?' Prince Mikhail's fastidiously trimmed eyebrows rose as much as a millimetre as he regarded the house servant who had delivered the request. 'In private?'

'Excellency, I understand the matter is – ah – a little unpleasant.'

'Very well. I'll see him in my study, where

unpleasantness can be dealt with quietly.'

Subsequently, in the humblest genuflection of respect, the steward's assistant bent almost double as he entered his master's presence with his hat doffed.

'Your Highness–'

'Get on with it.'

The man did so, unhappily and with many a wringing twist of his hat. It was like this. Pyotyr Czernin, the steward, had seen to the punishment of his son, but had refused to obey the order to watch the wielding of the knout, which was applied forty times by Burzak, the foreman. Unfortunately, very unfortunately, the steward's son collapsed on the thirtieth stroke, and received the balance while unconscious. Even more unfortunately, he did not come to, although more than one bucket of water was thrown over him.

'Alas, Your Highness, he is dead.'

Prince Mikhail looked more irritated than distressed. Serfs, in any case, were two a penny.

'Such a consequence might be unfortunate, yes,' he said, 'but is more to do with the victim's indifferent physique than with me. However, give Pyotyr Czernin my condolences and tell him and his wife to arrange the funeral.'

'Alas, Excellency...' Here the steward's assistant wrung his hat as if it were the most unwanted thing ever to have come to hand. 'I – I have to tell you that when Pyotyr Czernin discovered his son was lifeless, he drew his knife and stabbed Burzak in such a frenzied way that he too lies dead.'

'Good God,' said Prince Mikhail, 'do you peasants have no control over your primitive feelings? My steward has done the field workers' foreman to death, you say?'

'Your Highness – Excellency – it was because he saw his son lying dead in a pool of blood.'

'Go. Fetch him here, at once.'

'Forgive me, Excellency, but I cannot. He has gone, he has disappeared. With his wife and daughter.' The steward's assistant did not say the disappearance had happened an hour ago, or that the fugitives had ridden off on fleet, stolen horses. He was doing his best to protect the steward's back. 'Excellency, here is a letter I found in his office. It's addressed to you.'

'Is it written in blood, his son's blood?' Prince Mikhail was cruelly satirical as he took the envelope and ripped it open. The letter was not written in blood, but in essence it was red with fire.

'I curse you. I curse you now and for ever. By your evil orders, you have taken the life of my son. Watch over your own son, and others you hold dear. They too are cursed.'

Prince Mikhail, furious, despatched

servants to the four corners of the Crimea, but no traces of Pyotyr Czernin or his wife and daughter were found. So he widened the search to cover the four corners of mighty Russia, but perforce gave up the chase in 1909 when, after three years, his defecting steward seemed to have vanished from the face of the earth. The prince, forced to assume the man was dead, felt infuriatingly robbed of the pleasure of hanging him.

By this time his son, Prince Nikolai, was fifteen and his daughter, Princess Tanya, eleven.

A year later his son disappeared while the family was staying in their palace in St Petersburg. He was found after three days. By then he was merely a drowned and frozen body floating in the icy waters of the Neva. There were no marks on the corpse, nothing to indicate foul play, and it was assumed the unfortunate young man had accidentally fallen into the river during one more night of inebriated carousing with fellow students. It was a fact that no-one could have survived for more than a few minutes in the freezing flow. Assumption and fact did not afford the grief-stricken Prince Mikhail any consolation. He railed at fate for having dared to so wound the House of Yakanov. It had robbed him of his heir.

Three months later, during a ball given by the prince and his wife at their palace in St

Petersburg, Princess Mikhail suffered the misfortune of falling from the ballroom balcony to the ground below. The fall broke her neck, and the injury was fatal. No-one knew how she had come to fall, no-one had seen it happen. The great ballroom had been crowded with guests, every one of whom belonged to the flower of St Petersburg's aristocracy, and the attendant servants were all beyond reproach. True, a firm of caterers of the highest class had helped to provide the magnificent buffet of food and wine, but at no time were any of its employees seen near the balcony. They were all confined to the steam and heat of the kitchens.

So, by the late summer of 1910, Prince Mikhail had lost his son and his wife. He might have thought of the curse laid on him and his family by the man who had once been the steward of his vast Crimean estate, but he was not given to believing in such gypsy-like absurdities. All the same, he sent his daughter Tanya, then twelve, to England. He said, explaining this, that in Russia the future, and even the lives, of young aristocrats were threatened by ever-active revolutionaries and their homemade bombs.

The young lady, accompanied, of course, by a chaperone, ended up in a very circumspect and highly regarded finishing academy in the royal county of Berkshire.

That kept her agreeably secluded; she

liked the school, the countryside and her sister students. And when war broke out between Tsarist Russia and the Kaiser's Germany in 1914, Prince Mikhail decided she should remain in England until the war was over. Not that he was influenced in any way by the equivalent of a gypsy's warning. No, not at all, despite the inexplicable deaths of his wife and son. Their demise was due to fate, not the curse of a deranged peasant.

Alas, he met his own death on the battle-field only a few weeks after the conflict had broken out. The mighty Russian steamroller, advancing into East Prussia, was crushingly defeated by the Germans at Tannenberg. Prince Mikhail fell dead while at the head of his regiment during the fateful advance into the German trap. Strangely, his warrior's demise was caused by a bullet in the back, not the chest, a very odd thing considering he was facing the enemy, or so it was assumed. However, his relatives all insisted he had met a hero's death, as befitted a Yakanov, although later in the war rumours that dissenting soldiers killed some of their officers by shooting them in the back turned out to be true. But such dastardly acts were unknown during the early months of the war. Therefore, Prince Mikhail could only have been killed by the enemy, by a German soldier who had somehow managed to get behind him. So yes, the prince's battlefield death was deemed as heroic as the death of any fighting nobleman.

Thus, in late August 1914, Princess Tanya Yakanov became the sole surviving member of the late Prince Mikhail's immediate family, which was not what he had ever envisaged. She did not receive details of this fact until September, when her father's battlefield demise was made known to her. She was a mere sixteen then. Her faithful chaperone became father and mother to her. Back in Russia, an uncle took charge of the dead man's affairs, looking after the financial wants of his niece.

In 1915, not long after her seventeenth birthday, Princess Tanya met a British Army subaltern, newly commissioned. He was David, the brother of her best friend Sybil Tunnicliffe, daughter of General Sir Geoffrey Tunnicliffe. Due to be sent to France, David received permission to visit Sybil before he left. It was during this visit that he and Princess Tanya met. She was young and bewitching. He himself was only twenty-one, and a dashing type, a cavalryman. Classically, it could have been called love at first sight. Tanya and he were married when he was on leave from Flanders in August 1916. She had written to her uncle requesting him to release to her £20,000 to be used as her dowry. She did not hear from him until many months later, for communication with war-torn Russia was not of a speedy kind. In his reply, her uncle refused to release the money. Instead, he rebuked her for marrying a middle-class Englishman, when she should have known that only the son of a Russian nobleman could be her destiny. Arrange a divorce, he wrote.

Princess Tanya, now Mrs David Tunnicliffe, refused. She declared that under no circumstances would she ever contemplate parting from her English husband, and it was much to her joy and relief that he survived the ghastly war. Her uncle also survived, but he not only lost charge of her late father's estate, he lost the estate itself. It was confiscated by the Bolsheviks during the Russian Revolution, along with the palace in St Petersburg. Tanya subsequently discovered she was heiress to nothing, to neither money nor property. David assured her she was not to worry, since his family owned a very prosperous business in the City of London.

They settled down in Surrey, far from the grimness of Bolshevik Russia, and from the hand of fate that had robbed Tanya of mother, father and brother.

Chapter One

January 1959.

In a semi-detached, three-up, three-down house in Brixton, south-east London, Lulu Adams, wife of Paul Adams, looked cross. Well, she was cross, very much so. Even her spectacles held a glint of vexation.

'Consider yourself in receipt of ten black marks,' she said to her visitor. 'What made you lose your self-control to that extent, for God's sake?'

'Natural impulse,' said Miss Marjorie Alsop, activist on behalf of Brixton's Labour Party voters, more particularly those in favour of saving fur-clad animals from being skinned, indirectly, by the rich.

'Natural impulses are acceptable in the young and innocent,' said Lulu. 'But not in adults, particularly adults involved in the discipline of politics. You've got to attack problems with a clear and clinical mind. Smashing the office windows of a private company might light up the day for some of our working-class comrades, but won't win us the extra votes we need to form the next Government. In fact, it could lose us some.'

Miss Alsop, a robust young woman

mentally and physically, fought her corner, pointing out that she'd discovered the private company in question, Adams Fashions, owned retail dress shops that sold fur-trimmed coats. That same firm had led her to believe they were in favour of animal humanity, which meant helping to put a stop to the fur trade and its exploitation of creatures of the wild. Finding she'd been deceived, yes, she did give in to a natural impulse, leading a demonstration that resulted in some broken windows. Her indignation had been particularly aroused by discovering that the main deceivers were men she'd come to like and trust, to wit, Mr Robert Adams and his brother, Mr Sammy Adams. These two men had control of the firm, and therefore of its retailing of fur-trimmed garments.

'I considered my angry reactions to deception very natural,' she declared.

'Now look here,' said Lulu, 'I didn't help you to find a flat in Brixton and to get our local activists to back up your campaign so that you could rampage about like Boadicea. And what did it do for you? Got you fourteen days in Holloway without the option of a fine. Incidentally, what was the food like?'

'Bloody disgusting,' said Miss Alsop.

'Serve you right,' said Lulu, scowling a bit. She didn't believe in showing a fair face when vexation was biting. 'As I told you, Mr Robert Adams and Mr Sammy Adams happen to be my uncles by marriage.' They were also among her favourite men, and she had promised husband Paul that she'd sell Miss Alsop off any idea of making things unpleasant for them. Miss Alsop, originator of a movement in favour of collapsing the fur trade, had been a threat to Adams Fashions, and Uncle Sammy had needed help to get her off his back. Unfortunately, Miss Alsop had lost her marbles and Uncle Sammy had lost the plate-glass front windows of the firm's offices in Camberwell Green. Which was why Lulu was so cross. 'The last thing I wanted was for you to go to war on them. All right, so they're capitalists, but not the kind that ought to be shoved off Tower Bridge. If they exploited their workers, I'd go to war on them myself, uncles or not, but they don't.'

'Now look,' said Miss Alsop, by no means the kind of woman to let another woman tread all over her, 'what I did—'

'What you did didn't help anybody,' said Lulu, 'so shut up.'

'I beg your pardon?'

'Listen, Marjorie,' said Lulu, hoping one day to be a Labour MP and therefore knowing how to put more than two words together in commanding fashion, 'you've got to accept the need for discipline, for conducting demonstrations in an orderly fashion. Even if the UK is only a half-baked democracy under this Conservative government, it's still the only democracy we've got. Chucking bricks at office windows and fur-wearing countesses is out, out. That sort of violence might catch on and lead to the equivalent of a French Revolution and to half the population losing their heads. How d'you think I'm going to feel if I spot my uncles being taken to the guillotine in a tumbril? I won't even have the courage to wave them goodbye.'

'That's coming it a bit thick,' said the robust Miss Alsop, 'and I'd like to point out I've been told stories of how you've led aggressive demonstrations yourself.'

'That was in my wilful youth,' said Lulu. 'I've grown up since then. It's perseverance, sound argument and disciplined organization that'll carry the voters our way. Mind, I'll always back up any march on Downing Street by the workers, providing not too much injury is done to the bobbies. Now look, let's discuss a more orderly form of campaign for you and your cause. We'll have the discussion in the kitchen, where you can help me prepare a light lunch. My little daughter's with my mother-in-law, so time is all ours for the moment, and there's no point in parting on a bitter note. I daresay my uncles have recovered by now, and I know their office windows have been repaired. So come on then, let's see to lunch.'

'Lunch?' said Miss Alsop, who enjoyed food. 'How kind. I'll be delighted to help.'

'Well, between the two of us and what's in my larder,' said Lulu, 'I think we can provide ourselves with something better than anything the plod serve up in Holloway.'

While preparing the meal, they listened to a radio news bulletin which included the intriguing information that a member of the Soviet Union's visiting team of gymnasts had defected. It was something of a sensation, for the Soviet Union kept very tight control of all their athletes and orchestras during official tours in the West. For once they had lost out, and it seemed, said the broadcaster, that the Home Secretary, in accordance with international law, was duty bound to grant asylum.

'I should damn well think so,' said Miss Alsop.

'Don't get worked up,' said Lulu. Having once been a bit of a Commie herself, she was never keen on being reminded of those misguided days. 'Just scramble these eggs.'

'She's out now, y'know,' said Sammy Adams, mastermind of Adams Enterprises and its associated companies. He was in the office of his brother Robert, family peacemaker always known as Boots.

'Enlighten me,' said Boots. 'Who's out?'

'Mad Marj,' said Sammy.

'The Alsop headache?' said Boots.

'You said it, Boots. Out of Holloway.'

'Well, cheer up, Sammy, I've been given some good news by Gemma.' Gemma was his seventeen-year-old daughter, presently attending a college for young ladies in Dulwich. 'Well, she actually said thrilling.'

'Meaning Mad Marj is going to emigrate?' said Sammy.

'Not exactly,' said Boots. 'More to the effect that some young pop star by the name of Cliff Richard is giving a concert at a London venue next month. She says it'll be the event of our lifetimes.'

'Count me out,' said Sammy, 'I'm still collecting Marie Lloyd records, especially including "My Old Man Said Follow the Van". Listen, what's to be done if Mad Marj decides to smash the windows of our shops now that they're displaying fur-trimmed garments to keep customers cosy in winter?'

'Leave her to Lulu,' said Boots.

'Might I remind you you said that before?' Sammy made the point sorrowfully. 'And look what happened. Mad Marj used some of Lulu's own Labour supporters to help her make mincemeat of our office windows on behalf of skinned crocodiles, or some such. I tell you, Boots, it's going to get Adams Fashions some seriously injurious publicity, which won't do our balance sheet much good.'

'Hasn't Paul told you Lulu's having a word or two with Miss Alsop today?' said Boots. Paul was his and Sammy's nephew.

'He's told me right enough,' said Sammy, 'and I put it to you the same as I put it to him, what's the betting that Mad Marj won't end up making mincemeat of Lulu's own front windows?'

'I'll take the bet,' said Boots.

'You said that too quick, so I ain't playing,' responded Sammy. 'Anyway, apart from that I'm now about to lunch on a quick bowl of soup in the canteen.' The firm's canteen was open to all staff members, including managers and directors.

'I'm off to the pub,' said Boots. 'Joe the barman is retiring and I'd like to pay my respects. I'm meeting Polly there.'

'OK,' said Sammy, 'I'll make do with my bowl of soup in the canteen. I don't have time to eat or to wallow in a pint of old ale, I'm up to me eyebrows in work.'

'That's the price you pay, Sammy, for being the engine of the business,' said Boots, and off he went to the pub across the road, as he had on countless other occasions. Neither he nor Sammy knew that at this particular moment Miss Alsop was sitting down with Lulu to a very nice lunch they had prepared together. Lulu had the menace well in hand, at least for the time being. They were, in fact, talking about the benefits of socialism, not animal humanity.

Sammy would have been relieved. As a businessman, he was against socialism, naturally, but it didn't worry him as much as Mad Marj did, mainly because she was capable of aggravated assault and of causing the kind of bad publicity that would keep customers away from the firm's retail outlets. Well, who wanted to get in the way of a brick? Prior to bricks it had been squishy tomatoes, and they'd been bad enough.

Women. You just couldn't read them. Not unless they'd been born into or become part of the Adams family. Then, of course, his old ma saw to it that they behaved themselves. Wife Susie wouldn't dream of chucking bricks, or even a tomato. True, she'd waved her egg saucepan at him a few times, but that was a wife's privilege during an argument and purely a domestic matter.

'It beats me,' muttered Sammy to himself as he descended the stairs to the canteen. 'I tell you, God, I sometimes don't understand women at all.'

'Join the club,' said God.

At least, that was what Sammy imagined He said.

Chapter Two

Boots found himself a favourite corner table in the saloon bar of the pub. The Edwardian decor of the place still gave it a plush look, and its unhurried lunchtime atmosphere was always welcome to harassed Camberwell businessmen who needed an hour of calm to reorganize their lives.

Polly arrived only a minute or so after Boots had sat down. He came to his feet again as she looked around, spotted him and made her advance. Heads turned, eyes glanced. Polly had never lost her tall, willowy look, or the gliding ease of her walk, although she was now past sixty. She wore a fur-trimmed coat and a fur hat which, thought Boots, might have caused Miss Alsop to reach for her six-shooter.

'Well, here I am, old thing,' she smiled.

'So I see,' said Boots, settling her into a padded wall seat. 'Sometimes I can't believe what's in front of my eyes.'

'Heavens,' said Polly, 'am I beginning to look like a freak, then?'

'Perish the thought,' said Boots, reseating himself. 'Do you realize you could make a fortune from selling the recipe of how to look thirty at–'

'Don't mention the dread number,' said Polly, her light but careful make-up perfect. 'I'll just accept the compliment gracefully and without showing off. How's yourself, old scout? Haven't seen you since breakfast. And what's for lunch? Something light, I hope – oh, hello, Joe.'

Joe, the veteran barman, had arrived at their table. Table service was always offered to regular customers. Polly knew Joe well enough, and he showed a very appreciative smile at her welcome.

'Morning, Mrs Adams, good to see you,' he said. 'Morning, Mr Adams. Last time too, I reckon, more's the pity. Still, it happens to all of us, as my old dad said when he retired from the railways and they gave him a tin clock. What can I get you and Mrs Adams?'

'Your shout, Polly,' said Boots.

'Salmon salad by itself,' said Polly, un-buttoning her coat and letting it drop from her shoulders to reveal a jersey wool dress of light brown. The bodice was a marvel of tidy convex delineation. The secret may have lain within a delicate, fine-boned corset, the cultured descendant of heavy Victorian stays. 'That is, without a roll and butter, thanks, Joe.'

'Certainly, Mrs Adams.'

'I'll have the salmon salad too,' said Boots,

'but with a roll and butter, and a half of old ale. Polly?'

'Glass of your white house wine, Joe,' said Polly. The owners of this free house had added wine to its range of drinks a few years ago, an innovation of an unexpected kind but one that proved welcome to a good proportion of its regulars.

'I'll bring the drinks first,' said Joe.

'Fine,' said Boots, who had five new fivers in his wallet, earmarked as a retirement gift for Joe. The affable, grey-haired barman returned to his white marble counter to see to the ordered drinks. At which point in came a young man who looked as if he hadn't been brought up to make the most of himself. That is, he was wearing blue jeans, a tired anorak, and crêpe-soled suede shoes of a filthy grey, one with a brown stain. Further, his uncut hair was as bushy as a bird's nest.

'Pint of lager, mate,' he said to Joe.

'Lager?' said Joe, carefully filling a glass with white wine.

'Pint, chummy. And a plate of chips.'

'No chips,' said Joe, turning to the barrel of old ale, 'and no lager. Beer only.'

'Lager's beer, you silly old goat, or ain't you heard of it yet?'

'I've heard of it,' said Joe, tapping old ale from the barrel into a half-pint glass, while customers covertly inspected the hairy interloper and wondered about his origins. 'But it's not beer as this here establishment understands it. Try somewhere else.'

'Hold it, mate, hold it, you chucking me out?'

'No, just pointing you somewhere else,' said Joe, placing the orders on a tray.

'Well, you saucy old sod,' said the specimen of modern times, his eyes glittering. And as Joe came out from behind the bar with the tray in his hands, he was violently assaulted. The tray and its drinks crashed, a knife flashed, and Joe, stabbed in the chest, fell to the floor. A stunned silence ensued among paralysed patrons. 'That'll learn yer!' hissed the vicious young assailant, and made for the door. Boots, more incensed than paralysed, shot to his feet and rushed after him.

'Take care, old soldier, but get him!' urged Polly, also on her feet. 'I'll see to Joe.' It had been over forty years since, as an ambulance driver during the 1914–18 war, she had last attended to a wounded man, but all that she had learnt surfaced as she swooped to kneel beside the stricken barman. His white apron was already badly bloodstained. 'Someone find a phone and call an ambulance,' she shouted. A dozen and more customers were up and moving now, while Boots was well outside the pub.

He sighted the knife-wielder. He was

haring after a bus climbing Denmark Hill. Catching up with it, he swung himself aboard, the conductor standing aside for him, and the vehicle carried him away from Boots, whose shouts went unheard except by nearby pedestrians.

'What's up, mate?' asked a bloke.

'Can't stop,' said Boots, and raced across the road to his car, parked as always outside the offices. He unlocked the door, threw himself in and started the engine. He was consumed by a need to drive away in instant pursuit of the bus, but was held up by traffic coming down the hill. He fumed at being forced to wait, but was away as soon as the road was clear, knowing Polly would do her best for Joe. His chief hope was that the knife thrust wouldn't prove fatal, not for a man as likeable as Joe, and as close to a well-earned retirement as anyone could be.

As he passed the road named Champion Park on his left and approached the bend of the hill, the bus was out of sight, but when he had cleared the bend, driving fast, he saw it far ahead, climbing steadily towards the near reaches of Herne Hill. He raced after it, passing a van, and within a short while came up with the bus. It was at a stop and passengers were alighting. Boots pulled up ahead of the vehicle, then reversed to block it in. The driver thumped his horn. Boots quickly got out of the car. It did not occur to him that at the ripe old age of sixty-two he was well past this kind of caper. Normally very much in control of himself, his mood at the moment was one of fiery anger, his reactions all set on making every effort to catch the assailant. In any event, he was still sound of wind and limb, still in fine physical condition.

He ran round the bus to the boarding platform, where the conductor was ringing the bell to signal the all-clear to his driver. The driver, outraged, had turned in his seat to catch the conductor's attention and let him know some lunatic was blocking the way. Boots, casting a glance at the passengers who had alighted, noted they were all women with shopping baskets. Urgently, he addressed the conductor. 'Listen, what happened to that character who jumped aboard your bus at the bottom of the hill?'

'Eh?'

'He stabbed a pub barman. Is—'

'He did what?'

'A stabbing job. Believe me. Is he still aboard?'

'No, he ain't. Christ, he's that kind, is he? Well, call the police, mate, he got off way down the hill.'

'At an official stop?' said Boots. The bus driver was down from his vehicle now, and making his way round.

'I tell you, mister,' said the conductor,

'when he jumped on I ticked him off, letting him know it wasn't legal or safe to board a moving bus. He told me he was willing to buy a ticket, but when we slowed at the bend, the bugger did another jump. Off the bus this time.'

The angry driver, appearing, growled, 'Here, what's going on, eh?'

'I've been chasing a lousy maniac,' said Boots, swearing under his breath. He realized his quarry must have jumped off the bus while he himself was waiting for traffic to clear, traffic which had blocked his view.

'Maniac, what maniac?' demanded the driver.

'A demented young thug who knifed a barman,' said Boots, glancing restlessly about.

'Tell you what,' said the conductor, ignoring the frustrations of his driver, 'after he jumped off I did notice he turned into Champion Park.'

From the pub, the Champion Park road was second on the left off Denmark Hill.

'Right,' said Boots. 'Thanks – much obliged.'

'Collar the bugger,' called the conductor as Boots ran back to his car. Getting in, he made sure the road was clear, then did a U-turn that took him racing back down the hill. At the bottom, he turned right into Champion Park, once a causeway for trams heading for Nunhead. For fifteen minutes he drove slowly, searching, looking, but without any real hope of spotting his quarry. Eventually he turned back, drove to his offices, parked the car and ran across the road to the pub, noting the presence of a police car and a bunch of gawping people. At the pub door, a uniformed constable barred the way.

'It's out of bounds, sir, for the moment.'

'Yes, I know why,' said Boots, 'and I'm just back from a useless chase of the reason why.'

'Sir, you're—'

'Yes, my husband,' said Polly, appearing, and the constable stood aside to allow Boots entry. 'No luck, old lad?'

'The piece of garbage slipped me,' said Boots. The saloon bar's customers were still present, and a plain-clothes detective sergeant was talking to them and taking notes. 'Tell me the worst, Polly.'

'About Joe?' said Polly. 'He'll live, thank God. He was ambulanced to hospital a few minutes ago. Afraid I'm in a bit of a mess.' Her hands and the front of her dress were bloodstained. 'I did what I could to staunch the flow while waiting for the ambulance. Boots, you didn't actually run after the young swine, did you?' That, of course, was a reference to Boots's age and the wisdom of not punishing his body.

'Used the car,' said Boots, and while he gave all the details the police sergeant came across to listen and to make more notes. He already had a very accurate description of the assailant from everyone present, and now he had the information that the man might live in the vicinity of Champion Park.

'Very good, sir,' he said to Boots, 'very useful piece of information, that. Might I have your name and address in case we need to contact you?' Boots obliged, adding his phone number. 'And might I also have the pleasure of saying that your lady wife's first-aid work on the victim probably helped to save his life?'

'My wife,' said Boots, 'was once a wartime ambulance driver.'

The sergeant gave Polly a look of admiration.

'Did your bit on the Normandy beaches, did you, madam?' he said.

Boots, about to mention that it was actually on the battlefields of Flanders, tactfully changed his mind.

'You could say so, Sergeant, you could say so,' he said.

Polly, delighted by the flattery despite the circumstances, said, 'Yes, how charming of you to remark on that, Sergeant.'

Boots, now impatient at what he considered a lack of action, reminded the sergeant that time was of the essence, wasn't it? The sergeant closed his notebook, tucked it away and let Boots and Polly know he was now returning to the station to activate his inspector. Telling everyone they were free to go, he then left, accompanied by the constable.

Polly examined her stained dress and hands.

'I need cleaning up,' she said.

'I'll run you home,' said Boots soberly.

'No need, ducky,' said Polly, 'my own car's parked not far from yours.' Boots helped her on with her coat. 'I'm over the initial shock and can drive myself. But you can walk me to my car. My God,' she breathed, 'that's the first time I've seen attempted murder take place in front of my eyes.'

'I know how you feel,' said Boots, still carrying an unbelievable mental picture of the sudden and violent attack on Joe.

The pub owners, two white-haired brothers, were talking to the crowd of disturbed customers. Polly and Boots called goodbye and left. A voice reached Polly as she exited.

'Consider yourself a credit to the old country, Mrs Adams.'

'I'll second that,' said Boots. Outside, they passed the crowd of people drawn there by events, crossed the road and walked to Polly's car. Boots, certain she was still in some kind of shock, said, 'Are you sure you can make it on your own?'

'I think so,' said Polly.

'I'm not so sure myself,' said Boots, so he did the obvious. He took the wheel of Polly's car and drove her home himself. Polly thought that the act of a man who cared about her, and she was touched.

'Thanks, sweetie,' she said.

'Well, you're not an old tin clock, Polly, you're you,' said Boots. He glanced left as they reached and passed the entrance to Champion Park. He sighted nothing that looked like a walking jumble sale whose get-up hid a vicious temper. 'Proud of you, dear girl.'

Polly put her dress in the laundry basket when she and Boots arrived home, and then soaked herself in a hot bath. Their daily maid, Flossie Cuthbert, horrified when told of what had happened, turned her attention to Boots as soon as Polly was in the bath.

'Mr Adams, you'd best sit down yourself,' she said, 'you must be all wore out by everything. Yes, go on, sit yourself down and I'll make you some strong coffee, then come up with a bite to eat for you and Mrs Adams once she's out of the bath. I mean, you've both had no food, and you ought to have something a bit nourishing to keep body and soul together. And let's hope the police catch that murderous devil before the day's

37

out. Well, he's not the kind that ought to be free to walk about among decent people.'

'Very true, Flossie,' said Boots. He phoned Sammy to say he was being delayed, but would be back in his office later. Sammy said he supposed Boots had had too many of barman Joe's retirement pints. Boots let that go for the moment, then enjoyed the promised coffee. A little later he and a refreshed Polly each ate a light snack of a poached egg mounted on a slice of tender ham on toast. Then he phoned King's College Hospital to be told that Mr Joseph Turner's condition was stable. Satisfied with that, and feeling Polly was herself again, he took a bus back to the offices.

'Don't tell me, mate,' said Sammy the moment Boots showed up, 'you don't need to. It's all over Camberwell, and old Walworth too, I shouldn't wonder, that some lunatic tried to do Joe in and rob him of his retirement. It beats me that lunatics like that get born. I tell you, old cock, there ought to be some way of testing them at birth and drowning them.'

'Who's going to argue with that?' said Rosie. She and Rachel were both present, both very much concerned. 'But where does some way come from?'

'From an inventor of birth-testing equipment, if we can find one,' said Boots, and

38

Sammy asked him how he and Polly had coped with the situation. Boots gave all the details, and Rosie and Rachel listened spellbound. Sammy whistled, then pointed out that while Polly's first-aid act couldn't be faulted, it wasn't the best thing Boots had ever done, chasing after a lunatic at his age. He could have ended up being knifed himself, didn't he think of that?

'My life, yes, didn't you, Boots?' said Rachel.

'Rush of blood,' said Boots.

'Well, talk about the family's wise old owl losing his feathers for once,' said Rosie, a touch of lightness covering her deeper feelings.

'Still,' said Sammy, 'good going, Boots old mate, only I hope it doesn't get headlined. If it does, our old and respected ma will call round and let you know what she thinks about any of the family being mentioned in newspapers, that it ain't respectable.'

'I'll have to take my chances on that,' said Boots.

'Good luck,' said Rosie.

'By the way, Boots,' said Sammy, 'there's – um – there's some midday post that's wanting your attention, but if you're still out of breath I'll pass it to Rachel.'

'Let's have it, Sammy old lad, I'm not here looking for a couch and a nurse,' said Boots, which made Rosie think of all he meant to the family, and to herself especially.

'Well, I'll say this much,' said Sammy, 'you've survived one more war, Boots, and kept business in mind. Where would we all be if we only had to think about Monday washing?'

'We'd be in the position, Sammy, of thinking about who's up for doing the Tuesday ironing,' said Boots.

That evening, Boots's mother, known for many years as Chinese Lady, was listening to the six o'clock news in company with her husband, Sir Edwin Finch. There was mention of an assault on a pub barman by a knife-wielding young man in Camberwell. The victim's wound had been treated by a woman, an ex-ambulance driver of the war, and her action had helped to save the barman's life. Regrettably, the assailant had escaped, and the police were searching for him.

Chinese Lady sat up.

'Edwin, are you listening to this? In Camberwell, of all places. I can't think what's happening when there are wicked young men going about with knives.'

'Sad, Maisie, very sad,' said Sir Edwin. The name of the public house in question hadn't been given. Had the announcer mentioned it, Sir Edwin might have sat up even more stiffly than his offended wife, for he

40

knew the pub in question. As it was, it might have been any one of many, for Camberwell, of course, overflowed with pubs.

'You'll have to tell the family not to act careless when they go shopping,' said Chinese Lady. 'Well, it seems you never know what might happen. It wasn't like this in my day. I don't know, I just don't. I'm only relieved that the poor man's being looked after in hospital. When the police catch who did it, I hope he'll be hanged.' She brooded a little, then said firmly, 'That Hitler, he was someone ought to have been hanged well before he was born.'

'Before he was born?' said Sir Edwin. 'Hardly possible, Maisie my dear.'

'Well, it ought to have been,' said Chinese Lady even more firmly. She was still given to speaking her mind about Hitler, the man responsible for the death of millions, and in particular of Emily, Boots's first wife, who had once, way way back, been the helpful girl next door and the family's godsend. 'Young men using knives in public houses, I just don't know,' she murmured. 'But I do know I don't like the way things are changing, Edwin.'

'There are always changes, Maisie, some for the better, some for the worse.'

'Well, I've seen a lot in my time, Edwin, and I don't know I want to see a lot more if they're mostly going to be for the worse,'

41

said Chinese Lady. 'And I'm never sure that this wireless of ours was ever for the better. What's come out of it over the years has sometimes nearly been my death.'

'Let us all be grateful to Providence, Maisie, that you've survived,' said Sir Edwin.

That comment was delivered sincerely.

Polly's twins, Gemma and James, just seventeen, had been informed by Flossie of the part their brave parents had played in one of the day's unpleasant events. On arrival home from their respective colleges they had, as usual, entered the house by way of the kitchen, and there Flossie at once delivered the news.

'Flossie, you're kidding,' said James.

'Yes, having us on,' said Gemma.

So Flossie put them fully in the picture, which sent them galloping into the living room to congratulate their heroic mum.

And when Boots arrived home, a regular verbal free-for-all took place, which meant that Gemma, James and Flossie all talked at once about who had done this, who had done that and who deserved the biggest chestful of medals. Boots, attempting to retire early from the Tower of Babel in favour of attending to something or other in his study, was checked by Polly, who seized him by his tails and dragged him back.

'Oh, no, you don't,' she said, 'we're in this together.'

'That's it, Mama,' said Gemma, 'don't let him slip away to hide his light under a bushel.'

'True, we don't want him to turn out like Bossy Bullivant's dad,' said James.

'Who, dear boy, is Bossy Bullivant?' asked Polly.

'Head prefect,' said James. 'And whenever his parents appear at the school, his dad, who's terrifically shy and modest, hides behind his wife. Now, our dad – and our mum for that matter – shouldn't let modesty stand in the way of being decorated and so forth.'

'Spare us,' said Boots.

'Listen, Twinny,' said Gemma to her brother, 'we don't want anything like that to happen. I'd get looked at. Let's see if it's reported in the six o'clock news.'

It was, towards the end of the main BBC news, and Boots knew that if his mother was listening she'd probably be telling Sir Edwin that criminal incidents like this didn't happen in her day. Well, if so, he'd bet on Sir Edwin being too tactful to remind her of Dr Crippen and the shocking case of the Brides in the Bath.

'Family,' he said, 'as soon as we've finished supper we'll all call on my sister Lizzy and spend the evening with her.'

43

'Daddy, what for?' asked Gemma.

'I've a feeling,' said Boots, 'that by now at least one reporter has found out who the wartime ambulance lady is, and where she lives.'

'They'll come knocking?' said James.

'In case they do, let's all duck out,' said Polly, guessing that Boots felt publicity would do the twins no good with their contemporaries, no good at all. Television particularly could intrude unapologetically into people's lives and make public spectacles of them.

'I'll phone Lizzy first, of course,' said Boots.

So they sat down at once to supper served by a Flossie who was still in a state of trying to let admiration overcome agitation.

Afterwards, they took refuge with Lizzy, she happy to have them and enthralled by all that they recounted.

'But won't any reporters come back tomorrow?' she asked.

'Not if they read the note Dad left out for the milkman,' said James.

'What note?' asked Lizzy.

'Well,' replied James, 'it said, "No milk for a fortnight, please, we're visiting a close relative."'

Lizzy laughed.

'Me?' she said.

'Well, you're very close, Auntie,' said

Gemma, 'especially considering you're only just round the corner, more or less.'

The late-night news informed the listening public that the defecting Russian gymnast had been granted asylum, despite protests from the Soviet Embassy. It also mentioned that although a house-to-house search had been conducted, no arrest had been made of the man who had violently assaulted a Camberwell barman. Had the reverse of this been true, Polly and Boots, back from Lizzy's, would have slept content in the knowledge that Joe's vicious assailant was going to receive his comeuppance. As it was, they had unpleasant dreams.

Chapter Three

Earlier that day Sammy's elder son Daniel, on arriving home, had acquainted his favourite all-American girl with an account of what had happened to Aunt Polly and Uncle Boots. He had received the details from his dad at the office, with the injunction not to let them fly about in case they reached the ears of Grandma Finch, who was severely against any of her family looking as if they might make headlines in the *News of the World*. The details rocked Patsy more than a bit, and made her refer to barman Joe's assailant as a lousy specimen of humanity on a par with a leftover dog's dinner from Al Capone's Chicago.

'Fair comment, Patsy,' said Daniel. 'Let's catch the six o'clock news. I'd like to find out if the police have laid their hands on Al Capone's leftover. It seems he nearly did the barman in for good.'

'Sure, let's catch the news,' said Patsy.

Like others in the family at that particular moment, they learned from the news that the police still hadn't traced the man and were asking for help from the public. It was thought that one or more persons would recognize him from the very detailed description that had been issued, and that this would at least help to reveal his identity if not to secure his apprehension. But although people from various parts of southeast London had contacted the Camberwell police station to say they thought or were sure they'd seen a man answering the description, none said they knew him or his name.

A Soho photographer, one Charlie Ellis, might have phoned the police, but didn't. He kept quiet about the fact that for a while he'd employed a young bloke who sounded very similar to the description issued, though he'd had a normal haircut at the time, and was called Curly Harris. Charlie knew that wasn't his real name, and that he was always waiting for a new insurance card to turn up consequent, he'd said, on losing his old one. That hadn't worried Charlie Ellis. The bloke had been useful to him up to suddenly leaving about a year ago. Charlie suspected he'd done a job and that the police were after him. And if he'd now done a different job by slicing up a barman, well, Mr Charlie Ellis was going to keep quiet, since the young cuss knew too much about his photographic business, which was undercover porno. It wouldn't do to bear witness against him. He'd turn spiteful.

So Mr Charlie Ellis kept quiet.

Patsy felt upset for Polly and Boots, two people she rated as highly civilized. She also felt badly let down by the fact that such an incident could have happened in her adopted country, a land of teapots and cultivated back yards. She had long since assured American friends that the little old UK was completely free of the kind of homicidal hoodlums common to Chicago. So Patsy was very upset, and said so to Daniel. Daniel, an understanding guy, said yes, the deed was foul all right, but very unusual, and she could console herself by bearing in mind that the country was still primarily law-abiding and that the main pursuits of the people generally were still rooted in cricket, shopping markets, whist drives, jumble sales, village fetes and inviting aunts and uncles to Sunday tea.

'That's kind of reassuring,' said Patsy, 'and I just hope it lasts.'

'Well, you can bet Grandma Finch won't change,' said Daniel, 'and she sets the example for the whole country.'

'Well, you know that,' said Patsy, 'and I guess I do too, but outside of the rest of the family, who else does?'

'Not the rat who did the knife job, that's for sure,' said Daniel.

'Daniel, let's hope the police don't take too long to lock him up,' said Patsy.

At home the following day, Boots thought

about the fact that the assailant had been seen entering the thoroughfare called Champion Park. He wondered if the swine really did live thereabouts, or if the move had been a deliberately deceptive one. He'd have known he was in the bus conductor's sights. Certainly, the police had found no evidence that he was a known resident in the area covered by their house-to-house search. So exactly where did the dangerous lunatic hang out?

The twins wondered about that when the subject was being discussed over supper.

'Well,' said Gemma, 'it's my belief he's got to live somewhere near the pub.'

'Not necessarily,' said James. 'He might actually be a stranger. In fact, if he'd been familiar with that particular locality, he'd have known that that pub doesn't serve lager or chips.'

'Jolly shrewd point, James ducky,' said Polly.

'Yes, isn't he a clever boy?' said Gemma. 'Mind, he only knows about the pub because Daddy told us. Still, he could be right about the hairy beast being a stranger.'

'Agreed,' said Boots.

'I'm not too happy that he hasn't been caught yet,' said James.

'I share that feeling,' said Boots.

'But it was only yesterday,' said Gemma.

'I know,' said James, 'but all the time he's

out there somewhere, he could be thinking of doing Dad in the eye for chasing after him. An ugly character like that could turn up on our doorstep carrying an iron bar with foul intent.'

'Foul intent? Crikey,' said Gemma, 'that's Victorian stuff. Still, I know what you mean. Anyway, don't let's fear the worst. Remember, he wouldn't know where Dad lives.'

'For which, let's give thanks,' said Polly. 'I'm totally against this grisly and gruesome lump of evil arriving at our door. His rightful place is ten feet under in a black swamp.'

'Cathy talked about him,' said James. He was referring to Cathy Davidson, whose mother lived in Paris with her second husband. Cathy herself had come back to London to live with an aunt in Dulwich. She had resumed a cosy relationship with James. 'She suggested he might be a psycho-something who had escaped from an asylum.'

'Oh, you saw the young lady again this afternoon?' said Polly, still not sure she would ever want Cathy's maternal parent as James's mother-in-law. 'You walked her home from her college as usual?'

'Yep, as usual,' said James.

'Shout if you ever need help,' said Polly.

'Oh, let's be fair, Mama,' said Gemma, 'Cathy's really quite nice now, and it's not

50

her fault that her mother's Russian, and one of the show-off kind.'

'Part Russian,' said James. 'It's her aunt who's pure Russian.'

'I don't think I've had the pleasure,' said Boots.

'I won't pass judgement, since I haven't, either,' said Polly. 'But is she a little theatrical, James?'

'Like Eloise?' said James. Eloise was his half-sister, born of a French mother, and much given to excitability. 'No, she seems very civilized. Well, she's lived in England for years, so if she was ever inclined to be overdramatic, she's calmed down now. Mind, I've only met her for five minutes or so whenever I've seen Cathy home.'

'Well, if living in England has calmed her down, let's hand a deserved medal to our birthplace,' said Polly.

'Seconded, Mama,' said Gemma.

'Not forgetting, of course,' said Boots, 'that our birthplace has also been responsible for Jack the Ripper and Henry the Chop.'

'Henry the Chop?' chorused everyone else.

'Otherwise known as Henry the Eighth,' said Boots.

'Or Hairy Henry,' said James. 'Or Who's-Neckst-Henry.'

'Ugh,' said Gemma. 'I have to say, Mama,' she added, 'that I think our menfolk are going off a bit.'

'Oh, well, darling, we womenfolk do have to live with our occasional disappointments,' said Polly.

'Yes, and we do take the strain quite well, don't we?' said Gemma.

Cathy's Aunt Marie, a widow, was a few months over sixty, but still a graceful lady. Slim of figure and aristocratic of looks, she was addicted to fine clothes and, in the winter, to equally fine furs whenever she ventured out. Her temperament was even, her disposition kind, and she delighted in having Catherine, the daughter of a distant cousin, living with her. As a woman who had never known children of her own, she had love and affection to spare for Cathy, who simply did not get on with her French stepfather, an autocrat.

Aunt Marie's house in Dulwich was quite grand. It was looked after by her five servants, three of whom were well into their fifties, having been hired as long ago as 1925. These servants remained devoted, even though she and her late husband had moved house several times. Such loyalty was a cherished thing to Aunt Marie. So were memories of her husband, who had left her all his not inconsiderable worldly goods. She was never going to be in want.

She took lunch at midday, tea in the afternoon and dinner in the evening. Tea itself she drank with lemon. Tea with milk she considered peculiar to the natives, many of whom were slightly eccentric, anyway. All meals were cooked and served by her domestics.

Dinner was very welcome to Cathy, always starving at the end of her day at college. And Aunt Marie liked to see her enjoying her food. It was her conviction that a healthy intake of calories by young people contributed to the build-up of a sterling character as well as fine bones and firm limbs.

January had turned into February when at dinner one evening Aunt Marie, who spoke perfect English with scarcely any trace of an accent, asked an unexpected question of Cathy. Would she like to invite the parents of her boyfriend James to Sunday lunch sometime?

'Oh, I'm not sure I should do that, Aunt Marie,' said Cathy, bathed in the light of an electric-powered chandelier, a feature of the handsome dining room. 'Well, I mean, don't you think it would look as if I was trying to make more of things than I should? An invitation to Sunday lunch, well – oh, I'd love them to meet you, of course, but I'm not sure it wouldn't look as if – well, you know.'

'Yes, I understand, dear,' said Aunt Marie, 'as if they were expected to see me as a future relative of theirs. We'll leave it, then, but at least you can invite James himself to Sunday tea sometime, don't you think? I've only had the pleasure of speaking to him for a few minutes on one or two of the occasions when he's brought you home.'

'Oh, I'll do that, I'll ask him to Sunday tea,' said Cathy. 'That won't look too formal.'

'I've a feeling, my dear,' smiled Aunt Marie, 'that you're afraid his parents will think you're – let's see – yes, making the running? But don't modern girls do that now, haven't they given up being shy and modest?'

Cathy laughed.

'Oh, I'm not shy and modest, I know that,' she said, 'but with James, well, I used to be kind of gushing and pushy, and it's not my style now. Aunt Marie, his parents are lovely people, and I don't want them to think I'm still pushy.'

'At sixteen, dear Cathy, you're the sweetest girl,' said Aunt Marie, who had come to cherish Cathy's companionship and the girl herself. 'Tell me, have James's parents recovered from their dreadful ordeal of last week?'

'Believe me, Aunt,' said Cathy, who had received details from James, 'they're not the kind who go all limp and pale when something gruesome happens. They're both taking things in their stride, as they always do. They just don't fuss or fret. Of course, they're hoping for the unlovely brute to be caught and stretched on the rack, but so far he's dodged the Camberwell sheriff and his posse.'

'Dreadful man,' said Aunt Marie, indulging in a delicate shudder. The butler, Charles Rogers, came in then, accompanied by a maidservant, and he supervised the collecting up of the dinner plates and the serving of the dessert.

When that was done, Cathy said, 'By the way, Aunt, we've never heard whether the Russian gymnast who defected last week was a member of the men's or ladies' team.'

Aunt Marie let a little sigh escape. She rarely spoke of her homeland or her parents, and did not encourage questions about them.

'In these cases, I imagine only a very little information is given to the public in order to protect defectors,' she said. She sighed again. 'It's still happening, Cathy, people are still trying to get out of the country that was once mine. You can be grateful you were born here and not inside the iron walls of Communist Russia. It's a place of dreadful people and dreadful crimes.'

'James's father told me that Communism was invented to keep the workers in order by someone who was never a worker himself during the whole of his life,' said Cathy.

'Yes, Comrade Lenin,' said Aunt Marie, with visible distaste for the name.

'Well, I'm not a bit keen on Communism,' said Cathy. 'I like James's Uncle Sammy, who's a very enterprising capitalist, and I'm super-devoted to free beings like rock and roll stars.'

'I think you mean – let me see – yes, singers like Ethel Presley.'

Cathy shrieked.

'Elvis, Auntie, Elvis, not Ethel.'

'Elvis, yes, I see,' said Aunt Marie and smiled indulgently.

'Actually, he's in the American army now and serving in Germany,' said Cathy.

'Ah, yes? Then perhaps he's finding out there's one thing seriously wrong with Germany.'

'And what's that, Auntie?'

'It's too close to Communist Russia.'

Chapter Four

Lulu's husband Paul quizzed her about the present activities of Marjorie Alsop, the aggressive lady whose anti-fur campaign had threatened to turn Uncle Sammy grey. Lulu, having taken Miss Alsop in hand, said she was pointing her in the direction of Westminster, where dwelt the Minister of Trade, the man most likely to be influential in the matter of fostering a debate on the possibility of introducing relevant legislation.

'Relevant?' said Paul.

'Wake up,' said Lulu.

'Oh, you mean an anti-fur Act,' said Paul.

'Of course,' said Lulu, sitting down at the table with their little daughter Sylvia. Supper was ready. Supper was a working-class tradition. Dinner was the midday meal, which the middle classes called lunch. Lulu, naturally, was against anything that might make her Labour Party comrades think she and Paul were middle class. Not because she was an inverted snob, but because a working-class label was a practical must for any prospective Labour Party candidate. In any case, she was heart and soul in favour of improving the lot of the workers, especially the coalminers. 'A relevant Act would do far more for Marjorie's cause than chucking bricks.'

'An Act? No chance,' said Paul, whose turn it had been to prepare supper. His little woman had made marriage conditional on the sharing of various domestic tasks. He was presently serving up this evening's meal. 'Nope, not a chance in hell.' He addressed their infant. 'What d'you say to that, little pickle?'

'Oh, 'ell,' replied Sylvia, often called Sylvie by her doting parents.

'There, now see what you've done, put strong language into our child's mouth before she's even five,' said Lulu.

'Slip of the tongue,' said Paul, and sat down at the kitchen table to attack his food. 'But it's true, there's no Labour Minister or MP who'll promote an act that'll put the fur industry workers out of a job. Too many of them. You ought to know that, Pussy Willow.'

'Of course I know it,' said Lulu, watching Sylvia eating with relish. 'And what's this Pussy Willow stuff?'

'I like it,' said Paul, 'it reminds me of how fond I am of you.'

'Have you been reading Beatrix Potter?' asked Lulu.

'Not since I was six,' said Paul.

'Well, all right,' said Lulu, 'no hard feelings.' There would have been if he'd intimated he'd gone off her. Sometimes, as a woman looking at the possibility of a political career, she wondered what, as a wife and mother, she was doing to her prospects. Well, whatever it was, there were other times when she didn't actually dislike her home life, especially as she was pretty sure she had Paul well trained. It had taken time. Like all men, he'd had antediluvian ideas about what they all called wearing the trousers. Shame, really, when he was otherwise up to the mark. Still, he'd allowed her to re-educate him. 'But don't you realize that in pointing Marj at Westminster, I'm taking her mind off Uncle Sammy and Uncle Boots, and the contentious fact that the Adams shops sell fur-trimmed garments?'

'Well, you doll, good on you,' said Paul. 'I'm reminded I've got aunts, especially those like Aunt Polly, who look great in beaver. Of course, as a Labour Party bloke, I'm against the filthy rich and their furs as a matter of principle, but you couldn't ever call Aunt Polly filthy. Or Aunt Susie. Or Cousin Eloise. I know they've all got a few bob, but–'

'Don't go on,' said Lulu, 'take a look at my grilled kidneys. They're overdone.'

'Funny you should say that, mine are the same,' said Paul, refraining from exhibiting guilt. 'Still, our little pickle is enjoying hers. Anyway, with your help, Marj is happily organizing a visit to the House of Commons, is she?'

'It'll take time,' said Lulu.

'Lulu, you're not just a pretty face,' said Paul, 'you're a credit to me and Sylvie. I'll pass the good news to Uncle Sammy.'

'When you do, remind him to keep the firm's profit margins down,' said Lulu. 'I've got a suspicion that if my friends and activists were to get a look at last year's balance sheet, they'd think I belonged to a family of capitalist moneymongers.'

'Moneymongers? Is that a word?' asked Paul.

'Like it, do you?' said Lulu.

'It's got a telling touch,' said Paul. 'What d'you think about it, little one?'

'Oh, 'ell,' Sylvia replied once more.

'Oh, help,' grinned Paul.

Joe the barman was recovering well in hospital. Boots paid him a visit and they chatted about the incident. Joe said it was time the lunatic was caught. Boots said that considering a very accurate description had been circulated, discovery of his identity was overdue. Joe said as soon as the police did lay their hands on the geezer, he'd feel safer personally. As it was, his condition, steadily improving from hospital care, climbed towards a peak of healing when Boots slipped him the delayed retirement gift of twenty-five quid, with the compliments of himself and Polly.

'You're a gent, Mr Adams, and so's your missus,' said Joe.

'I'll tell her that,' smiled Boots, 'if I can rephrase it.'

The following morning, the police received an anonymous note by post. It was short but informative.

'You still want his name? It's Curly Harris, I'm not saying more.'

The envelope was postmarked Bermondsey.

'Do we know a Curly Harris?' asked Detective Chief Inspector Walters.

No-one did and, moreover, Scotland Yard had no record of any man of that name. Curly was obviously a nickname, so the Yard offered possibilities in the way of a Bernard Arthur Harris and a Sidney William Harris. Both men had done time more than once for burglary, but Camberwell should note that both were now in their sixties. Chief Inspector Walters did take note and dismissed both offerings. The description given by witnesses on the spot all pointed to a young man.

Since the incident, suggestions that the culprit might have been an escaped lunatic had caused inquiries to be made, but none of the contacted asylums had any knowledge of an escapee. Chief Inspector Walters now spoke of a resumed investigation into the whereabouts of their man, this time in Bermondsey.

'Are we sure, guv, that we can trust the postmark?' asked a detective sergeant. 'Anonymous letters aren't all that reliable, and if the writer was that keen to give us a name, what's stopping him telling us more?'

'He's probably a crook himself, Sarge,' said a constable, 'and some crooks won't go the whole way when passing information on a feller crook.'

'Still,' said the sergeant to the chief inspector, 'are we and our Bermondsey colleagues up for a house-to-house job in search of this piece of vermin? Only Bermondsey's a large area, guv, and full up with all kinds.'

'So all right, Bermondsey station needs an army, which I don't suppose it has,' said Chief Inspector Walters. He phoned his opposite number in Bermondsey about the anonymous note. It was agreed they couldn't afford to ignore it, and so a combined team was put together and sent out into the wilds of Bermondsey to plod around and ask around, in good old-fashioned police style. An artist's impression of the man was shown to people, who were asked if they knew him and where he lived. He was possibly known as Curly Harris.

Answers were various.

'Excuse me, I'm a respectable working

woman, I am, so you don't think I know anyone as 'orrible-looking as him, do yer?'

'Never seen any bloke like him in these here parts. Why doncher try the Zoo?'

'Don't know him meself, officer, but you could look in on the Black Horse pub. All kinds of dodgy customers use that place.'

The barman of the pub considered the question and the artist's impression.

'Curly Harris, you said? That's him, is it, with all that hair? I might've heard of 'im, but I can't remember where, and I can't say I recognize the cove from yer drawing. Wish I could. I ain't too bleedin' happy about what he did to one of me own kind. Sorry.'

There were other responses.

'Try Mrs Goodbody just down the street. I think she knows everyone in Bermondsey and she's a law-abiding old biddy.'

'Yes, I'm Mrs Goodbody, but kindly don't bother me, I got Mr Goodbody in bed with the flu, and I don't know nobody, anyway.'

'Eh? Curly Harris? Never heard of him. Try Parsons' Shelter.'

'What was Parsons' Shelter?'

'A charity dosshouse started by a funny old gent name of Percy Parsons years ago. It's down Jamaica Road.'

Hence a subsequent inquiry at this hostel for down-and-outs.

The warden, who needed a shave and a change of shirt, regarded the policemen unhelpfully. He didn't know anyone called Curly Harris, he said, and anyway no questions were asked of the kind of people who used the shelter, nor did they have to speak their names. Also, it was a principle not to give out information on any of them. What they were, and what they did, was their own business.

Including attempted murder?

Well, said the warden, he'd heard about what had happened at that pub in Camberwell, but was it officially recorded as attempted murder? More like grievous bodily harm, he'd have thought.

'You've definitely no recollection of a man of this description using your hostel?'

'No, I can't recollect no-one like that,' said the warden, who spent much of his time warming up with a nip of whisky and making sure he hadn't caught fleas from any of the misbegotten down-and-outs. A man emerged from one of the rooms. The two policemen both recognized him.

'Well, look at that, it's Dodgy Dan. What've you been up to lately, old nifty fingers?'

'None of yer business,' said the unwashed old tramp known as Dodgy Dan. He was about to set out for one of his favourite places of work, Waterloo railway station, in the hope that none of the ticket inspectors or porters would recognize him and threaten to call a copper unless he got lost quick.

'D'you know this man?' The police artist's impression was shown.

'Course I know 'im, don't I? It's Charlie Chaplin. Mind, I ain't actually ever met 'im.'

'You've never heard anybody here mention the name Curly Harris?'

'Who's he?' Dodgy Dan was no informer. He was too fond of his person to risk having it fatally injured by coves like short-tempered Curly Harris.

'Come on, Dodgy, I bet you've seen all kinds pass in and out of this hostel.'

'Some 'ostel. More like a home for bugs and fleas. Still, it's somewhere to rest me bones and they don't ask no rent. Well, I'm off now, I got to look in at the employment exchange to see if they've got anything to offer me, something that won't cripple me bad back.'

'You sure you can't help us with our inquiries?'

'I told yer, I don't know any Curly Barrett—'

'Curly Harris.'

'No, nor him, neither. So long, I gotter go now.'

All that was typical of the day, a big minus for the police team, which didn't go down well with the respective inspectors. Come to that, the arrival of the plod at Parsons' Shelter hadn't gone down well with its warden, since he at once thought they'd discovered his was the hand that had concocted the anonymous letter. It was a relief to find out it was merely a routine call. He'd named Curly Harris in that note because the bleeder, who obviously fitted the broadcast description of the wanted assailant, had done him down, lifting a full bottle of his whisky before bunking off to hide himself somewhere else. The warden, however, had stopped short of offering further information in the letter, or to the police during their call. Anything more might have made Curly Harris realize who'd shopped him. So he'd been relieved to see the fuzz turn their attention on Dodgy Dan.

Chief Inspector Walters, talking to his Bermondsey counterpart, said he had a feeling about the area, a feeling that it was definitely where the answer lay. He suggested continuing the search tomorrow. The Bermondsey inspector agreed, but offered the possibility that the name Curly Harris covered up the real one. Otherwise, some member of the public would surely have come forward to point an informative finger. That had to be considered, said Walters, and added that although this wasn't an inquiry into murder, as it might have been, the violence of the assault on the barman was such as to warrant getting the culprit convicted and behind bars as quickly as possible for the safety of the public.

Chapter Five

The resumed search in Bermondsey failed to give the police any satisfaction, following which the days ran on without the law coming anywhere close to apprehending the Camberwell assailant. Boots and his family settled hopefully for an arrest sometime in the not too distant future. And James secured his mother's immediate attention when he announced one evening that Cathy and her aunt, Mrs Marie Edwards, had invited him to tea on Sunday.

'Sunday tea?' said the once dizzy and exotic flapper of the Wild Twenties, now looking a little mettlesome.

'That's it, Sunday tea,' said James.

'It's a plot,' said Polly.

'Oh, I nearly forgot, Gemma's invited as well,' said James.

'That makes it not such a dark plot?' suggested Boots to Polly.

'Dear man, I simply can't help feeling James needs protection from any female with a Russian label,' said Polly.

'Mama, I do keep telling you Cathy's now harmless, even if she is part Russian,' said Gemma. 'As for her aunt, well, I'll keep my eye on James while we're there. I mean, I suppose you accepted for both of us, did you, James?'

'Yes, is that to your liking?' said James.

'Well, I simply can't wait to meet the lady,' said Gemma. 'Of course, it won't be like meeting Bill Haley or Tommy Steele, but it could be interesting.'

'Gemma,' said Polly firmly, 'if at any time during the visit you feel there's a trap closing around James, bring him home at once.'

'Do what?' said James.

'Darling, Gemma will make sure you don't wander into Russian quicksands,' said Polly. 'What think you, Boots old soldier?'

'I think,' murmured Boots, 'I think I was once told that no female at any age could be considered harmless. But I suppose there are exceptions. Let's rate Cathy as one.'

'But there's the unknown quantity, her aunt,' said Polly.

'Her aunt, yes,' said Boots.

'Yes what?' asked Polly.

'I pass,' said Boots.

'Mama,' said Gemma, 'I'm certain James will get out alive.'

'I'm falling about in the face of all this comic stuff,' said James.

'Well, as long as Gemma goes with you,' said Polly, 'your father and I will allow you to accept the invitation, James dear.'

'Well, that's great, Mother dear,' said

James. 'But parental permission at my age? For someone's Sunday tea? That's coming it a bit, isn't it? Of course, I make that point with all due respect.'

'Thank you, James,' said Polly. 'It's just that your father and I, as your caring parents, wish to preserve you for a happy future.'

'True, everyone's entitled to a happy future,' said Boots. 'I'm still locked into mine.'

'Supper's coming up, Mrs Adams,' called Flossie from the kitchen. With Flossie, sometimes it was supper, sometimes dinner. 'Any minute now.'

'Hooray, I'm starving,' said Gemma.

'Me, I'm always starving,' said James.

'Then with any luck,' said Boots, 'Cathy's aunt will provide you with a large helping of Russian caviar for Sunday tea, and not just bread and jam.'

Gemma put on her best frock for the visit. James put on a suit. Cathy's Aunt Marie received them with such natural old-world charm that Gemma at once felt she would be able to assure her mother the lady was quite unlike Cathy's flamboyant and extrovert maternal parent. Also, she was as charming in her looks as in her manner. It was no wonder Cathy showed an affection for her. Further, she seemed quite delighted when the twins presented her with a bouquet of flowers, due to a thoughtful suggestion from Polly that it was something they simply must do, never mind the lady's connection with Cathy's acquisitive mama.

As for the tea, it was served in an attractive room that fronted a conservatory. On this dull February day, wall lights glowed, and a log fire, crackling, issued little tongues of flame. The meal itself was not so much a tea as a repast of potted shrimps, hot buttered crumpets, cream pastries and an iced cake, the pastries and cake made by Aunt Marie's cook. And although Cathy had wanted everything to be informal, the laden table could hardly be called anything but grand. However, the lady herself continued to be so natural in her manner and so kind in her hospitality that Gemma and James tucked in without reserve.

She wanted to know if the young guests really were twins, since they weren't identical.

'No, but we're still twins,' said Gemma.

'We've got our parents' word for it,' said James, 'and we've never argued with that. Well, you don't, do you?'

'Actually,' said Gemma, piquant of features, 'it's a blessing we're not identical.'

'A blessing?' said Aunt Marie, glancing at James, firm of features. 'Is it?'

'Well, it is for me,' said Gemma. 'If you know what I mean.'

'Do we know, Cathy?' smiled Aunt Marie.

'I think so,' said Cathy who, at sixteen, was remarkably stylish. James reckoned her time in Paris had done that for her.

'I'm still a little foggy,' said Aunt Marie.

'I'm not,' said James with a bit of a grin.

'Well, to come to the point and to be frank without being unkind, what girl wants to look like my brother?' asked Gemma.

'Ah, now I see,' said Aunt Marie, and gave James the winning smile of a woman still deriving pleasure from life. She showed nothing of an ageing woman's mental or physical frailty, and her eyes, thought Gemma, were alive with quick, darting glances. 'Yes, James, you are very much a young man, and Gemma much the young lady.'

'Yes, you'll soon be able to grow a moustache, James,' said Cathy.

'I'll be giving that serious thought,' said James, dwelling on the lush, buttery texture of his second hot crumpet. 'Say when I'm twenty-one and need to look impressive.'

'Impressive for whom, James?' asked Aunt Marie, ringing a little bell.

'Whoever it might concern, I suppose,' said James. 'Like Judy Garland, if I happened to find her on our doorstep.'

'James, are you sure a moustache will make you look impressive?' asked Cathy.

'Weird, more like,' said Gemma.

In came the butler with a large teapot

swaddled in a cosy.

'The pot, ma'am,' he said, and placed it on a silver stand just to the right of Aunt Marie.

'Thank you, Charles,' she said.

The savouries and crumpets having been consumed, it was now time to introduce the young guests to the pastries and, accordingly, to pour the tea.

'Excuse me, Mrs Edwards,' said Gemma, as their likeable hostess began to fill cups, 'but could I ask–'

'Dear child, to all Cathy's friends I am Aunt Marie. It's how I like it. I don't care for too much formality when in company with young people.' She mused a little. 'I can remember very stiff and correct behaviour, and being told that anything I really wanted to do was not permitted. I was happy to escape such restrictions. Ah, well, that was long ago. Cathy, see that Gemma and James help themselves to the pastries. Oh, forgive me, but what was it you were going to ask, Gemma?'

'I hope you won't think it's impertinent,' said Gemma, as accomplished as James in the field of chat. Well, within the ranks of the Adams family it was no good being inarticulate. One quickly learned to use one's tongue. If one didn't, one kind of sank without trace at a family gathering. 'But what I wanted to ask was when did you actually leave Russia and come to England?' She put the question while accepting a pastry from the dish offered by Cathy.

'Nowadays I give that very little thought,' said Aunt Marie, who practised privacy to the point of being ex-directory as far as her telephone was concerned. 'But it was before the outbreak of the First World War.'

'Did your parents bring you?'

'No, Aunt Marie came here with only a chaperone,' said Cathy. 'She was happy to be here, but it meant parting from her father. We don't talk about it very much, do we, Auntie?'

James thought there was a little protectiveness about Cathy's comment, so he changed the subject by saying how much he was enjoying the tea. Great, he said.

'Thanks for saying so,' said Cathy, careful these days not to give the impression she had any special claim on James, although one could truthfully say that among the girls he knew she was tops. 'Yes, thanks.'

'It's super, it really is,' said Gemma, much taken with the perfection of her cream pastry.

'Well, I'm always happy to see young people enjoying themselves,' said Aunt Marie. 'Cathy brings some of her schoolfriends to see me from time to time, and they light up the house.'

'I've met the kind,' said James, 'so have my parents. Gemma brings them home. Light

73

up the house? I'll say. We're lucky we don't live in a smoking ruin.'

Cathy laughed, Gemma rolled her eyes, and Aunt Marie smiled before busying herself refilling teacups. She was eating modestly herself, while all three young people were doing full justice to what was before them. The conversation took natural turns, with the indulgent hostess wanting to know how Gemma and James were doing academically. A flow of information arrived from the twins, while Cathy compared college notes with them. Funny moments were frequent, each of which brought forth a smile from the hostess, although there were other moments when she seemed a little far away.

Gemma and James were acquiring quite a liking for the Russian-born lady, anglicized to the point of understanding English colloquialisms and being able to discuss the country's politics if required. That boring subject was out, however, as far as Cathy and the guests were concerned, so no-one raised it. The Sunday tea, therefore, was harmonious from start to finish, and not once did Cathy show any trace of her former eager and breathless self. James thought her pretty super and much more the great-niece of her elegant aunt than the daughter of her exhibitionist mother, now safely tucked away in Paris with her rich French husband.

Safely, that is, as far as his own mother was concerned. Mother Polly had a thing about the danger of allowing the ex-Mrs Davidson to get too close to her family, especially to Pa. A little grin chased itself across James's face. It came and went unobserved.

It was Cathy who saw the guests out after they had said goodbye and thank you to their delightful hostess.

'Aunt Marie is so pleased you came,' said Cathy, 'and so am I.'

'Our pleasure,' said James. 'Super tea and your aunt's a lovely lady.'

'Seconded,' said Gemma.

'See you after classes tomorrow, James?' said Cathy.

'Yup, I'll walk you home,' said James, and gave her an impulsive kiss. Its unexpectedness turned her a little pink. James was always very sparing with his salutations. 'So long now,' he said, 'and tell your aunt thanks again.'

'Oh. Yes. Yes, I'll tell her,' said Cathy, and was still slightly pink when she delivered the message.

Walking home with Gemma, James agreed with her that Cathy's Russian aunt was the kindest of ladies. He thought, however, that she had a nervous streak. Gemma wanted to know what he meant by that. He said that now and again she gave sudden quick glances, as if expecting someone to appear at her elbow.

'Oh, yes, I noticed that,' said Gemma. 'But I remembered Cathy telling me her aunt does suffer a bit from nerves. She thinks it's to do with the fact that when her husband was alive their house was broken into one night while they were sleeping. Her husband went down to investigate. Halfway down the stairs, he met the intruder coming up. There was a terrific fight, apparently. Aunt Marie phoned the police, but just before they arrived the burglar or whoever he was escaped, leaving her husband battered and bleeding. The police never traced the man.'

'I've not heard that from Cathy,' said James.

'Well, I have,' said Gemma.

'It would account for her aunt's nerves being a bit twitchy, you bet,' said James, and walked on with his sister through the biting air of the wintry evening.

'Well?' said Polly on their arrival home.

'It's filthy cold outside,' said Gemma.

'Minx, I don't wish to hear about the weather,' said Polly, 'and you know it.'

'You'd like to hear what we think of Cathy's aunt?' said James.

'In case you haven't guessed,' said Boots, 'your mother's agog.'

'Traitor,' said Polly. 'Have you no feeling for the blood I've spilt in protecting this family from a Russian invasion?'

'Um, part Russian, I think,' murmured Boots.

'Still, the lady was a bit gone on you, Pa,' said James.

'And we didn't want to lose you,' said Gemma.

'Yes, don't you remember how Gemma and I used to rush to raise the drawbridge to keep the lady out?' said James.

'I can remember your mother playing Lady Macbeth,' said Boots.

'Oh, yes, "Out, out, damned blot",' said Gemma.

'However, I'm grateful, of course, that the drawbridge was always raised in time,' said Boots.

'Dee-lighted, old top, to hear you say so,' murmured Polly.

'Anyway, Mama,' said Gemma, 'you'll be ecstatic to know that Cathy's aunt is a kind and lovely lady. She gave us a super tea, starting with caviar and prawns, just like Daddy told us to expect.'

'Caviar?' said Polly.

'Then we had hot crumpets, cream pastries and iced cake,' continued Gemma. 'Mama, you'd never believe the lady was Russian, she has hardly any accent and is as gentle as a lamb.'

'True,' said James.

'Quite true, James dear?' said Polly.

'Utterly, Mother dear,' said James. 'I don't

think she'll start landing on our doorstep, so Pa's quite safe. We won't need to worry about the drawbridge.'

'Cease this mockery,' said Polly. 'Remember the real dangers your father faced. If we hadn't taken those precautions, he'd have been eaten ages ago.'

'Roasted or grilled?' enquired James.

Chapter Six

A cold but bright morning. February was well advanced, windy and chilly March waiting to blow in. 'Girls, attention now.' Miss Judith Stanton, headmistress, addressed the assembled students of Maiden Hall, the independent college for young ladies, either boarders or day girls, south of Dulwich Village. Here it was that young hopefuls took their university entrance exams, and it was much to the credit of the teaching staff that the pass rate was excellent. It has to be said, however, that the boys of the nearest state school considered the girls to be toffee-nosed and pretty useless, which wasn't the case at all, although it was true none had so far opted to try for a degree in engineering. On the other hand, they wanted nothing to do with the outdated and gruesome custom of being turned into gentlewomen. The world had become a lot more open for their sex, and the idea of being merely ladylike and ornamental was out, full stop. 'Attention, please.' Miss Stanton made herself heard this time.

Two hundred and thirty-two teenage girls became quiet.

'All present and correct, ma'am,' called the head girl. That wasn't quite true, since four girls were absent with flu. However, all those in good health were definitely present.

On the assembly hall dais, Miss Stanton, a cultured lady but formidable in her ability to control the heathenish element, turned and drew forward a girl who was slim to the point of thinness, her silky black hair parted down the middle, her eyes large and lustrous.

'Girls, here is a new friend, Irena Leino, already known to boarders. She has come from Helsinki, in Finland, in the hope of perfecting her English and entering Oxford University. We will do all we can to help her. She will join Senior B Class. Please give her a warm welcome.'

'Welcome, friend Irena, welcome!' chorused the girls.

The slender newcomer, looking cool rather than nervous, gave little bows right, left and centre in acknowledgement of the greeting. The head girl then took charge of her and introduced her to the students who were to be her classmates. After all that, she took her place at a desk in her allotted class, that which was the province of Senior B students, due to sit university entrance exams next year. Senior A girls, very advanced (academically), included many who would sit this year.

Sharing the desk with Irena was a very

likeable and outgoing student, who happened to be Gemma Adams. The head girl had felt that Gemma, naturally communicative, was the best bet to help the new student fit in quickly. Gemma, incidentally, was not the most ambitious of scholars. That is, instead of three brilliant years at a university, she had hopes of a place at the Chelsea College of Arts and Science in September the following year. She fancied making a name for herself in fashion design. Her Uncle Sammy, founder of Adams Fashions and its retail outlets, was offering encouragement.

Turning to the new girl, Gemma said, 'I'm happy to know you, Irena.'

'Thank you, you are very kind,' said Irena, her foreign accent quite strong.

'Do you really come from Finland?'

'Yes, from Finland I come.'

'Well, imagine that,' said Gemma, 'you're the first person from Finland I've ever met. I'm fascinated. Have you come especially to study here?'

'Yes, that is so.' Irena's smile was responsive, her large eyes alert to her surroundings. 'English and English theatre.'

'Are your parents here with you?'

'No.' A little sigh. 'They died during the war.'

'Oh, I am sorry, how sad for you,' said Gemma.

'Young ladies.' Miss Taylor, English literature teacher, rapped her desk with a ruler. The sharp sound brought chattering students to attentiveness, and the day's first lesson began, with Gemma thinking that Irena Leino, although obviously mourning her late parents, was kind of cool and intriguing. Was there something one ought to know about Finland? Oh, yes, like David against Goliath, that little country had been at war with Russia while Russia was at war with Germany. Gemma remembered that from recently introduced lessons touching on the history of the Second World War.

During the afternoon a gentleman from a Whitehall department called on the headmistress. They conducted their conversation in her study over tea, with the door closed, the subject being the new student, Irena Leino.

'Her embassy has ceased fussing and has officially accepted the situation,' said the gentleman. 'We have their assurance that there'll be no attempt to reclaim her.'

'We can trust that?' asked the headmistress.

'An official assurance is officially accepted,' said the gentleman a little drily. 'My department, however, is keeping an open mind. Certainly, it's our wish to protect the young lady from being forced to return, especially as she informed us she lost her parents and their comforting arms in one of Stalin's purges.'

'It's abominable to be denied freedom,' said the headmistress, 'and admirable to have escaped the chains. Civilization took many steps back when the Russians succumbed to the ideology of Lenin, and even more when the Germans accepted Nazism as their religion and Hitler as their god.'

'A sad reflection on the intelligence of certain sections of the human race,' said the gentleman.

'Unfortunately, yes. Do have another biscuit.'

'Thank you. On behalf of my department, I must also thank you for accepting the young lady as a student boarder and for allowing her to – yes, shall we say to lose herself amid all the other students?'

'She has adjusted very well as a boarder, although a place in a quiet country village might have enabled her to lose herself completely.'

'Is there such a thing these days as a quiet country village?' murmured the gentleman thoughtfully. 'Not if one reads Agatha Christie.'

'Fictional mayhem can hardly be considered a serious factor,' said the headmistress.

'I made the point lightly,' said the gentleman. 'Regarding the young lady's residence here, on the outskirts of London, she has long wanted to see our capital together with its theatre and ballet. It was while she was there, in the heart of the West End, that she chose to make her escape. As you know, she expressed a wish to live within reasonable reach of theatres such as Drury Lane and Covent Garden. We went along with that wish, while letting her know it would be too risky for her to return to London's theatreland yet. As I intimated, we're not yet quite ready to believe the Soviets have no further interest in her. We were delighted when, after making various enquiries, we discovered you were willing to board and care for her, and to advance her education.'

'One must do what one can to help asylum seekers such as Irena Leino,' said the headmistress, happy to know the costs were coming out of the public purse. 'I've thought it wise to agree with you in the matter of her identity. Until your people are able to inform me with certainty that she really is safe to become herself, I'll keep my promise not to reveal her real name. She has a natural intelligence, and a wish to study for the Oxford University entrance exam next year. Having tested her academically, I think next year might offer her that possibility, and I can inform you she finally started her first classes today.'

'Splendid,' said the gentleman. 'Of course, when she feels life really is safe for her, she may wish for the chance to resume her career. That could well bring her into the public eye. We shall consider that wish at the right time. Meanwhile, on the assumption that her embassy might still be interested in her whereabouts, despite assurances to the contrary, we're using means to point them in the direction of Edinburgh. One can't, however, guarantee they'll take the bait.'

'Well, Maiden Hall college is happy to be the protective factor of her present existence,' said the headmistress.

'We are grateful, Miss Stanton. You can assure me our charge has settled down to a reasonable extent?'

'I do assure you. She's a very composed and sensible young lady, and as I've already said, she's attending her first classes today.'

'Excellent. We must provide help and protection to any individuals who risk their lives to escape tyranny.'

'I could not agree more,' said Miss Stanton.

That wrapped up the conversation, and the gentleman departed soon afterwards, having enjoyed a second cup of tea and another biscuit.

At the end of the day's classes, the new student repaired with other boarders to their living quarters. Gemma, as a day girl, went home with a friend, while Cathy Davidson, also attending the college, had the usual pleasure of being walked home by James, who met her outside the gates. It was a dull and chilly afternoon, the grey sky beckoning the deeper grey of twilight. The old and the crotchety might be hugging their firesides or keeping close company with their central heating, but Cathy and James, vital with the quick blood circulation of healthy youth, took little notice of the cold. Cathy, intrigued by the advent of the student from Finland, simply had to tell James about her, that she was very stylish, and also very cool and composed. Well, most Scandinavian people, she suggested, were pretty cool, weren't they? They weren't temperamental, like Italians, for instance.

'So is this Finnish girl a bit of a stunner, by the way?' said James.

'To look at?' said Cathy. 'Well, she's so slender she looks boyish.'

'Boyish? Alas, poor woman,' said James.

'Poor woman?' said Cathy. 'What do you mean, poor woman?'

'I'm quoting Grandma Finch,' said James. 'It's what she always says about any female who's a bit lacking in – um – well, what can I say?'

'Don't bother, just fall over yourself,' said Cathy, far from boyish herself. 'Listen, have you heard your granny actually say what you said she says?'

'Well, no, I've just heard my dad mention

86

it,' said James. '"Alas, poor woman". Yep, that's it, that's what he said she says about any female a bit lacking.'

'I'm going to ask your dad if your granny actually uses the word alas,' said Cathy as they sauntered through the wintry grey. Neither of them thought of hurrying. They were at the stage of being very happy in each other's company. 'Honestly, James, I bet no-one's used it since Jane Austen finished writing her novels.'

'You sure?' said James. 'I mean, it's a useful warning that something woeful or dramatic is going to hit your ears.'

'But except for the way you've just said it, I've never heard you use it.'

'I could do.'

'Go on, then.'

'Alas that you couldn't make Cousin Jennifer's birthday last week.'

'But I did, you know I did.'

'So you did,' said James. 'Well, then, alas that I forgot.'

Cathy laughed. The sound travelled lightly through the dusk.

'Very witty, James,' she said.

'By the way, you looked great,' said James. 'Was your dress something from Paris?'

'No, something from Selfridges.'

'Well, what you brought back with you from Paris is pretty noteworthy,' said James. 'It must be your acquired French *oo là là*.'

'Have I heard of *oo là là?*' asked Cathy.

'Sure,' said James, 'it's the same as American oomph.'

'I've heard of American oomph, of course,' said Cathy.

'You've got a fair old share of both,' smiled James.

Cathy laughed again. This time the sound seemed to make the cold air tingle.

'How much d'you want for that kind of compliment?' she asked.

'Not a penny,' said James. 'Just tell me more about this Finnish girl.'

Cathy said Irena Leino had come from Helsinki in the hope that the college would help her to qualify for the Oxford University entrance exam next year, and James asked if she couldn't have qualified back in Finland. Cathy said well, it seemed she preferred to sit the exam here as soon as she was ready to, and the headmistress and staff would help her along. Mind, she was older than all the Senior B girls, being nineteen, but apparently she wasn't advanced enough in some subjects to sit for the exam this year.

'But she's very bright and eager to learn.'

'Well, I daresay you'll give her a helpful leg-up,' said James, and they stopped, having reached Cathy's home, the handsome retreat of her Aunt Marie. 'So long, then, Cathy, see you tomorrow.'

'James, thanks for walking me home so

often,' said Cathy.

'My pleasure,' said James, and they parted on that equable note. Their friendship wasn't one of teenage cuddles, kisses and pop talk. It was based on an earnest liking for each other, not on adolescent vibrations. If Cathy had once exaggerated matters in suggesting she and James were destined for the altar, those particular vibrations were now out of sight, sound and hearing. Cathy had grown up. That wasn't to say she didn't sometimes draw imaginative pictures about her future.

'James walked you home again, my dear?' said Aunt Marie, putting a book aside and looking up from her cosy armchair as Cathy entered the sitting room.

'Yes, James again,' said Cathy, bending to kiss her aunt.

'Is there something exciting going on between the two of you?'

'Well, if a happy friendship is exciting, Auntie, the answer's yes.'

'I see.' Aunt Marie did not pursue the subject. She knew that Cathy, since the resumption of her relationship with James, preferred to let it develop in its own way and not to push it. 'Have you enjoyed a worthwhile day at college?'

Cathy referred to the new student, a girl from Finland, and asked her aunt if she knew anything about the Finns. Aunt Marie said she had never known any, she only knew that Peter the Great conquered Finland and brought it under the control of Russia for a while. But regarding this Finnish girl, why was she attending Maiden Hall?

'She wants to sit an entrance exam to Oxford University,' said Cathy.

'Commendable, I suppose,' said Aunt Marie, 'although I'm not too fond of my adopted country allowing in too many strangers. The United Kingdom should remain exclusive to those who wish us well.' She was a naturalized British subject, with what Chinese Lady would have said was proper respect for the monarchy. 'Of course, I don't mean your new student from Finland wishes us ill, only that one can never tell these days what is in the mind of a stranger within our gates.' She meant these days of the cold war. 'However, shall we have some tea and biscuits, Cathy?'

'Super,' said Cathy. 'I'll pop along and tell Charles, shall I?'

'Thank you, dear.'

Gemma, of course, acquainted her parents with details of the new student while everyone was waiting for the evening meal to be served by Flossie, queen of the kitchen.

'From Finland, you say?' said Polly.

'Yes, kind of weird,' said Gemma.

'The young lady, she's weird?' said Polly.

'No, of course not, Mama,' said Gemma. 'I mean, it's weird because no-one at school has ever met a Finn or been to Finland or even had a Finnish penfriend.'

'How tragic,' said James ironically.

'What's the young lady like?' asked Boots.

'Oh, striking,' said Gemma, 'with long silky black hair parted down the middle, huge eyes and an Ingrid Bergman accent.'

'But not much of a figure,' said James.

'Cheeky ha'porth, how do you know?' asked Gemma.

'Cathy told me,' said James. 'That is, she mentioned that this young version of Greta Garbo hasn't–'

'Greta Garbo's Swedish, soppy,' said Gemma.

'I can't help that,' said James. 'I only know from what Cathy told me that this one's very boyish-looking on account of not having much of a figure.' His characteristic little grin escaped. 'Alas, poor woman,' he murmured.

Boots laughed. Gemma looked as if her dad and brother both needed a psychiatrist. Polly, however, was smiling. She knew how the saying had come about.

Gemma put in a good word for the student from Finland.

'Never mind that my brother's a bit strange sometimes,' she said, 'Irena Leino is very nice, even if she is a bit older than most of us in Senior B. We're all going to help her reach entrance exam standard. She's in love with all she's heard about Oxford's colleges for women. She told me so, and–'

'Dinner's coming up,' called Flossie, and the subject was dropped as the family made tracks for the dining room.

Boots brought it up again when he was preparing for bed that night. Coming out of the bathroom after his ablutions and the cleaning of his teeth, he spoke to Polly. Polly was already in bed and looking forward to the kind of sleep that would help to preserve her health and strength and keep wrinkles at bay.

'I've been thinking about Gemma's new classmate,' said Boots, slipping on his pyjama jacket.

'Spare me, old scout, if you're going to tell me the story of her life,' said Polly.

'She comes from Finland, Gemma said.'

'So?'

'She has long black hair.'

'So?' Polly yawned.

'The Finns are Scandinavian, and fair,' said Boots. 'Generally.'

'So?'

'Irena Leino, according to what Cathy told James, is not only dark but pretty flat-chested.'

'Should that young lady be talking about bosoms to our innocent son?' asked Polly.

'Scrub innocent, old girl,' said Boots, 'it's

1959, and young people are beginning to know it all. Some have already got there. Now, regarding the fact that this Finnish girl apparently lacks a bosom–'

'Yes, alas, poor woman, as James pointed out, but so what, old scout?'

'Many female gymnasts develop sinews instead of flesh,' said Boots.

Polly blinked.

'Ye gods,' she said, 'now I know what you're thinking, but could it actually be, and almost on our doorstep?'

'Out of pure curiosity, I'll make a phone call tomorrow,' said Boots. Switching off the bedside light, he slipped in beside Polly. Despite their shared moment of curiosity, after one more long day of active life, natural tendencies of the body drew them both into slumber quite soon. Boots dreamt dreams of the old days in Walworth, and Polly dreamt mathematically. That is, she found herself trying to count how many times she had shared her nights with Boots since their marriage. The answer eluded her, numbers tumbling about in hundreds of thousands but never staying still enough to be readable. But there was a moment when a million flashed up, and somehow that brought her awake.

A million? A million? Heavens, that would make them about five hundred years old.

Mr and Mrs Methuselah.

A little murmur of sleepy amusement made itself heard.

Then Mrs Methuselah went back to her slumber.

Chapter Seven

'Daniel,' said Patsy at breakfast on Thursday morning.

'Hearing you, Patsy,' said Daniel.

'Oh, super show, Daddy,' said ten-year-old Arabella, well into her cereal and orange juice. 'Mummy likes it when you're listening.'

'Daniel,' said Patsy, 'have you remembered that while the children are at school and you're at the office, I'm going up to town, and by train because Cousin Matthew is giving my car its first service?' She was referring to Cousin Rosie's husband, who owned and ran a garage. 'I'm having lunch with my old childhood buddy, Sadie Bergenbaur.'

'How d'you spell that?' asked Daniel, gulping hot coffee.

'Now, Daniel–'

'OK, I know you're going to have lunch with her,' said Daniel. 'Why not bring her home and have her stay for a couple of days?'

'I've been trying to persuade her, but she insists she's too busy,' said Patsy. 'As I've told you, she writes one-liners for a radio series back home, and is picking up material in London prior to the producer bringing an English character into the series. I'm lucky she's finding time to lunch with me today, as she hasn't even been able to keep a promise to visit old family relatives in Devon.'

'You're telling me an American Bergenbaur has got relatives in Devon?' said Daniel.

'I guess it happened somehow,' said Patsy. 'Anyway, we'll be having the roast beef of good old England at Simpsons in the Strand, and exchanging stories of how we've survived the earthquakes of war and change.'

'Is she married?' asked Daniel.

'Too busy for that,' said Patsy. 'Listen, good guy, so that I don't have to cut short my get-together with Sadie, you promised to leave the office early and be here in time to see to Arabella and Andrew when they arrive home from school.'

'Mummy, we can see to ourselves,' said Arabella.

'Well, I can,' said eight-year-old Andrew, now an outgoing lad after threatening for a few years to develop into a bit of an awkward and dour type, very uncharacteristic of an Adams offspring. Patsy had thought he was going to take after her pa's Midwest farming folks, who rarely spoke more than six words to each other during the course of a whole day.

'Done good?'

'Yep.'

'Hay dry?'

'Yep.'

'Tired?'

'Nope.'

That was their kind of conversation, but then life was good and solid out there in Kansas, so who needed talk?

Some people thought the Adams men, women and kids needed it every minute of every day.

Patsy smiled at her son's declaration. 'Sure you and Arabella can see to yourselves,' she said, 'but I'm reminding your pa he's still got certain obligations.'

'Noted, sugarbush,' said Daniel, rising to his feet. 'You have a great time in Simpsons with Sadie Whatsit, and I'll be back home by three thirty to take care of the kids.'

'Well, thanks, Daddy,' said Arabella, objecting to 'kids'.

'So long now, everyone,' said Daniel, and delivered kisses all round before departing in the direction of the firm's offices. Once there, he asked his Uncle Boots if he'd ever met any people by the name of Bergenbaur.

'One or two,' said Boots.

'Down in Devon?'

'Devon?' said Boots, who'd been thinking of his time in Germany.

'Devon,' repeated Daniel.

'I pass,' said Boots, which was his usual

thinking of response to questions he considered unanswerable.

During the morning, a member of the staff of a daily paper took a phone call from a reader. He listened to an enquiry.

'No problem,' he said, 'hold on and I'll give you the answer in a couple of ticks.' He came back on the line after only forty-five seconds, which was a very acceptable equivalent for a couple of ticks. Sometimes, under some circumstances, a couple of ticks could last for half an hour in the hive of a national daily, where the spoken word was as prolific as the written. 'Hello there?'

'I'm here.'

'Good,' said the newspaperman. 'I can tell you they came to London from Helsinki, where they'd competed in a meeting. In London they gave a display at Olympia.'

'Many thanks,' said Boots.

'You're welcome.'

So, thought Boots as he replaced his phone, the Russian gymnastic teams reached London from Finland, and it was in London that one gymnast defected and asked for asylum. Very interesting. Very.

The work-shy old tramp known as Dodgy Dan was talking to himself as he set out from a Bermondsey hostel to the bus stop. I think I'll try Waterloo station again, he mused. Me life's been a corblimey hard luck story this last year or so, starting with nearly being done to death by some raving female cow up by Herne Hill, and followed by interfering ticket inspectors shutting me off from making an honest living on their railway platforms. (His idea of an honest living was to wait for a train to come in and then to nick anything left behind in an overhead rack, but railway officials had been onto this lark for more than a few months now.) I ain't been able to get anywhere near a standing train since I don't know when. I dunno I fancy going back to picking pockets, the law's ruddy criminal in what it does to a bloke if he's fingered. It's the Scrubs for six months, and no option. It's me personal belief that the law ought to be done away with. Well, who's going to miss it? Only rich toffs that lose a bit of their oof to hard-up blokes like Spiky Lemmon now and again. (Spiky Lemmon was an incurable burglar who had done over burglarproof houses in districts as posh as Ascot, and was now unfortunately doing seven years in Brixton Prison on account of same.) Don't they have no feeling for the poor and starving?

'It's a ruddy liberty,' he murmured to the cold morning air of Bermondsey, once a place of huge bomb sites and now a rising phoenix of redevelopment, mostly concrete.

'Watcher, Dan.'

Dodgy Dan quivered as someone fell into step with him. He took a look.

'Fornicating Eskimos if it ain't you,' he said. It was too. It was young Curly Harris the Knife all right, never mind that other people might not have recognized him dressed up in a high-class raincoat and with his hair barbered. The raincoat was one Dodgy Dan himself had sold to Curly after swiping it off a rack in a standing train. 'Here, you've 'ad yer hair cut.'

'Shut yer gob about that.'

'All right, all right, but been on a week's 'oliday, have yer?'

'Mind yer bleedin' biz.'

Dodgy Dan, not wanting to get partially sliced by the quick-tempered Curly, humbled himself.

'Sorry, sorry. But you after something, are yer?'

'Just a chat.'

'What about?'

'The Old Bill. You been talking to 'em?'

'Me? Talking to the fuzz?'

'Have yer? I heard something I didn't like.'

'Now listen, Curly–'

'Button yer lip.'

'All right, so you don't want yer moniker mentioned.' They both slowed as they approached the bus stop, taking care not to come within hearing distance of the small queue. 'Listen, the cops talked to me, didn't

100

they? That ain't the same as me talking to them, which I never do, nor ain't since I was seven and asked one of 'em to see me across the road in Peckham. And what 'appened? Nearly got run over, didn't I?'

'Did they talk to you about me?'

'Asked if I knew a bloke by the name of Curly Harris. Never 'eard of him, I said. And of course, I ain't, have I?'

'Not if you don't want yer left leg chopped off.'

'Which I don't. 'Ere, they asked Spongy as well.' Spongy was the hostel's warden, well known for soaking up his drink without it making any difference to his legs. Real name, Arthur Gumbridge. 'And he said what I said, that he'd never 'eard of yer.'

'Nor will he. I had a word with him, like I'm having with you.'

'Listen, I'm one of yer mates, ain't I? Didn't I sell yer that high-class raincoat for just a couple of bob? Suits yer too, I 'ardly recognized yer–'

'Shut yer face, button yer lip and keep it buttoned,' growled Curly Harris. And off he went, much to Dodgy Dan's relief. Well, the young bleeder was bound to still be carrying that knife of his, the knife he was a bit too handy with. That and his short fuse made him the kind of cove no-one wanted as his best friend. It was a flaming miracle that so far he hadn't got a police record.

Dodgy Dan, still musing, reached the bus queue and joined it. The queue immediately pushed forward in a small body, since the newcomer definitely looked like one of those down-and-outs noted for passing on their fleas.

'Problems?' whispered Gemma Adams to Irena Leino. The class was engaged in the study of early twentieth-century history, and had been set an essay on the campaigns of the suffragettes.

'Problems, ah, yes,' whispered Irena. 'Please to say the name of the leader.'

'Mrs Emmeline Pankhurst,' breathed Gemma.

'Yes, but 'ow to spell it?'

Gemma whispered the spelling. Miss Burnaby, history teacher, looked up from her desk.

'Unauthorized talking during my classes is out,' she said. 'Kindly note that, Gemma Adams.'

'Yes, miss.'

'Tell Irena Leino so.'

'Yes, miss.'

The two girls had a word during the mid-morning break, when Irena said she would like to get out of the college sometimes. Gemma said boarders had to ask permission and to say where they were going and when they would be back. Irena would find, however, that they wouldn't be allowed to go up to the West End unless it was with someone as responsible as a parent or one of the teachers.

'No, no, the West End I am not permitted,' said Irena. She meant not yet. 'I would simply like to go for a walk.'

'After classes?' said Gemma. 'Not much fun in this winter weather, and pretty dark as well by five.'

'I think a Saturday would be nice,' said Irena.

'That's more like it,' said Gemma, 'I could walk you to the nicest parts, and Cathy could come with us to make a jolly threesome. Let's ask her.'

'Most kind,' said Irena.

Cathy, when approached, said next Saturday morning would be fine with her, and mornings were best, anyway, at this time of the year. Irena only needed to ask Miss Stanton for permission.

'Ah, yes, a nice woman,' said Irena, 'and like a mother to me.'

'But she wouldn't let you out by yourself,' said Cathy, 'not while you're so new to everything.'

Irena, big-eyed, smiled.

'She has said I would lose myself.'

At that point a ringing bell called all students back to their classrooms.

'Hoppit,' said the ticket inspector at the barrier of Platform 4, Waterloo railway station, south of Waterloo Bridge. The concourse was a place of hustle and bustle beneath the vast iron and glass canopy. 'Hoppit, d'you hear?'

'Here, I got a platform ticket, ain't I, and I'm expecting to meet a relation on the next train in, ain't I?' complained Dodgy Dan amid the sounds of hissing steam.

'You've got a platform ticket, but you're not expecting any relation. More like a gent's brolly or a valuable parcel, or some such item left behind by a passenger. Listen, old clever clogs, you wore that lark out long ago. Consider yourself lucky you haven't been run in. Just hoppit.'

Dodgy Dan protested in effect that he was being unlawfully victimized. What he actually said was, 'Here, don't come it on an innocent party.' He went on to complain that it was getting ruddy hard for a bloke to make an honest living, and if things didn't improve he'd think of emigrating.

'And I ain't joking,' he said bitterly.

'Emigrating to where?' asked the ticket inspector.

'Monte Carlo, where else?'

'It's full up, Dan, try Dartmoor. They've got free board and lodging there.'

'Think I'm daft, do yer?' said Dodgy Dan, noting through the barrier the slow approach of the expected train. If there was something to be picked up, he could hide it under his jumble-sale overcoat, and the law, as represented by this bossy ticket inspector, need never catch sight of it. 'Here, come on, let me see if me Cousin Vi's aboard, she's sort of dear to me and I ain't seen her since I got back wounded from Dunkirk.'

'For the last time, hoppit.'

'Now look–' Dodgy Dan let it go then, seeing the ticket inspector was signalling to a member of the railway police. Off he went at a kind of shambling trot. If this sort of thing keeps happening, he told himself, I'll starve to death, unless I can click for a bit of social welfare, which I could if I had a doctor's certificate. If not, ruddy suffering orphans, I might even have to take a job cleaning up pavements, which won't do me no good at all. I could fall down dead. I think I'll try Charing Cross. It ain't far and it's me last hope for the morning.

The train, chugging in from the wilds of the south-east suburbs, came to an unhurried stop. Passengers already on their feet opened doors and began descending to the platform. Those alighting from the far coaches passed a bristly-chinned citizen wearing a shapeless hat and an overcoat that could already have been well past its best at the time when King Edward VIII was making up his mind to abdicate the throne in favour of bedtime with Mrs Simpson.

Dodgy Dan had made it onto the platform with a ticket, and was now beginning to do his stuff, putting his peepers to work on vacated compartments. Talk about instant luck, and good fortune favouring the poor and starving, like. In only the third compartment from the end, a superior-looking white carrier bag sat forgotten on a rack. The name of its source was printed in Oxford blue: Allders of Croydon.

Into the compartment went Dodgy Dan, and out he came again in the twinkling of an eye, the bag under his coat. He joined passengers heading for the barrier. Out from a compartment midway down the standing train stepped an attractive woman in a round black fur hat and a fawn-coloured coat with a black fur collar. Her movement was spring-heeled.

Dodgy Dan spotted her and his recognition was immediate, even though it had been well over a year since he'd last seen her. Holy cows, he hissed to his startled self, it's her, it's that mad female bruiser from Herne Hill, the one that nearly done me to death when all I was after was a look around her fully detached to see what her silver was like.

As for Patsy, saints alive, she thought, I know that face and that shifty look. It's him.

Who'd have thought I'd ever see him again? What's he after, picking a few pockets or doing a handbag snatch?

Amid the outgoing stream of passengers, she followed him, although more out of curiosity than malicious intent.

Dodgy Dan, however, sensing she was on his tail, thought she was going to do him a bit of no good again, such as calling for a cop and charging him with attempted breaking and entering. So he got a move on, hustling his way through the crowd of passengers. He did a hasty feel for his platform ticket with the idea of making a quick handover at the barrier. The movement caused the superior-looking carrier bag to fall from under his coat. It dropped at his feet and nearly tangled them up. He did a quick if clumsy shuffle and kept going. Best not to be found with the goods on his person if that spiteful female put the railway cops on him.

'Hi!' Someone called after him. 'Hi, you've dropped your carrier bag!'

He still kept going. Patsy still kept her eyes on him. He reached the crowd milling at the barrier and he flashed his platform ticket at the inspector.

'Here y'ar, mate,' he said.

'Half a mo, mister, here's your carrier bag,' called the someone who had picked the bag up. A young man. 'You dropped it.'

'Hey, that's mine! I forgot it, I left it on the train!' The cry came from a well-dressed woman.

'No, sorry, lady, I saw this old gent drop it,' said the young man as the milling at the barrier thickened. The inspector was ignoring Dodgy Dan's outstretched hand and proffered platform ticket. It wasn't a discriminatory gesture. He was ignoring all tickets and calling for a bit of order. The woman was having none of that, obviously suspecting that a bit of order would result in the complete disappearance of the bag. She began to push her way into the mill.

'I tell you, that carrier bag's mine,' she shouted at the young man. 'And I tell you again, I left it in my compartment in the last coach of the train.'

'Well, come on, mister, is it yours or hers?' bawled the young man to the back of Dodgy Dan's head. It was noticeable that people closest to the tramp were doing their best to back off from his whiffy self. Patsy, an interested spectator, was hovering on the edge of the bunched passengers. 'Come on, listen up!' yelled the young man.

Putting on a deaf act, Dodgy Dan addressed the ticket inspector, while Patsy kept her eye on him from the perimeter of the crowd.

'Here, look, mate, can't yer let me through?' he said. 'I got an urgent appointment to keep with me lawyer.'

'I'm not letting anyone through until the rightful owner of that carrier bag is found,' said the railway official.

'It's me, I'm the owner!' shouted the woman, now wedged in but still purposeful. 'It's a purchase I made at a Croydon store.'

That, of course, was obvious. The name of the store was clearly visible. A City type spoke to the ticket inspector.

'May I suggest the rightful owner can be established by naming what the purchase was?'

'Madam?' said the official to the woman.

'I object,' she said.

'There you are,' said the young man to Dodgy Dan, 'she's objecting, so you name the goods.'

'Someone talking to me?' said Dodgy Dan to no-one special.

'Oh, all right,' said the woman, 'it's a black corset, but I'm not inviting anyone to wave it about.' She glanced at the official. 'You take a look.'

The ticket inspector, receiving the bag from the young man, paused to give Dodgy Dan a keener perusal.

'I know you,' he said.

'Me?' said Dodgy Dan plaintively. 'Me?'

'Come on!' howled an irritated and frustrated passenger. 'Get cracking and let us through!'

The ticket inspector opened the carrier bag. He saw a white cardboard box.

'Don't you dare touch it!' called the woman.

'Just taking a look, madam,' said the ticket inspector, and peered. He noted printed details on the box, details that satisfied him. 'Right, it's yours.' He handed the bag over the heads of people and the woman reclaimed it. 'Sorry for the delay, ladies and gents, you can all go through now.' He stood aside. 'No, not you.' He tapped Dodgy Dan on the shoulder, then signalled to another official. As the delayed passengers surged through, he said, 'You'll have to explain how you got hold of that lady's goods.'

Dodgy Dan simply did a bunk. Patsy, free of the barrier, watched him doing a shambling gallop. Unfortunately for his peace of mind, the alerted official blocked his path. Patsy, a smile on her face, might have stopped to tell the official that she knew something shady about the tramp. But as she heard him protesting that he was a wounded war hero trying to earn an honest living, she allowed her sense of humour to prevail, and she simply passed by, leaving the official to deal with the old humbug as he thought fit. She herself was content with the walloping she had handed out some time ago.

Chapter Eight

'Patsy, I never did see you looking so good,' said Sadie Bergenbaur. She and Patsy were lunching on roast beef at Simpsons in the Strand. Sadie was Patsy's age, thirty-one, and they had known each other since their high-school days in Boston, but whereas Patsy had elected, in effect, to disappear from the mainstream of Boston life by going to the UK with her pa and then marrying some old-fashioned English guy, Sadie had launched herself into the excitements of a career on the airwaves, and was now a scriptwriter for radio shows. Patsy in appearance still retained much of the health and vitality of an all-American cheerleader, while Sadie looked keen, sharp and inquisitive, as if she was invariably nosing her way into something she could make use of in a script. She had been regaling Patsy with her experiences of London life and London characters during her week-long search for material that would give a humorous English angle to an established radio sitcom series. 'Living in the UK suits you, Patsy?'

'Sure,' said Patsy, 'as long as I'm not asked to sort out its problems.'

'You wouldn't run for President, then?' said Sadie.

'President?' said Patsy, helping herself to a little more horseradish sauce.

'I heard tell that when Queen Liz's time is up, the UK will turn into a republic, with a female president following the female monarch, and setting up office in Buck House.'

Patsy laughed.

'Sadie, you've been taken in by one of London's born comics,' she said. 'Let me guess, you heard that from a bus conductor or a doorman.'

'Do I count for the booby's prize if I tell you it was confided to me by a cab driver?' said Sadie, cutting herself a portion from her sliced beef and forking it home. She chewed with the relish of a woman who hadn't yet allowed pressure of work to upset her appetite and give her ulcers. 'I've spent a week making myself palsy-walsy with Londoners, and picking up what I've come for, material for a genuine English angle to this radio series that still goes out in prime time. Genuine, I guess, only if I've understood the natives. Darned if I can make out what some of London's famous cockneys are saying. It all reaches the ear in a hell of a hurry.'

'Daniel will tell you—'

'Daniel?'

'My guy.'

'Oh, yes, sure. So?'

'He'll tell you cockneys talk their own kind of lingo. You get to understand it, given time. Farther up, in the north-east of this old island the people there are called Geordies, and I can personally vouch for the fact that the English they speak is definitely understood only by other Geordies.'

'Patsy–' Sadie paused to allow their waiter to refill their wine glasses. 'Thanks.'

'My pleasure, madam,' said the waiter, one of the well-trained stalwarts of this dining establishment of unfailing Edwardian decor and enduring popularity.

'Patsy,' said Sadie, 'I believe your pa mentioned to me that the family you married into has connections with London's cockneys.'

'Oh, sure,' said Patsy, 'the family elders. They were brought up by Daniel's grandmother in a cockney district called Walworth, on the south side of London Bridge. But I guess you could say they've talked themselves out of the basic accents. They're easy to understand.' She went on to mention that one of the uncles, nicknamed Boots, had the kind of mellow baritone that would slay most American women. Also, as she had gradually found out during her time as one of the family, all the children of the aunt and uncles had had what the British called a grammar-school education, which helped them do justice to their own language. A British grammar school was the equivalent of an American high school. The improved way of life of the Adams clan was due to their perseverance in working to better themselves. They'd made the grade from working class to middle class. Grandma Finch–'

'Grandma Finch?' said Sadie.

'Yes, Daniel's paternal granny,' said Patsy, refraining from mentioning that the matriarch was actually Lady Finch. Sadie might think she was upping her standing as a granddaughter-in-law. Or, more likely, she would want to meet the redoubtable old lady in the hope of catching some jewels falling from her lips. Grandma Finch, Patsy went on, was the fount of the family's ability to make the most of life. She had watched and supervised the progress of her descendants from the time her daughter and sons began to fight their way out of the UK's breadline to become the prosperous, civilized and encouraging parents of their own children. Daniel, for instance, was the eldest son of Grandma Finch's youngest son, Sammy, a natural entrepreneur and the driving force behind the family business. As for Daniel himself, not even on the campus of Boston University would Sadie find a more outgoing fun guy.

'That's your Daniel?' said Sadie.

'Oh, we're equally lucky,' smiled Patsy. 'I have him and he has me. I'm not just a sugar doll.'

'I like it, Patsy, that you're aware of your own worth,' said Sadie.

'Sure,' said Patsy. 'Incidentally, as well as each other we have our kids. That makes for some kind of happy ever after. Listen, are you thinking of using a London cockney character in your radio series? Is that why you're concentrating your research here?'

'Oh, nothing will be decided until I get back to Boston and talk to our producer,' said Sadie.

'Outside of your scriptwriting, you're still unattached, Sadie?'

'You know me, Patsy, I'm hooked on my job. But I'm pleased you're doing fine with Daniel and your kiddos. I know you've been back home with them a few times, so how does Daniel rate America?'

'He's given it top marks,' said Patsy, finishing her main course and taking an appreciative swallow of wine. 'He mentioned to me once that he wouldn't have minded being born a Wild West cowboy along with John Wayne, except that then he might have missed meeting me. In which case, he said, he'd never have known if his horse and saddle would have been as meaningful to his life as me and my cooking.'

'I like that, I could work on how to use it,'

said Sadie, still looking sharp and keen despite the well-being that lunch or dinner at Simpsons usually induced in its patrons. 'And I'm getting a feeling I'd make a mistake if I didn't get to meet Daniel and interview him.'

'There you are, then,' said Patsy, 'why not come home with me and stay for a couple of days? We'd be happy to have you before you fly back to Boston.'

'Patsy, I'm gonna take you up on that,' said Sadie, 'and not just because it'll be great seeing you alive and well in your UK home. It'll also give me the opportunity to catch the sights and sounds of an English middle-class family in their daily round of living. That's if we can first call in at my hotel for me to pick up a few things.'

'Of course,' said Patsy, and the decision so pleased both of them that they allowed their waiter to tempt them into enjoying a dessert consisting of ye olde English syrup pudding served with cream. The cream countered the sweet richness of the syrup.

It has to be mentioned, however, that when they were lingering over coffee and liqueurs, Sadie did say she'd have to fast for a week.

By the time Patsy arrived home, with Sadie in tow, Daniel had achieved the upper hand with Arabella and Andrew, and they were

116

both in the kitchen, helping him to prepare supper for the three of them, Patsy having let him know in advance that she wouldn't be interested in food herself. The kitchen didn't look as it usually did. It was full up with father, daughter, son, youthful enthusiasm and potato peelings, half of which were in a bowl on the table, and half on the floor.

'How's it going, folks?' said Patsy, breezing in. 'Looks fine from here. Carry on, Daniel – oh, meet my old buddy Sadie Bergenbaur. She's here to stay with us until first thing Sunday morning. Then she has to scoot. Sadie, meet Daniel.'

Sadie saw a lanky man with dark brown hair, lively blue eyes and an easy smile. He wore no jacket. In its place was a plain and practical apron. For his part, Daniel saw a slender dark-eyed woman with sharp but pleasant features. She wore a brown leather coat and a soft-peaked black leather cap.

'Hi, Daniel,' she said.

'And how's yourself?' said Daniel, shaking hands with her.

'How's myself?' said Sadie, taking note of his vocal vibrations. 'I'm great right now.'

'Personally, I look better out of this apron,' said Daniel. 'But never mind that, meet the kids, Arabella and Andrew.'

'Hi, kids,' said Sadie, 'treat me as an aunt.'

'We've already got lots of aunts,' said Andrew.

'OK,' said Sadie, 'count me as one more.'

'Oh, thanks,' said Arabella.

'Don't let's hang about, folks,' said Patsy, 'Sadie needs a shower and a change, so we'll talk later. Come on, Sadie, this way.'

She took her guest upstairs, Sadie carrying a valise containing some of her belongings. In the kitchen, Arabella said, 'Daddy, can we really call her Aunt Sadie?'

'Well, it'll be easier than calling her Miss Bergenblower,' said Daniel, cutting up leeks.

'Crikey, all that?' said Andrew.

'Correctly, I think it's Bergenbaur,' said Daniel.

Patsy re-entered the kitchen. She'd left Sadie to make herself at home in the spare bedroom, after pointing her at the bathroom and shower.

'What's cooking for your suppers, Daniel?'

'The leftovers of yesterday's meat pie, but the veggies are fresh,' said Daniel.

'And what are you two doing to help?' asked Patsy of Arabella and Andrew.

'We've peeled the potatoes,' said Arabella.

'Silly question,' murmured Patsy, noting the evidence. 'Daniel, sometime Sadie would like to meet Grandma and Grandpa Finch. She wants to find out if your most revered relatives can provide her with a real old-fashioned English angle to her radio scripts.'

118

'Well, if they can't,' said Daniel, 'nobody can, not even Sir Francis Drake.'

'Daniel, you kook, Drake's long gone,' said Patsy.

'Is that a fact?' said Daniel, placing the leek segments in a cooking dish. 'Nobody told me. I get a feeling sometimes that I'm short of information. I'll end up dead ignorant. Oh, well, if Drake's gone, we still have our revered ones. Sadie couldn't ask for more.'

'Arabella sweetie, Andrew honey, take note that your father's still cute,' said Patsy.

'Mummy, I don't think Daddy likes being called cute,' said Arabella.

'I know,' said Patsy, 'but it's the only way I can get even with him for being a smarty-pants.'

By nine, Arabella and Andrew were in bed, and Sadie was deep in converse with Daniel, liking the sound of his vowels and his aptitude for making the kind of comments that held a promise of being turned into one-liners for an English character. Patsy, having had a long day, was happy enough to relax and to let Daniel take the full weight of Sadie's enthusiastic venture into the life of her family. She actually drifted off a little after ten and had a jerky dream about a flea-bitten tramp trying to insinuate himself into her house by way of the letter box. His head kept poking through, and she kept knocking

119

it back with her egg saucepan. Eventually the letter box expanded and all of him tumbled in, only for the ceiling to fall on him and smother him beneath a mountain of plaster. At which point she woke up, found it was nearly eleven and that Sadie and Daniel were still talking to each other, Sadie as keen as ever.

Patsy blinked.

'Where am I?' she asked.

'At home,' smiled Daniel.

'And back with Danny and me,' said Sadie.

'So sorry, I don't usually nod off, especially if we're entertaining,' said Patsy.

'Not to worry,' said Daniel.

Patsy, yawning, said, 'Well, while I've still got the strength, I'll take myself up to bed. OK to leave you two to carry on with your happy talk?'

'It's OK with me,' said Sadie.

'Is Daniel pointing you at some useful English one-liners?' asked Patsy.

'By the dozen,' said Sadie.

So Patsy left them to it and retired to bed. She did not wake up until the alarm went off.

Chapter Nine

Over breakfast.

'Exactly what time last night did you two call it a day?' asked Patsy of Daniel and Sadie.

'A little after midnight,' said Daniel, 'by which time I was cuckoo, and Sadie was still a powerhouse.'

'I'll take that as a compliment,' said Sadie, still keen and alert.

'You and my pa are two of a kind,' smiled Daniel. 'Your engines never blow.'

'Crikey,' said Arabella, 'what's that mean, I wonder?'

'Search me,' said Andrew, making himself sound grown-up.

'Sadie's meeting Pa this morning,' said Daniel to Patsy. 'And Uncle Boots. She's coming to the office with me for the morning, and I'll get Pa to let her wander round picking up office one-liners. The family can't do less for your old school chum, Patsy.'

'I'll be tickled, you bet,' said Sadie. 'Patsy, you sure you don't mind if I bomb off with Danny? I'll find some lunch and then get back to you.'

'You go ahead, I'll just stay home myself

and have an exciting time defrosting the fridge,' said Patsy, feeling slightly miffed. 'Oh, and maybe I'll sweep the garage out as well.'

'Mummy, Daddy did that last weekend,' said Arabella.

'Well, I'll see if he did the corners,' said Patsy.

'Watch out for the cobwebs,' said Daniel.

'Cobwebs like garage corners,' said Andrew.

'So do the spiders,' said Patsy.

'Patsy, garage corners count as grounds for an argument?' commented Sadie, breakfasting on cereal and some of Patsy's homemade fruit buns. Like many New Englanders, she enjoyed a sweet breakfast. 'I like that, and I'll make a note.'

'Glad to be an inspiration,' said Patsy.

However, some time after the children had set off for school, and Daniel had gone to the offices with Sadie, there was no thought in her mind about defrosting the fridge. Instead she phoned Polly, and Polly invited her to coffee.

Dodgy Dan woke up late. Well, yesterday had been a gorblimey strain. It had begun with Curly Harris the Knife threatening his wellbeing, then being chucked out of Waterloo station, good as, and then getting mixed up in all that worrying stuff at Charing

Cross, which included being spotted by that aggravating and dangerous female who'd tried to put him in hospital a while ago. She'd followed him down the platform, and there'd been all that argy-bargy at the gate, which resulted in him losing a nice parcel of goods that he'd honestly won by finding it lying about in a rack. After which he'd been stopped by a bossy piece of railway fuzz and asked all kinds of interfering questions about his private life and his source of income. Talk about a liberty-taking carry-on. If a parcel or two had come his way at somewhere like a railway station now and again, it was nobody's business but his own. Finders keepers, that was what honest people believed in. Of course, the fuzz couldn't hold him, but they kept on at him until he was fair worn out, and had had to go to the station buffet and pay for a hot cup of char to stop himself falling down and being swept up.

But what finally turned the day into his worst ever was getting back to the hostel to find his locker had been broken open. A feature of this particular hostel was that its founder, some geezer called Percy Parsons, had provided for every inmate to have a free room, a free bed, a free breakfast and a locker in which to safely stow any kind of valuables a bloke might just possess. And only the warden had the keys, an individual one for each locker, so if you wanted to open it he had to do it for you.

There'd been money in his locker. Not just a quid or two, but real oof. As much as nearly fifteen quid, in fact. Savings for his old age and all honestly come by from what he'd found in train compartments, and in ladies' open handbags when they were shopping down Petticoat Lane or other street markets.

He'd gone to the office of the warden, the beery geezer name of Arthur Gumbridge but known as Spongy.

'Here, d'you know me locker's been busted?'

'Eh? What?' Spongy looked worried. One of his chief responsibilities was to make sure no inmate's locker was interfered with. That meant he had to watch the movements of anyone entering and wandering. 'Listen, that sort of thing ain't allowed. What did yer bust it for when you know I've got the key?'

'If that's supposed to be funny, I ain't laughing,' said Dodgy Dan, issuing blue sparks. 'Come on, who's been 'ere while I've been out? Answer up, warden, or I'll report yer to the Board for allowing illegal entrance to me room and me locker.'

'Here, don't you come the old acid with me,' said Spongy, but he was sweating a bit, aware that his vigilance could never be called sharp. 'All right, listen, there's only been one visitor – your old mate that told

124

me he was leaving a keepsake on your bed for old times' sake, like. If it was him that did your locker over, he didn't tell me. And knowing you and him were mates, I trusted him, didn't I?'

'Who yer talking about?'

'I told you, your old mate. Curly.'

'Curly Harris?'

'That's him.'

'He's no bleedin' mate of mine, I've just sold him one or two things, that's all. And now he's done me for me goods and chattels, 'as he?'

'Don't look at me,' said the warden, 'I'm only telling you I think it was Curly, but I'm not reporting it official. Curly's got a nasty temper, and the Board's strict about me duties.'

'That's your 'ard luck,' said Dodgy Dan, his heart bleeding.

'Look, I'll give you five bob not to report it to the Board.'

Dodgy Dan took the five bob, of course, but it didn't cure what was lying heavy on his mind. His locker busted and done over by that young bleeder Curly Harris. Well, sod that, Curly Harris had got to be done over himself, never mind who he might suspect and go after.

Point is, how do I keep out of his way once he's out of clink? Or if he slips the fuzz? Blackpool, yus, that's the answer. I can soon learn to speak the language, and I'll be able to sleep at nights, seeing the place is hundreds of miles from Curly when he's in an aggravated state, which he will be. I ought to be able to get there by train without buying a ticket. Well, a platform ticket at the most. And besides, with Easter not more than a month or so away, the holiday season will be starting, and Blackpool's railway station will be full up with arriving trains several times a day, and who knows what might be up for a bit of honest loot on overhead racks? Enough, I reckon, to pay a landlady for me rent and leave a bit over for me living expenses and me new piggy bank.

I suppose I'd better have a shave before I go, when I go. I've heard some Blackpool landladies are a bit fussy. Best to look a bit of all right, I suppose.

'Daniel's taken her to the offices so she can spend the morning tuning into English office chat?' said Polly, gracefully draped over a settee upholstered in ruby-red velour.

'Well, I did promise her that Daniel and I would do what we could to help her build up a portfolio of comments and customs that she'd use to convert into English one-liners,' said Patsy, comfortably at ease in an armchair that matched the settee. She enjoyed a lively relationship with Polly. Unlike most younger members of the

Adams clan, she found her stimulating. 'American situation comedies on the radio are built around one-liners. Our radio's built around *Mrs Dale's Diary*.'

'I'm fascinated,' said Polly, sipping coffee made by Flossie. 'Boots has strong views on how people in radio and television earn their money. The dear man feels they generally favour bad news over good when looking for a major story. Let me say, Patsy old thing, it might be better if your friend Sadie, very much a radio personality, it seems, didn't cross His Lordship's path.'

'That could turn out to be an eye-opener for Sadie,' said Patsy, 'and the prospect certainly tickles me, although if I know Boots, it's my guess he'll let her down lightly.'

'Hello, I thought you might drop in, Miss Bergenbaur,' said Boots, rising to greet the lady keen to pick up usable quips and sallies from the staff and executives of a typical English business house.

'Call me Sadie, Mr Adams. Great to meet you. I've already heard from some of the girls here that you're the equivalent of every woman's dream man.'

'Every woman's dream man with a reasonable amount of sense knows he couldn't live up to the dreams of a real woman,' said Boots, 'which is why he does a

127

bunk as soon as she wakes up.'

'Excuse me?' said Sadie. Then, 'Oh, right. Sure.' She laughed. 'I get it.'

'Hang on to it, then,' said Boots, and Sadie regarded him with quickening interest. Daniel had told her he was over sixty, but she'd have put on her very best outfit if he'd asked for a date. Come to that, she'd have done the same for Daniel.

'Do you have any funnies I could note, Mr Adams?'

'I don't know if this one is funny,' said Boots, 'but it's in your own field. The radio announcer had a little son who said his prayers every night and always concluded with, "And here, dear God, are the headlines again."'

Sadie trilled with receptive delight.

'I like that, you bet I do,' she said, 'but I was thinking more of a typical English funny taking in an English office boss.'

'Believe me, Miss Bergenbaur,' said Boots, 'anyone able to take in my brother Sammy, overall boss of this business, could be voted in as the first President of Trafalgar Square and its pigeons.'

Sadie trilled again, while wondering if his wife could spare him for a quick weekend in Paris, which thought impelled her to let him know she'd had a great time during her visit to the French capital two years ago. She'd found it very much as it was during her first

128

visit in '38, when her parents had taken her on a vacation to Europe.

'It hadn't changed, not by one brick, Mr Adams.'

'I'm not surprised,' said Boots, 'it was the only capital in Europe that escaped bombing raids.'

'Well, I guess that's something to note. Mr Adams–'

'Hi there.' Daniel interrupted, as pre-arranged. He was at the open door. Boots gave him a nod.

'Yes, we've finished, Daniel.'

'Fair enough,' said Daniel. 'This way, Sadie, and I'll take you to see my Uncle Sammy for a quick chat now that he's free.'

'Oh, sure, but–'

'This way,' said Daniel, and relieved Boots of her hungering presence.

As for Sammy, after haunting her for five minutes with his electric blue eyes and obligingly exchanging some bright repartee with the keen lady, he informed her he knew not a monkey's uncle about one-liners. In fact, he didn't even know what they were, he said, but supposed them to be something like detachable paper inner linings for spring coats on a cold day, and that they were thrown away after a single wearing. So if Miss Bigginbare would excuse him he'd get down to looking after the firm's overheads and the current profit and loss situation. All of which sent Sadie pie-eyed in a fascinated kind of way, although she did wonder if he was real and if, accordingly, she could work in an anecdote based on an English boss who'd run his head against a wall sometime during his developing years.

Daniel then took her up to the top floor to see the bookkeepers. He'd leave her there, he said, to digest their comical comments on invoices and petty cash vouchers.

On the way, Sadie said, 'I guess I can talk again with your two bosses?'

'Don't bet on it,' said Daniel, 'they're always up to their eyeballs in work.'

Sadie sighed a little, then said, 'OK, I'll stick with you, Danny.'

'I'll be going out after lunch to visit our shop in Streatham,' said Daniel. 'We're having it enlarged, and I'm meeting our architect there. Before I go, I'll call up a taxi that'll take you back to Patsy.'

'I appreciate that, Danny,' said Sadie, stopping on the landing with him, 'but I think I'll pick up more for my notebook if I go to this shop with you. You're a sweetie, and I can't miss the chance of meeting up with an English architect.'

Daniel asked if she really wouldn't prefer to spend the afternoon with Patsy, and Sadie said she'd spent nearly all day yesterday with her, so she'd still stick with him. So Daniel perforce had to invite her to join him for lunch in the firm's cafeteria before making the journey to Streatham. For which Sadie gave him the kind of smile she usually reserved for men who could take her mind off her work and make her think positive about what a moonlit bedroom was for.

Daniel, putting himself at a safe distance from her smile, showed her into the book-keepers' office and left her to pick up anything that would help her give birth to hilarious one-liners on the double entry system.

'Hi, folks,' said Patsy when Daniel and Sadie arrived back from their day at the office at six o'clock. Daniel landed an affectionate smacker on Patsy's lips, then went at once in search of the kids, much as if what he most needed in place of a sophisticated American scriptwriter was five minutes of being alone with childish simplicity. 'What kept you, Sadie?' asked Patsy.

'Oh, this afternoon your guy took me to one of the firm's stores in a suburb called Streatham,' said Sadie. It was a great outing, she said, and a real cute little fashion store, where Danny chewed the fat with an architect and she did the same with the manageress, the assistants and the customers. Danny, she said, was just about the most helpful guy ever, giving up a lot of his working time to put her in line with the English way of life. She was owing a lot to Danny.

Patsy, a little cool, said, 'I'd like to mention he doesn't usually answer to Danny. We both prefer the name he was born with, especially as he's always had a great admiration for the biblical Daniel, the one who went into the lions' den to face up to being eaten.'

'Who's complaining?' asked Sadie.

'I am,' said Patsy. Sadie rode over that with a hugely friendly smile, the kind that looked like a winning commercial for somebody's toothpaste. Americans did take great care of their teeth, so they were never afraid to show a smile. And the one Sadie showed Patsy was to let her know she was still her long-time best friend.

'I guess I'll take a shower now,' she said, and made her way upstairs. Patsy found Daniel and separated him from Arabella and Andrew.

'What's the idea?' she asked.

'Come again?' said Daniel.

'Listen, chummy, you're my guy, not hers.'

'Patsy, nobody could be more thankful for that than I am,' said Daniel, 'and I've an idea that when I arrive at the offices on Monday, my good old pa is going to read me a lecture about never again darkening his door with the heroine of American radio. Patsy, you said never a word to me that when your old school mate sticks to someone it's for ever.

Well, today felt like for ever.'

'For ever in her case lasts for just a week-end,' said Patsy, 'and even then she probably calls her producer on her bedside phone every ten minutes. Well, OK, so her life's her own, and I know I was the one who persuaded her to stay for a few days, but it's as well she's going back to town on Sunday.'

Today was Friday.

'OK, sugarbush, you start putting supper on the table while I go and freshen up.'

Several minutes later, Patsy, overseeing the washing of hands by her children, heard voices from upstairs. She took herself to the foot of the stairs and quickly realized that the sound of friendly chat was coming from the marital bedroom.

'No, I shan't go back to my hotel on Sunday morning, Danny, I'd like to stay until Monday. It's still a week before I make tracks for home.'

'You're thinking of spending the whole weekend with us?'

'I sure am, honey, and maybe you and I and my notebook can squeeze in some more time together.'

Up went Patsy, and there just inside the door of the marital bedroom she found Sadie, wrapped only in a bath towel, loose hair engagingly framing her face, bosom on the up and up, doing her best to let Daniel see how stunning she looked when improperly dressed. Shades of treachery, thought Patsy, my old schoolfriend is obviously considering ways and means of enjoying some quick sessions in private with my fun guy, say in the broom cupboard.

'Sadie, go away and get dressed.'

'Oh, there you are, Patsy. I was just letting Daniel know I'd love to stay until Monday morning.'

'Well, hard luck, friend, you're going back to your hotel right now.'

'Now? Now? Patsy, am I hearing you?'

'As soon as you're dressed and packed,' said Patsy, 'I'll take you to our local railway station and put you on a train to Charing Cross, and I won't quit the platform until I see the train move out. Then you'll be in time to have dinner at your hotel.'

'Patsy, what's steaming you up?' asked Sadie, trying to look upset and mystified all at once.

'Don't ask or I'll really sound off,' said Patsy. 'Daniel, we'll go down now and have supper with Arabella and Andrew. Sadie will be dressed, packed and ready to move out by the time we've eaten.'

For the first time in her life Miss Sadie Bergenbaur, famous in Boston for her witty one-line contributions to a radio show, was stuck for words, and while she was still suffering from numb tonsils, Patsy took Daniel by the elbow and led him out of the danger zone.

'Patsy,' he said, as they began to descend the stairs, 'I've got a feeling you've fallen out with your old school chum.'

'My old school chum is now wondering how she lost this part of her script,' said Patsy. 'And listen, don't you ever let any other woman get close to you. If you ever do, I'll alter the shape of your head. With a shovel. You hear me, Daniel Adams?'

'There was never any problem as far as I was concerned,' said Daniel, pretty sure that Patsy steamed-up had to be taken seriously. 'I'm yours faithfully, believe me.'

'Lucky for you, old boy,' said Patsy.

'Come on, Mummy,' said Arabella, as her parents entered the kitchen, 'Andrew and me are starving.'

Some time later, Patsy stood on the platform of Herne Hill station watching a train depart. Sadie did not appear at a window to wave to her, and Patsy did not want her to. She was thinking that among one's best friends were some who weren't. Deciding to accept that as a proven fact, she left the station to make her way home.

Home. Daniel and the children.

All her own.

She quickened her step.

'I'd like to say something,' said Mrs Felicity

135

Adams to her husband Tim, Boots's son by his first wife, Emily.

'Does that mean I should turn off the telly?' asked Tim, ex-commando and stalwart support to Felicity during her years of blindness. Caused by a bomb blast during the blitz on London, the damage to her eyes, thought incurable, yielded to a natural healing process over the course of seventeen years. Natural was considered the equivalent of miraculous by all concerned, and especially by Felicity herself.

There she was, relaxing in an armchair and too dreamy, apparently, thought Tim, to be paying much attention to the television programme. He felt she sometimes took time off from everyday matters to dwell silently on the joys of restored sight, particularly the joy of daughter Jennifer at last becoming visible to her.

Jennifer, just fourteen, was up in her bedroom at the moment, listening to her record player. Athletics and other sports were Jennifer's preferred recreations, but she shared most young people's craze for pop music. Tim was well aware that record players were prized gifts these days for teenagers, who spent their pocket money buying records featuring their favourite rock 'n' roll stars or popular jazz bands like Louis Armstrong's. Still at the top of the rock 'n' roll charts were the songs recorded by Elvis Presley to the

136

accompaniment, said some people, of his well-toned pelvis. Just listening to him on a record player could send teenagers swoony, even if repeated playings sent their grown-ups barmy. Speaking of grown-ups, Adams teenagers fell about when told that Uncle Sammy's favourite record was still of Marie Lloyd singing 'My Old Man Said Follow the Van'.

Tim smiled to himself. Felicity interrupted his musings.

'Yes,' she said.

'Mmm? Oh, right, yes, turn off the telly.' Tim did so. 'Now, what's on your mind, Puss?'

'I've been thinking, I never saw what my daughter was like until she was thirteen,' said Felicity.

'Agony for you, I know that,' said Tim, 'but you did a superb job with her.'

'We decided it would be too much for me to have any other children,' said Felicity. 'But now I think I'd like the pleasure and privilege of having a child I could see day in, day out from birth. That, old son, would more than make up for all I missed with Jennifer.'

'You're serious?' said Tim.

'Never more so,' said Felicity, still a healthy and supple brunette at thirty-seven, the same age as Tim. 'What d'you think, Tim, do you like the idea? Well, I need your help, of course.'

'You're sure you'd really like another child?' said Tim. 'There'd be a lot of years between it and Jennifer. She'd be fifteen or on the way to it when a little brother or sister arrived.'

'I know, yes, but let's try, Tim,' said Felicity.

'Without losing time?' said Tim.

'Yes, lovely idea,' said Felicity.

'Right,' said Tim. Six foot and easy-limbed, much like Boots, he came up from his chair and moved towards the door of the living room.

'Tim, where are you going?' asked Felicity.

'Well, Puss, if you must know, to find out if there's a bottle or two of Guinness either in the larder or in the nearest pub,' said Tim. 'And I'll check with our fishmonger if oysters are in season.'

Chapter Ten

Saturday morning.

Chief Inspector Walters of the Camberwell police was shown another anonymous letter, one that had arrived at the station by the morning post. By post, however, did not mean the envelope had been stamped. It hadn't, and double payment had been asked for and given.

The address, 'Police Station, Camberwell', had been made up of letters cut out of a newspaper. And the message in the letter, made up likewise, was brief: 'CH at 21A Blackfriars Rd'.

'Any fingerprints?'

'None, guv.'

'What's CH mean?'

'Curly Harris?'

'Who's shopped him, would you say?'

'His landlady, guv?'

'Not a mate with a grudge?'

'That's possible.'

'Right, get after him.'

The new boarder at Maiden Hall college had received permission from the headmistress to enjoy a morning walk with Cathy Davidson and Gemma Adams, but was strictly forbidden to be out for more than an hour and a half. Was that understood? Oh, yes, ma'am. So by ten o'clock the three girls were sauntering around the avenues of Dulwich Village, the weather conditions kind in that the air was bright and crisp. It was up to Cathy and Gemma to show Irena the quiet and attractive nature of the area, and indeed there was a country village aspect to be taken in, especially around the old-established boys' college. Irena, keen to acquaint herself with the neighbourhood, showed a particular interest in residential avenues, and in who the residents might be.

'There, such lovely houses. Do you know who lives in them, Cathy?'

'Well, no, they aren't close to where I live.'

And, 'Look, how grand. Who lives in this road, Gemma?'

'Well-off families, I should think.'

Gemma and Cathy mentioned after a while that Dulwich was quite a large area, and they only knew near neighbours. Irena said that in places the houses were so very grand she could not help wondering what the people who lived in them were like. Were some of them, for instance, related to the rich and famous, or perhaps to foreign princes?

'Help,' said Gemma, 'I don't know anyone like that, I only know my Uncle Sammy once had a stall in a Walworth market, that my mama was a giddy flapper in the Twenties and Daddy grew up as the Lord-I-Am of all he surveyed in the back streets of Walworth. Mind, Cathy has posh relatives, like her Anglo-Russian mother.'

'Anglo-Russian?' said Irena, intrigued.

'Yes, and she lives in Paris with Cathy's French stepfather,' said Gemma.

'Oh, Paris,' said Irena, seemingly dismissive of France's much-admired capital.

'But I don't see my mother as posh,' said Cathy.

'Still, your French stepfather is, isn't he?' said Gemma.

'Posh, what is posh?' asked Irena, as they strolled on.

'High-class,' said Gemma.

'High-class and a bit snooty,' said Cathy.

'Ah, I think you mean proud aristocrats,' said Irena, and Cathy and Gemma didn't argue. The morning and the outing belonged to the young lady from Finland.

It was a happy outing, Cathy and Gemma having become fast friends, and Irena having become attached to them, although always a cool and composed figure compared to their outgoing selves. They did what they could to be responsive to her interest in the kind of people who lived in the area.

'See that house, Irena? We do know who lives there, old Mrs Francis. She's eighty-four and still rides a horse around the green.'

'Eighty-four? Gemma, that is so?'

'Yes, and they say the horse is even older.'

'No, no, Cathy, I do not believe that.'

'I don't, either, but it's what people say.'

There were several moments like that during the girls' unhurried excursion, and one of a different kind when they were passed by a group of Dulwich College boys out for an athletic training run. One boy forsook all school rules and whistled at them.

'Ah, boys,' said Irena, 'they take a long time to grow up, I think.'

'Yes,' said Gemma, 'but my mother will tell you that when they do get there, that's the time to start running.'

'And my mother will tell you,' said Cathy, 'that that kind of running is just the thing if you like being chased.' She laughed. 'And if you like being caught.'

'Count me out,' said Gemma, 'I don't yet know any boy who fits that kind of picture.'

'Ah, you and Cathy are very funny, Gemma,' said Irena.

The morning air was invigorating, Irena showing no lessening of interest, her large eyes busy espying this, that and the other. Towards the end of the outing, Cathy was able to point to a particular house when they reached the entrance to a very handsome avenue.

'See, Irena, that's where I live with my aunt. That house a little way up, the one with the double gates.'

'Ah, such a lovely house,' said Irena.

'Yes, my aunt and her husband moved several times before they ended up here,' said Cathy. 'She's a widow now. Would you like to meet her one day?'

'Well, it certainly can't be now,' said Gemma, 'we have to be back at Maiden Hall by eleven fifteen, and we all know how awesome Miss Stanton is about punctuality. Cathy, we'd better start walking Irena back.'

'Irena, I'll invite you to meet my aunt sometime in the future,' said Cathy. Her aunt always liked notice of possible visitors.

'So kind,' said Irena.

On arriving back at the college, she said goodbye to Gemma and Cathy, and went to the headmistress's study to report her return. Miss Stanton, temporarily absent, appeared five minutes later to find the young lady from Finland consulting the London telephone directory that lay on her desk.

'Irena?'

'Oh, Miss Stanton.' Irena, straightening up, showed a slight flush of embarrassment. 'Excuse me, please, I was thinking to find the telephone number of the Theatre Royal in Drury Lane. It is most famous.'

'Irena, if you were thinking of ringing the box office, I must remind you that for your own safety the London theatres are forbidden to you for the time being.'

'Yes, madam, that is so. But theatres are so attractive to me.'

'Be patient, young lady, and the time will come when it will be safe for you to go to a theatre every week, if you so wish. Did you enjoy your outing with Cathy Davidson and Gemma Adams?'

'Oh, yes, madam, very much.'

'Good. We'll allow you to repeat such excursions in their company until the day when you'll be free to venture out by yourself.'

'Thank you, madam.'

When the girl had gone, Miss Stanton referred to the phone directory, still open. And yes, at the section covering names that began with a 'T'. So the girl had been looking for the Theatre Royal, Drury Lane. Well, she had made no secret of her wish to enjoy London's theatres, but she must be kept from them for the time being. In that area, eyes were everywhere and no-one was sure that the Soviet Union's embassy had genuinely lost interest in her.

The sharp-eyed passenger in a raincoat and peaked cap came to his feet as the bus on which he was travelling began to slow down on its approach to a scheduled stop in Blackfriars Road, south of Blackfriars Bridge. He glanced across the road, casually at first, then intently. He swore beneath his breath.

The rozzers had come around.

There was their official car, parked outside 21A. A uniformed constable sat at the wheel, and two plain-clothes busybodies were entering the house. The door closed behind them. The bus came to a stop. He hesitated, then descended the stairs and alighted. He now had his back to the police car. He slipped a hand inside his raincoat and drew out a spectacle case. When he turned around to cast a new glance at 21A, he was wearing horn-rimmed glasses. He looked up and down, and when traffic had cleared he crossed the road, passing in front of the car to reach the pavement. He did so without hurry, giving the constable driver time to look him over, and to make a move. But no move was made. He hadn't been recognized. He turned left, and sauntered very casually past the closed door of 21A as if challenging it to open and to disgorge the hairy fuzz. Nothing happened. So, considering what to do next, he kept going until he reached a bus stop for vehicles going south.

There he waited, all the while directing glances at the house where he'd been lodging since leaving Parsons' Shelter immediately after the incident at that Camberwell pub. Now, obviously, his landlady, Elvira Figgins, was being questioned. Well, he could rely on Figgy to tell the cops nothing that would land him in the dock. Figgy, fortyish, had a sour opinion of cops. They'd been responsible for her doing time. It had first happened during the war, when she'd been charged with two offences of shoplifting. For each she'd been sentenced to a whole six months without remission in a female slammer. Just because it was wartime and her laden bags of goodies had contained mostly rationed items. Bloody spiteful use of the law, she always reckoned. A caution would have been fairer. Then, some years ago, she'd been picked up by the cops for pocketing a client's wallet after spending a couple of hours with him somewhere in Soho. Everyone on the game always reckoned that sort of thing was fair pickings, but not the rozzers. So Figgy hated the law. Himself, Curly hadn't yet done time and he wasn't in favour of doing any now.

A couple of buses came, stopped and picked up passengers. He stayed waiting, casting glances, and interesting himself in the traffic and people. When one more bus approached, he glanced again at 21A, and there the heavies were, emerging. They returned his glance as they moved towards the waiting car. He played the innocent onlooker. Disinterested, they ducked into their transport.

So, he thought, as he boarded the bus, they

hadn't recognized him. Well, now that he looked like a fancy Soho ponce, who would? Still, it had given him a lift, challenging them head-on, good as. But what a gorblimey nuisance they were, trying to hunt him down and bottle him up, all on account of that lousy barman treating him like a kid who didn't know an onion from a turnip. And now someone had obviously shopped him. There could only be one name in the hat. Well, with the plod probably arranging to keep a watch on Blackfriars Road and its immediate area for the time being, he reckoned he could safely pay Dodgy Dan a call, slice him up a bit, and then find new lodgings.

Gemma was home after her outing with Cathy and Irena. James was playing rugby for his college's first fifteen. If Boots had made the most of his years at a south-east London grammar school, without ever remotely rubbing shoulders with rugby players, James was profiting from his time at Dulwich's famous college. He was being turned into a well-educated young sport without ever taking on any hint of the superior. His mother, in any case, was an engaging example of a woman who, born into the upper classes, could mix as easily with East End dustmen and Billingsgate fish porters as with lords and landowners. James had a great fondness for his gregarious mum and any amount of admiration for his easy-going dad.

Gemma treated her parents like her best friends. She was a girl growing up, happy to let life reveal its quirks and perversities in the same way that her father had during his teens. Unlike some young women, she did not rush about in search of the ultimate in a relationship. She was like her mother in that respect. Polly had never thought seriously about any marital relationship until she met the one man who mattered. A bitter blow it had been to find he was some other woman's husband.

'Hi, Dad, hi, Mama,' said Gemma, going into the garden on her arrival. The morning still being bright and crisp, her parents were working there, preparing vegetable beds for spring planting. Gardening was yet another recreation they shared, and Gemma often thought their easy air of togetherness was born of common interests, whether they related to yesterday, today or tomorrow. Neither ever bored the other, nor did Gemma ever think they would. Nor did she regard them as old.

'Welcome home, sweetie,' said Polly, clad in a thick woollen sweater, warm skirt, wellington boots and an old felt hat. She might have looked all anyhow, but didn't and never would. Polly had flair, whatever she dressed herself in.

'How did it go?' asked Boots, wearing an ancient roll-top jersey and trousers even more ancient. Now he did look all anyhow, yet still had appeal for any woman who wandered into his life either by accident or design.

'Lovely walk,' said Gemma, and told them how interested the girl from Finland had been in what kind of people lived in the really handsome parts of the village.

'Does she talk about Finland?' asked Boots.

'Hardly ever,' said Gemma. 'Daddy, I suppose you know those old gardening trousers of yours ought to be banished to the nearest bonfire?'

'Darling,' said Polly, digging in locally harvested manure, 'I personally banished them to a prepared bonfire only a month ago, but when morning came Flossie found they'd walked back home to the kitchen door. I'm afraid they've become your father's oldest and most faithful friend.'

'Crikey, Daddy,' said Gemma, 'if they're as faithful as that there might come a time when you might not be able to get them off.'

'If that happens,' said Polly, 'your father will have to live in the shed.'

'I'll give that serious thought,' said Boots, forking the manure from a wheelbarrow and spreading it. 'Finland, I suppose, isn't everybody's idea of a topic for conversation. I believe it's a very civilized country, but not many people take their holidays there, do they?'

'No-one I know,' said Gemma, 'and I must say Irena seems happy enough to be here in our little bit of England, even if everything's foreign to her. Still, we all do our best for her, although Miss Stanton strictly forbids her to go wandering out and about in case she gets lost. Bless us, folks, imagine anyone getting lost in the wilds of Dulwich Village.'

'Calamitous,' said Boots. 'But Miss Stanton takes really good care of her, does she?'

'Oh, yes,' said Gemma, 'she's strict all the time about where Irena is and what she's doing. By the way, we showed Irena the house where Cathy lives with her aunt, and she thought it super grand. But would you believe, she knows a great big nothing about Elvis Presley or Tommy Steele. Or rock 'n' roll. Or Bill Haley. Isn't that sad? I mean, without Elvis Presley and rock 'n' roll, you're simply not living. Mama, I'm going to make myself some coffee. Would you and Daddy like a cup?'

'We've had ours, poppet,' said Boots.

'Oh, jolly good show, old things,' said Gemma, taking off Polly.

Waiting until their daughter had disappeared into the kitchen, Polly said, 'Boots, you still think this girl Irena might be the defecting Russian gymnast?'

'I've a suspicion,' said Boots, 'and it fits the information given to me by the newspaper, and the fact that Miss Stanton is taking extra special care of her. Like another forkful?' He let a large amount slide from his fork onto the plot.

'Dear old bean, you're so kind,' said Polly who, in her wildest days, had never dreamt she would end up as a middle-class house-wife growing her own middle-class onions. But then, what woman ever suspected she'd end up potty and brainless about a male being? 'Tell me, what d'you make of the fact that Gemma at seventeen doesn't have a boyfriend?'

'In this particular day and age when boy-friends seem to be ten a penny,' said Boots, 'count it as a blessing that Gemma's dis-criminating in favour of athletics and a spot of tennis. Put your faith in that, old girl, and take happy note that James is just as wise in the easy relationship he's enjoying with Cathy.'

'I'm beginning to like Cathy,' said Polly.

Boots smiled.

'I think you find it easier to like her now that her mother seems to be permanently out of sight in Paris,' he said.

'I can't help it, I feel jaundice coming on whenever there's any mention of the man-eater,' said Polly. 'By the way, exactly when are the police going to lay their heavy hand on that frightful cut-throat who nearly put paid to dear old Joe?'

'Good question, Polly,' said Boots. 'I'll drop in at the police station on Monday and find out how near or far they are in respect of collaring that hairy young son of Satan.'

'Well, do that, father of Hercules,' said Polly, 'but kindly don't go running after any other antisocial blot – oh, look here, you stinker, what's all this around my feet?'

'More muck,' said Boots.

'I'm right, you are a stinker,' said Polly.

'All in a day's work,' said Boots.

Chapter Eleven

Arthur Gumbridge came out from behind his cubbyhole at the sound of the main door being opened and shut by someone. That someone turned out to be not the usual kind of down-and-out but a young bloke in a cap and raincoat, and wearing horn-rimmed spectacles.

'You looking for a room?' said the warden. 'If you are, we're full up and you'll have to try the Army.' He meant the Salvation Army.

'I ask yer, tosh, have I asked for a room?' said Curly Harris.

The warden peered, then realized the raincoat was familiar, that it was the spectacles and smart cap which had foxed him.

'Is that you again? You were here a few days ago. What've you come back for?'

'Some bleeder's talked about me.'

'Talked about you?'

'Yes, he bleedin' has.'

'Wasn't me, I don't talk about nobody.'

'All right, so where's Dodgy Dan? At 'ome, might I ask?'

'Not any more. He's hopped it.'

'Where?'

'How do I know? I ain't his mother. All I do know is that he took all his belongings, such as they were, which wasn't much, 'specially as he found someone had broke into his locker and emptied it, which didn't do me much good, seeing the Board holds me responsible for that kind of thing.'

'Spongy, you lookin' at me?'

'You?' said the warden. 'Listen, I got more sense than to look at any of you. I mean, if I was asked, I wouldn't remember you visiting a little while ago, would I? No, course I wouldn't. I've got me health to think about, haven't I? And I work to the rules of the Trust, don't I? Which means I don't ask questions of nobody, and that includes not giving anyone looks that they don't like.'

'All right,' said Curly Harris in surly vein, 'so where's Dodgy Dan now?'

'I just told you, how do I know? I mean, if any of me lodgers ever leave a forwarding address, it'll be the first time, won't it?'

'Did he quit this fleapit with a packed bag?'

'So he did, this morning and – here, wait a bit. Now I come to think, he asked me what Margate was like this time of the year. Then he said no, forget it, there wasn't nothing for nobody at Margate except in July and August, and off he went.'

'Well, I got to find him, I owe him a bad turn.'

'What's he done?'

'Talked. I just told yer, didn't I?'

'What would he want to do that for?' asked Spongy, as if he didn't know who Dodgy Dan suspected of rifling his locker.

'Never you mind. I'll find him. You just keep yer gob shut.' And Curly Harris, quite sure Dodgy Dan would be on his way to Margate if he'd said there was nothing there for him, departed from the hostel, hands in his raincoat pockets. The warden, watching him, reckoned that in one of those pockets was Curly's best friend. His knife.

There goes a nasty piece of work, he thought, and still only twenty and a bit. Time he was put away, but I'm not giving any more information to the cops. I don't fancy the way he looks at me. He's suspicious of everybody, and there's no-one he likes. Someone ought to say a prayer for Dodgy Dan right now. I'd say one meself, but I can't remember ever being religious. What did I mention Margate for when it was Ramsgate? And was it this morning he left or was it yesterday? Looks like I went a bit unconscious on his account. Oh, well, time for a nip before I check on whether old Beanbag's done his stuff with the Harpic today.

Old Beanbag was the hostel's resident cleaner and maintenance man.

The phone rang in Aunt Marie's palatial

residence. Cathy beat the butler to it.

'Hello, yes?'

'That's you, Cathy?' said James, home from his rugby and a spell in the pavilion's hot bath. He was one of the few who had Aunt Marie's ex-directory phone number. 'It's only me.'

'Hello, only you,' said Cathy.

'Well, yes, I was all over mud an hour ago after the rugby match,' said James, 'and in that state you don't feel or look as if you matter very much to civilization. Your one need is a hot bath.'

'Oh, tough,' said Cathy.

'I'm improving minute by minute,' said James. 'Anyway, I'm ringing to confirm our date for the Brixton hop this evening.'

'James, as usual I'm looking forward to it,' said Cathy.

'Good-oh,' said James. 'Look, Dad's going to do us a favour and pick us up in his car outside the hall at ten thirty. He says it's time he did something Christianlike on Saturday nights instead of leaving us to fight for a bus home.'

'Honest?' said Cathy.

'Honest,' said James.

'Your dad's a dream,' said Cathy. 'One day I'll fall in love with him.'

'I won't mention that to my ma,' said James, quite sure she would load a blunderbuss at this possible threat from a part-

156

Russian young lady. 'Gemma tells me you enjoyed your walk with Irena Whatsit this morning.' Which comment prompted a typically lengthy chat between two young people who saw a phone for what it was, an instrument of cosy communication, and not just something for the benefit of a housewife and her grocer.

And while that was going on, Polly asked Boots if he thought they should invite Cathy and her aunt to Sunday tea sometime, in return for the tea Gemma and James had enjoyed with them. Boots said it might be best to leave it to James to come up with the suggestion.

Gemma cut in. 'It's no go, anyway, Mama, not with Cathy's aunt. She never socializes, never goes out anywhere, except to the shops about one morning a week, when her butler drives her and carries the shopping basket for her. Well, she orders most of her groceries from Fortnum and Mason. Cathy told James, and James told me.'

'Good heavens, the lady's a recluse apart from popping in on her local shops once a week?' said Polly.

'Perhaps, when she lost her husband, she also lost her sense of security,' said Boots. 'It happens.'

'She's still sweet,' said Gemma, 'and she never interferes with Cathy's comings and goings.'

'Well, if James wants to invite Cathy herself to Sunday tea,' said Boots, 'we'll organize a dish of hot buttered crumpets, shall we?'

'Daddy, I'm not sure how you organize a dish of crumpets,' said Gemma.

'We might have to,' said Boots, 'it'll be the first time for your mother.'

'I've seen that old layabout more than once,' said the railway official in answer to an enquiry from a young man, 'but not today.'

Charing Cross station was enjoying a Saturday afternoon of relative quiet. Enjoyment for Curly Harris, however, was nil. He'd asked every official in sight if Dodgy Dan had been seen, and every answer had been negative. If that old fleabag had gone to Margate, it would be no problem to find him and jump him. He'd be standing out like a hairy old goat in a well-kept chicken run. And before sawing his left leg off, Curly wanted to know exactly what he'd spilled to the cops. But there was no point in going to Margate himself unless he was certain the useless old heap had arrived.

'Look,' he said to the official, 'I got to catch up with him and give him an urgent message, and I know he was after going to Margate today.'

'Well, if he was here catching a train, I didn't notice. Asked at the booking office,

158

have you?'

'Twice. No luck.'

'Well, keep trying. Now, if you don't mind, I've got a job to do.'

It took Curly Harris another hour of asking around before he came to the conclusion he was wasting his time. He'd come back tomorrow, because he was certain it was Dodgy Dan who'd given the Old Bill his new address, the house rented by Elvira Figgins. Well, Dan was the only one who knew it, and the lousy old sod knew he'd put himself in the way of a slicing by handing the address and maybe other info to the coppers, which was why he'd decided to hide himself in Margate. He had to be done over, either there or here in Charing Cross station, say down in the station toilet.

That's a point, is he hiding himself there right now?

He wasn't.

Bugger it, said Curly Harris to himself, I ain't after inspecting the insides of every other public convenience in London, I'll come back here early tomorrow. But what to do for the rest of the day? Look for new lodgings somewhere, I suppose, seeing I can't go back to Spongy's dump or get Figgy to put me up, not while the plod are still sniffing around Bermondsey and Black-friars. And I got to give pubs a miss, with all the lousy publicans still looking out for me on behalf of the rozzers. Half a bleedin' tick, though, who's going to recognize me? Good question, that.

'Get yourself off this train, or I'll have you run in,' said an inspector of the London and North Western Railway to an artful nonentity.

''Ere, where's yer manners?' protested the artful nonentity, otherwise Dodgy Dan.

'And where's your ticket, eh?'

'I told yer, I've gorn and mislaid it,' said Dodgy Dan who, although he'd had a shave and a wash, looked much like his usual messy self. At the moment, he had a compartment on the Blackpool train all to himself, but no-one could have said he was decorating it, any more than his old luggage case, tied with string on account of the age of the lock, was decorating the overhead rack.

'Our man at the gate informed me you only showed a platform ticket.'

'Can I help it if he's got a bad memory?' Dodgy Dan sounded upset, which he was. It was always the same, there was always some lousy geezer in uniform trying to interfere with his right to be alive. This one wanted him off the train, which wasn't even moving yet. It was still in the station, getting steam up. 'In any case, I challenge yer to prove I'm gettin' a free ride. I'm just sitting 'ere, ain't

I? Considering I been up all night nursing me sick old mother, you ain't refusing me the comfort of a sit-down, are yer?'

'I'm after making sure you don't get a free ride to Blackpool or wherever. In fact, I'm ordering you off this train. So, are you leaving or do I have to summon a constable?'

Dodgy Dan sighed and heaved himself up.

'I dunno, there ain't a bit of Christian charity on offer these days,' he said, pulling his case from the rack. 'There's me old mother near to dying of antirinus—'

'Antirinus? What's that?'

'How do I know, except if I catch it meself I don't suppose you'll come to me funeral,' grumbled Dodgy Dan, who could see himself sleeping on an Embankment bench when night fell. He couldn't risk going back to Parsons' Shelter, not until Curly Harris was behind bars. 'I dunno you can look yer own mother in the face after what you're doing to me. Strewth, I was nearly better orf in a Jap prisoner-of-war camp and wounded as well – all right, all right, don't rush me, I'm moving, ain't I?'

He was off the train and down on the cold platform seconds later.

'Don't let me catch you here again,' said the station official.

'Well, seeing as you want me right out of the place,' said Dodgy Dan, now heavily laden with his case, 'do I get me money back for me platform ticket? It might only be tuppence to you, but it could make the difference to me between staying alive or dying of starvation.'

Not even the tiniest semblance of Christian charity was offered in response to that heartbreaking appeal, and when Dodgy Dan eventually left the station he was utterly disillusioned with humankind. His immediate priority was to avoid running into Curly Harris's knife, and his next priority was still to get himself far away. Mind, if the fuzz had fingered Curly by now, getting away wasn't all that urgent. He could take his time about finding a bit of Christian help from some landlady in Blackpool. But right now, could he risk making a few enquiries to find out if Curly was in the nick or not? No, best not to show himself in a police station, best to get hold of an evening paper and find out from that. He realized, bitterly, that if the bugger hadn't swiped his savings, he'd have been able to afford to buy a train ticket to wherever and been halfway there by now.

Pointing himself in the direction of Whitechapel, he thought of dozy females taking their handbags for an outing down the East End markets. Mind, he'd had to give up bag-dipping on account of the law getting spiteful about it and committing him to the Scrubs. But trying instead to earn an honest living off overhead train racks, on the basis that finders were keepers, wasn't paying so good these days.

So he'd risk trying a market or two, and a handbag or two, and perhaps earn himself enough oof to keep body and soul together for a week or so. But he needed to dump his belongings somewhere safe for the time being.

Where was the nearest Salvation Army hostel that was safe from Curly Harris's unfriendly peepers?

And where was that young bleeder himself if not in the nick? If Spongy had dropped a hint, he might be in Ramsgate.

Chapter Twelve

At ten twenty that night, Boots was well on
the way to Brixton to pick up Cathy and
James, along with Gemma. Polly was with
him, having said she'd prefer a ride out into
the starry night instead of being left alone.
Boots was onto that, of course.

'Starry night?' he'd said. 'Are you sure it's
nothing to do with the possibility that when
I drop Cathy off there might be an invitation
to come in and meet her aunt?'

'Listen, chummy,' said Polly, 'I'll lose faith
if you turn into one of those inquisitive old
buffers known for asking awkward questions.'

'I'll rearrange my thinking,' said Boots.

'There's a good old scout,' said Polly, and
Boots thought that most people who had
known Polly in her wild days would never
have seen her as a caring mother, concerning herself with every aspect of the twins'
lives without, however, becoming an interfering nuisance.

Now she was seated beside him as they
headed for the dance hall.

At the bar of a pub, Curly Harris had sunk

four pints of light ale followed by two rum-and-Cokes. He'd also eaten some hot sausages on sticks. Neither the publican nor his barman had recognized him. The only thing irritating him was the crush at the bar, where he'd been sitting ever since arriving, challenging recognition. Irritation for Curly Harris was all too easy to come by during a drinking session, since that was the effect alcohol had on him from the time when he first introduced himself to it at the age of seventeen. His temper was rising as a man, accompanied by a woman, crowded him in an attempt to get attention from the publican.

'Here, come on, Charlie, gin and tonic for Sally,' the bloke kept calling. The publican, busy attending to other customers, wasn't playing for the moment.

'Listen, you,' hissed Curly Harris into the bloke's ear, 'you're sitting on me bleedin' lap.'

'You talking to me, mate?'

'Yes, I bleedin' am,' said Curly Harris, and followed up by inviting the bloke and his bleedin' Sally to get lost. What he actually said contained the worst kind of four-letter word, and he backed that up by digging the bloke viciously in the ribs with his elbow. The bloke turned on him. The publican, who hadn't missed the lead-up to the fray, was onto the cause of it immediately.

'You,' he said, pointing a finger at Curly, 'out, out. Now.'

For a moment, Curly thought about leaping the bar, jumping the publican and slicing off a large part of his left ear. But could he risk the cops being called? Besides which, the publican was a six-footer built like an ox. He ducked out. He walked, cursing and swearing, amid crowds coming out of cinemas, pubs and other places of entertainment. He walked deliberately into a group of young people emerging from a dance hall, just at the moment when a car pulled up at the kerbside. His violent contact split the group and sent a young man sprawling to the ground. Cries of indignation filled the night air.

From the car, Boots and Polly saw the incident by the light of the illuminated facade of the dance hall. They saw a man in a cap and raincoat barge a quite brutal way through the teenagers, sending one of them flying. He barged on, stopping neither to apologize nor to help Giles to his feet. Giles it was, Rosie's son.

'Ye gods, was it like this in our day, Boots?' breathed Polly in disgust.

'At any time,' said Boots, opening the car door, 'there's always some misbegotten hooligan spoiling life for the unoffending.' Then he and Polly were out of the car. The bruising character was well away, lost in the

166

night, while James and Cathy were helping Giles to his feet. Around them were Gemma, Emily and her Teddy-boy friend, Bradley Thompson, Cindy Stevens, Maureen Brown and some other young people.

Boots and Polly, edging in, were instantly spotted.

'Hi, Aunt Polly, hello, Uncle Boots,' called Emily. None of the related young people ever addressed Boots and Polly as Grandpa and Grandma. While it wouldn't have kept Boots awake at night, Polly would have considered it the equivalent of a death knell. In any case, Grandma to the young Adamses only ever meant Grandma Finch, and Grandpa only Grandpa Finch.

'Oh, hello, parents,' said James. 'Giles caught an unsolicited shove in the back from some bloke short of manners, and we're livid about it.'

'Yes, we saw,' said Boots. 'Giles?'

'I'm OK, Uncle Boots,' said Giles, brushing himself down.

'Are you sure?' asked Polly.

'Sure,' said Giles, and happily accepted congratulations from Cindy on surviving his encounter with the pavement. A bus passed, slowing down on its approach to a scheduled stop. Some of the young people, the upheaval over, made a dash for the vehicle. Boots offered to find room in his car for Cindy, James, Gemma, Emily, Giles and

Cathy. The offer was received with noises of undying gratitude, and when Boots drove off Cindy and Giles were squashed up on the front bench seat with himself and Polly, and the other four teenagers were wedged along the back seat. They all talked of the uncouth bloke without realizing, any more than Boots and Polly did, that he was actually the vicious young assailant who'd put barman Joe in hospital with a knife wound.

Boots drove to Denmark Hill, where he dropped Cindy off at the home of her dad, Harry Stevens, an author, and her step-mother Anneliese, once a German army nurse and now a fully integrated British national. Giles got out of the car with Cindy.

'I'll just see her to her door,' he said to Boots.

'Don't lose her on the way there,' said Boots.

At her door, Cindy rang the bell and then received a good-night kiss from Giles. When Harry opened the door, he caught them at it.

'Am I interrupting?' he asked.

'Oh, nothing secret, Dad,' said Cindy, blushless. Seventeen, she was known to be making a study of boys in general before she decided which one was the most civilized and the most manageable. She was coming to the conclusion that she'd have to revise her requirements, since most didn't seem to understand what being civilized meant, and those who did, like Giles and James, kind of talked their way out of being manageable. 'Just Giles saying good night.'

And Harry, a Navy man during the war, recognized, not for the first time, that the teenagers of today were much more outgoing and far less conservative than those of his day. In his day, if you kissed a girl outside her front door, you were expected to declare your intentions. And if they weren't honest, her dad would come knocking on your door.

'Yup, good night, Cindy,' said Giles. 'Good night, sir,' he said to Harry, 'I'll borrow Cindy again next Saturday evening, if that's OK with you.'

'With me, you mean,' said Cindy.

'Right,' said Giles.

'I see, you approve of her, do you?' smiled Harry.

'She's a great mover, Mr Stevens, great,' said Giles.

'Exactly how great is great?' asked Harry.

'Oh, just a couple of steps from being super,' said Giles, and, dodging a blow from Cindy, returned to the car.

Boots next dropped off Giles and Emily at their Red Post Hill address. Rosie came out to the car to thank Boots and Polly for bringing her young ones home. Boots said it would be no bother to do the same thing each Saturday while the winter lasted.

'Well, you're a sweetie,' said Rosie. 'It's always a relief to have Emily arrive home on time. The young madam seems to think parents are surplus to requirements, apart from providing board and lodging.'

'Hang on to your own beliefs, Rosie,' said Boots, 'they're what you fought for in the war against Hitler and his lunatic hordes.'

'Noted, and good night, old soldier,' said Rosie, 'good night, Polly.'

'So long, ducky,' said Polly.

Cathy was next off. Boots pulled up outside the tall ironwork gates of the handsome mansion on the south side of Dulwich Village. James got out and Cathy followed, thanking Boots and Polly for the lift. Polly watched with interest as James, having pushed the gates open, escorted the stylish young lady to her front door. Cathy used her key to let herself in. A man appeared, framed by the open door against the background of the illuminated hall.

'Hello, hello,' murmured Polly, 'a gentleman friend?'

'No, Mama, the butler,' said Gemma.

Cathy and the butler disappeared as the door closed, and James, on his way back to the car, pulled the gates to. A distinct click followed moments later, after which James re-entered the car.

'Why that loud click, dear boy?' asked Polly.

'Oh, the butler always locks the gates electrically at night,' said James. 'Cathy says it's to keep the burglars out.'

'But they opened when you pushed them,' said Polly.

'Yes, the butler always seems to know when Cathy gets home from her Saturday night outings,' said James. 'So he makes sure the electric lock is off just at the right time.'

'Second sense,' said Boots, as he began to drive home. 'As for taking precautions, very wise. This area of Dulwich has always been a favourite hunting ground for Bill Sikes and his mob.'

'The kind who leave the place all messed up?' said Gemma.

'That kind, yes,' said Boots, 'although I've heard the more polite ones also leave a note saying "Hope you don't mind, but what was yours is now ours."'

'Daddy, don't you know that joke's as old as the dodo and ought to be buried with it?' said Gemma. Sighing, she added, 'Mama, Daddy really is going off a bit.'

'Let's look on the bright side, darling,' said Polly, 'and hope it's only temporary.'

After dipping his fingers unsuccessfully into a handbag or two in an East End market, and having nearly been caught out, Dodgy Dan decided it just wasn't his day. So he sneaked back to Bermondsey and Parsons'

Shelter, where Spongy the warden owed him a favour for not reporting the busted locker. Spongy, informing him that Curly Harris hadn't been around since yesterday, returned the favour by finding him a room. Dodgy Dan took himself to bed to dwell on his future, which he knew might be non-existent unless he could put himself far away from Curly and his evil intentions. There hadn't been any news to say the fuzz had got him in the nick.

That particularly unpleasant young man, having upset a group of teenagers by barging into them, lurched about ill-temperedly, a surly threat to anyone who offended him just by being in his way. Brixton was his location at the moment, an area of home-going people after an evening out. They were all in his way and, accordingly, they were all a bleedin' nuisance. He began to feel sick. He lurched into a side street and there he threw up on a doorstep.

He felt better after that, and began to think about where to rest his head for the night. He hadn't found any new lodgings and he missed the kind he'd enjoyed with Elvira Figgins after the spat in that Camberwell pub, when he'd been staying at Parsons' Shelter. He'd been a bit skint at the time, but had cracked a crib in the morning, a house from which everyone was absent. It was that successful piece of quick work, with no fingerprints left behind, that had sent him round the pubs at lunchtime to celebrate, and to come up against that saucy barman. Now, could he chance going back to Figgy's just for the night? It was a fact he couldn't go home. His old man, backed up by his old lady, had kicked him out two years ago, with a promise to break every bone in his body if he ever showed up again. Parents, who'd have 'em?

In the end he tried Parsons' Shelter again, where Spongy, having told him the place was full up, came over a bit faint on account of knowing Dodgy Dan was back in residence and that more grievous bodily harm might be done if Curly found out. Well, there was Curly, cleaning his fingernails with the point of his knife while waiting for an answer. So Spongy thought a bit quick, told the young cut-throat the shelter was still full, but that he'd phone the nearest Army hostel to find out if they could fit him up with a bed. It was very late, but he'd make the call, he said, out of friendship. Which he did, although not out of friendship, and the Salvation Army said yes, they could find a bed for one more of God's unfortunates in their Tooley Street hostel. Tooley Street was this side of London Bridge.

'You could chuck out one of yours to make room for me here,' said Curly.

'Now come off it,' said Spongy, watching the play of the knife, 'you know I can't do that without getting meself reported and sacked.'

'Well, all right,' said Curly. 'Listen, has that bleeder Dodgy Dan shown up?'

'Him?' said Spongy. 'No, I told you, didn't I, that he'd gone off with all his belongings, that he'd talked about trying his luck in Ramsgate–'

'Hold on, you bleedin' told me Margate.'

'Did I? Well, with all the comings and goings I get confused, don't I, and who wouldn't? Margate or Ramsgate, I can't remember exactly which. Anyway, there's a room for you at the Army shakedown in Tooley Street, like I said. Now, would you mind if I closed this shelter up for the night and went to bed?'

'All right, off yer go, Spongy, but about Margate or Ramsgate. By morning when I look in again, you'd better know which one it was. I ain't going to Margate if it was Ramsgate, and I ain't going to Ramsgate if it was Margate. So think about it, eh? You know I ain't in favour of being mucked about.'

I ain't arguing with that, thought the warden, who knew he'd got to tell Dodgy Dan it would be better for his health to quit Parsons' Shelter first thing in the morning and to keep away from the Tooley Street area for the time being. This job's beginning to give me the kind of headache I don't like, he realized.

Without sparing time for his usual lick and a promise, Dodgy Dan was off as soon as Spongy woke him up and gave him the bad news. He didn't even put his boots on until he had turned the nearest corner.

Chapter Thirteen

Sunday night.

At Maiden Hall, some boarders were relaxing in the common room prior to retiring to their dorms. In one dorm two were relaxing on their beds. One student rolled off and stood up.

'Where are you going, Irena?' asked the other.

'I am starving,' said Irena Leino, 'so am going down to the kitchen to see if there are any biscuits in the larder.'

'Well, if there are, bring me some, but don't get caught.'

Down went Irena. The staircase led into a well of relative quiet, the only sound being that of the murmur of conversation coming from the lounge in which resident teachers were gathered. Irena did not descend all the way to the kitchen. She stopped on the first-floor landing, listened for a few moments, then slowly turned the handle of Miss Stanton's study door. The door opened. Darkness greeted her. She stepped in, closed the door and switched on the light. She looked around. The study in its tidiness and good order was typical of the principal's organized outlook. Beside the telephone on the right-hand corner of the desk lay the London directory. Irena made a quick consultation of it before extracting a piece of thin pasteboard from the top of her stocking. There was a number on it, followed by two digits representing an extension.

She picked up the phone and dialled, alert for the possibility of interruption. Her call was acknowledged and she gave the extension number. Someone answered, a deep-voiced man.

'Yes?'

'Lioness calling. Listen, I cannot find the address. Without an entry in the phone directory I have nothing to help me, and I cannot keep asking questions without arousing curiosity or suspicion.'

'You have called at the right time. We now have the address. It was obtained from a clerk of a removal firm. We also know she has changed her name. Take note.'

The name and address were given, and Irena memorized them.

'That is all I need,' she said.

'It's your privilege, one you asked for. Honour your ancestor. Goodnight.'

That ended the conversation, spoken in a language quite foreign to that which was usually heard in Miss Stanton's study.

Irena switched off the light, closed the door quietly and proceeded down to the kitchen. There, in the larder, she found a tin of mixed teatime biscuits from which she helped herself to five. One she ate on her way back to her dorm. Two of the remaining four she gave to the other boarder.

'Oh, super show, Irena, no bother?'

'None,' said Irena.

'Four whole biscuits – well done. It made your risky trip worthwhile.'

'Yes,' said Irena.

A little later, when she was in bed, she thought about the name she'd been quoted and experienced a feeling that it was not unfamiliar to her.

Monday morning.

Boots stopped off at the Camberwell police station to ask about the search for Curly Harris. Chief Inspector Walters came out of his cluttered den to talk to the man who had made a determined effort to catch the hairy piece of no-good. He told Boots that although the miscreant wasn't yet in custody, his lodgings were known.

'But he's not in residence?' said Boots.

'He wasn't when we made our swoop on Saturday morning, Mr Adams. We interviewed the tenant, but could get little out of her. She said she didn't interest herself in her lodger's business, or his comings and goings, that all her time was taken up trying to keep herself alive in this lousy country.'

'The lady's not happy with our green and pleasant land?' said Boots.

'She said it was a pity Hitler didn't win the Battle of Britain and take us over.' Chief Inspector Walters, an old-time cop, allowed himself a smile. 'It turned out she had a record for wartime shoplifting, for which she did two spells in Holloway. She's also known to the Yard as a lady of the night. So I don't think she's the kind of citizen who'd help us to jump Curly Harris. But we're keeping a watch on the place.'

'Well, I hope you nab him before he gets handy with that knife again and makes a real killing,' said Boots, and left.

On arriving at his office desk a little later, he was opening up his post when Rosie entered.

'Morning, old love,' she said, 'you've got a visitor. Rachel and I are holding her down in our office. Sammy did a bunk as soon as he knew she was here, so I'm afraid she's now your exclusive problem.'

'If Sammy did a bunk I suspect you mean Miss Marjorie Alsop is once more on the premises,' said Boots.

'And spitting,' said Rosie. 'Apparently the manageress of our Brixton shop was foolish enough to put on display a fur-lined winter jacket matched with a fur hat.'

'Window display?' said Boots.

'So it seems,' said Rosie.

'Doesn't Miss Alsop live in Brixton now?' asked Boots.

'Yes, and not far from Lulu and Paul,' said Rosie.

'And the shop,' said Boots, and Rosie saw a smile flicker. Her adoptive father could always see something amusing about over-earnest characters like Marjorie Alsop, just as the vicious or the insufferable could always arouse a glint of steel. 'Yes, I see,' he said, 'the manageress did have a thoughtless moment.'

'Our uninvited visitor wants to see you,' said Rosie, 'and to let you know she's bitterly disappointed in Adams Fashions. We're criminally two-faced, she says.'

'I thought Lulu had sold her off the feverish aspect of animal humanity and pointed her at a political solution,' said Boots.

'Well, perhaps you'll be happy to know I've phoned Lulu and she's now on her way to relieve us of Miss Alsop,' said Rosie. 'At the moment the lady's making life a burden for Rachel.'

'Now it's my turn, is it?' said Boots. 'Well, I'd better take my fair share of bruises, so wheel her in, Rosie.'

'All you have to do, old thing, is to stay alive until Lulu gets here,' said Rosie, and went back to the office she shared with Rachel.

Miss Marjorie Alsop, referred to as Mad Marj by Sammy, almost bounded into

Boots's presence a minute later. Simult-
aneously she burst into fiery speech.

'Mr Adams – I protest – your shops are
selling garments that aren't simply trimmed
with fur offcuts – it's far worse than that and
I have to tell you your word is worth very
little – very little – and let me warn you, yes,
let me tell you your two-faced attitude is
putting the windows of all your shops in
danger of being reduced to splinters – and
that's no–'

'Something is bothering you, Miss Alsop?'
Boots interrupted on a fairly mild note.

Miss Alsop jumped up and down, good as.

'Bothering me? Yes, yes, aren't you listening?'

'Something about our shops?'

'About the fact that you and your brother
assured me your shops only stocked garments with a little fur trimming. Your
brother, in fact, led me to believe these trim-
mings were only made up from manu-
facturers' offcuts. Mr Adams, I hate being
disillusioned by people I've come to like. It's
shattering.' And Miss Alsop threw her hands
into the air like an MI5 chief discovering all
his agents were Russian spies who took afternoon tea at the Ritz with the granddaughters
of Lenin.

'Take a seat, Miss Alsop, while I finish
opening my post,' said Boots, 'and then
we'll have a chat.'

'No, I won't be mollified, Mr Adams. Or patronized. Don't you ever think of how you would feel if evolution had taken a reverse turn and you were being skinned by polar bears to make parchment for their lampshades?'

'Polar bears?' said Boots.

'Or beavers. Or any other animal that today suffers death from the traps and guns of capitalistic fur-hunting traders.' Miss Alsop really was on her mettle. 'Yes, Mr Adams, how would you like being trapped and skinned by a furry creature?'

'I'm not sure my imagination will stretch that far,' murmured Boots, 'but I congratulate you on yours.'

'Mr Adams, will you or will you not give me your serious attention?'

'Miss Alsop, you have it,' said Boots, doing his best to turn away her wrath.

'Well, then, will you–' The flushed Miss Alsop broke off at the sound of a voice from without.

'No, never mind fussing about, let me get at her.'

And in came Lulu, all vibrations and steamed-up spectacles.

'Yes, do come in, Lulu,' said Boots, and his hint of a smile flickered again.

'Marjorie, what's going on?' Lulu demanded, her bosom heaving a bit. 'You're supposed to be at my place this morning, not here battering my uncles.'

'Battering? Battering?' Mad Marj spluttered. 'I'll have you know that if I were, they'd deserve it. I'll also have you know–'

'I already know,' said Lulu, 'so put a sock in it and come home with me. Stop letting matters of small importance divert you from your career as a political activist.'

'Small importance?' Mad Marj attempted to stand her ground. 'That might be how your uncles look at it, it's not how I do.'

'We've been through all that,' said Lulu, 'and we're grown-up now. Come on, stop standing around looking like Henry the Fifth working himself up at Agincourt and let's get back to Brixton. You'll be meeting my father later, he's dropping in for a bite of lunch and he'll let you know how you and I can get to meet the Minister of Trade.'

'Genuine?' said Mad Marj.

'Of course,' said Lulu, 'but don't expect my father to support you. His first priority in a case like this would be the interests of the workers, not the polar bears. Right then, stop all this Red Indian hatchet stuff and let's go.'

'Well, all right,' said Mad Marj, 'but I stand by my conscience and reserve the right to take unilateral action in the event of being further deceived by Adams Fashions.'

'Spoken like a true activist, but a daft one,' said Lulu. 'Anyone with sense would go after the big guns, not the pea-shooters. Come on. Sorry you've been bothered, Uncle Boots, hope Marjorie hasn't offended you.'

'Not a bit,' said Boots, 'I'm not an over-sensitive pea-shooter. Goodbye, Miss Alsop, and I wish you well.'

Mad Marj, yielding, sighed as she left his office and his man appeal in company with Lulu.

Boots returned to his morning mail. Rosie put her head in.

'Did you win?' she asked.

'As you can see, I'm still alive,' said Boots.

'Happy day,' said Rosie, and went back to the office she shared with Rachel.

'Well?' said Rachel.

'All clear,' said Rosie.

'Sammy can come out of hiding now?' said Rachel.

'Yes, where exactly did he bunk off to?'

'He's down in the canteen, hiding himself behind a cup of coffee,' said Rachel. She herself went down to give Sammy the glad tidings, that the latter-day Boadicea was now safely departed in her chariot. Sammy stopped turning grey and went back up to his office. There he phoned the Brixton shop and told the manageress to take the fur-lined winter jacket out of the window, and to keep in mind the fact that Marjorie Alsop, the dangerous female tomato-thrower and window-breaker, lived close by and was, accordingly, always likely to take a look at what was on display. The manageress fell over herself in assuring Sammy all would be put right and kept so.

From then on the morning was peaceful for him. That is, ringing phones, queries on overheads, debatable profit margins and arguments about the final costs of rebuilding the firm's burned-out shop in Southend were all part of the everyday business carry-on that kept him happy.

Sammy Adams was a man who might have made a fortune as the executive head of an international corporation, but he had never thought in those terms. His fulfilment and satisfaction were in being his own boss, founding and running his own business. As for making a fortune, he had accomplished that. A modest fortune, perhaps, compared with a millionaire's, but there it was, vested in his own house, in the money he had in the bank, and in the shares he owned. And in his own wife, not someone else's, as was the case with Monte Carlo types. Susie alone made him feel rich.

Over the evening meal, Polly asked Gemma how the Finnish girl was coming along.

'Well,' said Gemma, 'although she's been a bit po-faced lately–'

'Moody, you mean?' said Polly.

'Yes, I suppose you could call it that,' said

Gemma, 'and when I asked her what was up, was she homesick or something, she said it was just that she kept having doubts about passing the Oxford entrance exam, and that her doubts made her feel gloomy.'

'I've heard of gloomy Swedes,' said Boots. 'A gloomy Finn is news to me.'

'It's the Scandinavian link, Dad,' said James.

'Anyway,' said Gemma, 'I kept telling her she wouldn't be forced to take the exam until Miss Stanton was sure she was ready to. Fact, I said. That finally cheered her up. So I'm taking the credit for doing away with her gloom. Is that worth increasing my pocket money, Daddy? I mean, when strangers cometh among us, blessed are those who give them kindness.'

'Well, I've got to admit it, Dad, cometh among us is worth an extra bob or two,' said James.

'A gem,' said Boots.

'And what d'you think Miss Stanton went on about at morning assembly?' Gemma continued.

'Wrinkled stockings?' said James.

'Daddy, you'll have to do something about your son,' said Gemma, 'he's kind of falling apart. I really don't know what Cathy sees in him that she couldn't see in a seaside donkey with cloth ears.'

'James, remind me to talk to you sometime,' said Boots.

'Hearing you, Pa,' said James. 'I hope it'll be about starting a bank account for me if you're going to up Gemma's pocket money.'

'Never mind your finances, James,' said Polly, 'let's hear what it was that Gemma's principal went on about at morning assembly.'

'Biscuits,' said Gemma.

'Biscuits?' said Polly, noting that her children's pork chops had been gnawed hungrily to the bone.

'Yes,' said Gemma. Miss Stanton, she said, had informed the students that the teachers' biscuit tin was being raided, and that she suspected this was taking place regularly at night. Which pointed to boarders. Did any of them wish to own up? No-one did. 'And no-one pointed a finger, either,' said Gemma. 'Well, one doesn't, does one? I expect some boarders wake up at night feeling hungry. Mama, what's for afters?'

'Strawberry jam tart,' said Polly.

'Yours, Mum?' enquired James.

'Don't ask awkward questions, dear boy,' said Polly, whose affinity with a cooker and a recipe book was still as vague as when she had served up lumpy custard to Boots during the first months of their wartime marriage.

Chapter Fourteen

Lulu and her dad had calmed Marjorie Alsop down. Accordingly, Lulu informed Sammy he could now dwell in peace. Sammy said now and for ever? Lulu said she couldn't promise for ever, but she could for the next month or so, during which time Marjorie would be moving closer and closer to a meeting with the Minister of Trade at teatime on the Parliamentary terrace. Well, after that, said Sammy, do your best to get her to fall down a hole somewhere. Lulu said she would.

A more welcome caller than Miss Alsop arrived at the offices on Friday morning in the shape of Mr Eli Greenberg, friend and business help to Sammy for many years. Sammy noted that the old one-time rag-and-bone man still looked hale and hearty, despite his bushy beard being liberally sprinkled with white, his round rusty hat rustier than ever and his ancient coat sagging a bit. He was in his seventy-ninth year, and apart from observing the Jewish Sabbath, he hadn't spent any day of his adult life doing nothing.

'Welcome, Eli, take a seat.'

'Vell, that's kind of you, Sammy, ain't it? I vas passing, vasn't I, and thought I might have a little talk vith you.' Even if he lived to be a hundred, Mr Greenberg was still going to speak his own kind of English. 'My vord,' he said, seating himself on the other side of Sammy's large and handsome oak desk, 'ain't it alvays a pleasure to see you up to your eyes?'

The desk was laden with all that appertained to Sammy's daily grind, letters, invoices, estimates and notes.

'All in a day's work, Eli old cock,' said Sammy. 'Now, what's on your mind?'

'Business, Sammy, business.'

'You're going to talk my language, Eli?'

'I hope so, Sammy. Now, ain't I alvays heard you don't believe in standing still?'

'Eli,' said Sammy, 'when you're standing still in business you're actually moving backwards.'

'My own sentiments, Sammy, ain't they? Vell now, there's your clothes store by the Elephant and Castle, vhich store is managed by young Freddy Brown and doing fine business, ain't it?'

'True,' said Sammy, passing over the fact that young Freddy, his brother-in-law, was now forty-four.

'And ain't I also heard you vould like to expand it?'

'If I said no, I'd be telling a porkie,'

189

confessed Sammy.

'Vell, Sammy, next door is an Italian cafe, ain't it? Now run by a Polish gentleman vunce of the Free Polish Army.'

'Italian cafes run by Polish gents ain't common to me, Eli,' said Sammy, 'but I've got a feeling you're up and ticking, so carry on.'

Mr Greenberg pointed out that if Sammy's property company acquired the Polish-run and Polish-owned Italian cafe, it would enable the clothes store to enjoy a pleasing amount of expansion.

'I von't say it vill look like Selfridges, Sammy, but it von't look like peanuts, either.'

'Not the way we'll window-dress it,' said Sammy, 'but will the Polish gent sell his premises without asking a price that would ruin the property company's balance sheet? Further and so on, is he thinking of selling?'

'Vell, Sammy,' said Mr Greenberg happily, 'it so happens–'

'Ah,' said Sammy just as happily.

'It so happens, Sammy, that I'm acquainted with the gentleman, Mr Robinson–'

'Robinson?' said Sammy. 'A Polish Robinson?'

'Vell, no vun could get their teeth round his Polish moniker, or spell it,' said Mr Greenberg, 'so he changed it to Robinson, vhich is as English as yours and mine, ain't it? Now, Sammy, about his inclinings.'

'I'm listening,' said Sammy, the electric blue of his eyes bright with pleasurable anticipation.

'His good lady being Scottish, she vishes to go back to Glasgow,' said Mr Greenberg. 'Vell, she don't have much understanding of cockney, not like you and me, Sammy. Ain't you and me been understanding of it all our lives? But Mrs Robinson, she don't know vhat Elephant and Castle people are saying, vhich gets up her nose, poor voman. So for the right price, Joe vill sell and move to Scotland.'

'Joe?'

'Joe Robinson, ain't it?'

'What's the right price, Eli, d'you know?'

'Vell,' said Mr Greenberg, 'he's only just made up his mind about selling, vhich I think his missus made up for him. As soon as I got to know, I thought now vhat about my old friend Sammy, vould he be interested? So didn't I have some little talks vith Joe, and ain't he asking two and a half thousand for freehold of cafe and upstairs living rooms? But of course, asking ain't exactly the same as getting.'

'We'll name a fair price,' said Sammy.

'And between you and me, Sammy, seeing it's business mixed vith pleasure, I von't ask for more than a little commission. In Bank of England notes, say?'

'Eli old cock, count on fair do's,' said

Sammy, 'and seeing you're talking my language concerning Polish Joe, would you like to join me in a cup of coffee?'

'That's kind, Sammy, ain't it, but might I say tea vould be more to my liking?'

'No problem,' said Sammy, and phoned the canteen to ask for a pot of tea for two to be sent up, with biscuits. By the time it arrived, five minutes later, Sammy had arranged for Mr Greenberg to introduce him to Mr Joe Robinson from Poland. And by the time his old friend was ready to leave, Sammy said to hang on a few more minutes so that Boots could come and say hello. Boots, receiving the invitation by office phone, came in to shake hands with Mr Greenberg, and to tell him he was looking as fit as a new fiddle.

'Ah, you're a kind man, Boots, like alvays, and don't you and Sammy still make a man feel the vorld ain't only for villains and scallyvags?'

'The world at present, Eli, is an exciting treasure chest for the young,' said Boots, 'which is a welcome improvement on what it offered in Hitler's time. But what brings you here today?'

Together, Mr Greenberg and Sammy acquainted Boots with the details of their discussion. Boots said the prospects of an expanded store in that well-populated locality of south London, the family's old stamping ground, were certainly worth serious consideration, as long they didn't keep Sammy awake at night.

'Vell, ain't new business prospects meat and drink to him?' said Mr Greenberg.

'They help to charge his electricity,' smiled Boots, 'and I'd take a bet that he'll never blow a fuse.'

'Listen, you two,' said Sammy, 'stop talking about me behind my back in front of my face.' Which made Mr Greenberg depart with a twinkle in his eye and a curl to his beard.

'Sammy,' said Boots, 'if this expansion goes through, it'll mean more responsibility for Freddy and taking on more staff.'

'And laying on a real spread of window displays, as well as opening up an upper floor,' said Sammy. 'We'll turn it into Walworth's Selfridges without giving it a posh label. Posh labels ain't favourite with Walworth people. It makes 'em think prices are posh too. Now, about change of usage for the Italian cafe, we'll need a promise that we'll get planning permission before we contract to purchase. I'll get Tim and Daniel working on that.'

'Have a nice time, Sammy,' said Boots.

'Blind O'Reilly,' said Sammy to himself as his brother went back to his office, 'he's still giving me a pat on the head. Talk about Lord-I-Am.'

'What d'you think, Puss?' said Tim to Felicity over dinner that evening. 'Sammy's after expanding our store at the Elephant and Castle.'

'Sammy never stops pushing out the boundaries of the business,' said Felicity.

'Uncle Sammy's a humdinger,' said Jennifer, at fourteen as tall, vigorous and vital as any girl of sixteen. Supple limbs and enthusiasm meant she was already her school's fastest sprinter. 'A real go-getter.'

'He's all of that,' said Tim, 'and he's always wanted to make more of the store, with quite separate men's and women's departments, and a wider range of wear. He has a chance now if the property company can purchase the cafe next door. Daniel and I have to find out if the council will grant change of usage.'

'Hasn't the Elephant and Castle seen major post-war development?' asked Felicity. 'If so, I can't see why the council would refuse permission to turn a cafe into part of a store.'

'Daddy,' said Jennifer, 'isn't the Elephant and Castle in Walworth where Grandma Finch brought up her family?'

'Walworth, yes, that's the place,' said Tim, 'and their old house is still standing.'

'I'll go and explore one day,' said Jennifer. 'I mean, it's where our Adams roots are. I've been to Mummy's home in Streatham,

194

where our Jessop roots are.'

'And where your maternal grandma's pot plants are a credit to all of us,' said Tim.

'Watch it, matey,' said Felicity, to whom restoration of sight had meant that life was once more a bright canvas of colour, movement and people. In the forefront of that canvas were her husband and daughter, each such a strength to her during her years of blindness.

'Perhaps we'll drive to the store tomorrow morning,' said Tim. 'I know Pa and Uncle Sammy are going, and I'd like to refresh myself on its layout and make a guess at its potential now that the rebuilding of our Southend shop is nicely under way. The improving economy is all in our favour.'

It was true that in many areas of commerce and industry wages were better, threadbare pockets a thing of the past. Indeed, Prime Minister Harold Macmillan had assured the British people they'd never had it so good. Well, fancy that, remarked an underpaid coalminer of Kent, I'd never have known it if he hadn't said so.

'Daddy, yes, I'll come with you tomorrow,' said Jennifer. Then, in similar vein to her cousin Gemma, she asked, 'What's for afters, Mum?'

'Apple pie,' said Felicity.

Glad cries from Jennifer, as healthy of appetite as any of her cousins.

'I say, you're not going down to pinch more biscuits, are you?' enquired Irena Leino's dorm mate. It was close to ten o'clock and both girls should have been preparing for slumber, not sitting on their beds and chatting.

'Ah, just one more go, I think,' said Irena, and she slipped out, with no more sound than that of a foraging mouse. Down the stairs she went, by the glow of landing lights, down to the door of Miss Stanton's study. There she paused, listening for unwanted sounds. The resident teachers, however, were all gathered together in their lounge as usual, along with their principal, and none thought of popping down to check for goings-on. Or goings-out for that matter. The student boarders of Maiden Hall did not indulge in out-of-bounds larks.

Opening the study door and entering, Irena switched on the light, closed the door, then quickly searched for what she had come to know was there, a street map of Dulwich and the surrounding area. She needed to look at it carefully, to be able to make her way to the right station for a train that would take her across the Thames to Victoria. Yes, that was it, West Dulwich, that was the right one. She knew so from information given. Now, how did one get there from Maiden Hall?

She studied the map intently.

She did not get back to her dorm for quite a while, and when she did her companion boarder was in bed.

'Irena, you've been ages.'

'Yes, there were teachers close by, I think. So I hid myself until it was safe, and did not go into the kitchen.'

'Just as well. I'm sure Miss Stanton has set some kind of trap for the biscuit raider.'

'Perhaps you are right, yes, perhaps you are, but such biscuits are very tempting.'

That, possibly, might have meant that the biscuits Irena was used to were inferior to Huntley and Palmer's rich tea assortment.

Chapter Fifteen

Saturday morning.

Elvira Figgins was in a ratty mood. Coming up to forty-one, she was finding that competition from younger members of her profession, an extremely long-established one, was limiting custom of the better kind. Most of the time she was having to make do with second-class punters. On top of that she'd lost her paying lodger, which was seriously aggravating. Well, he had not only paid her generously for use of two rooms and for keeping her mouth shut about how he earned his oof, he had also paid at least once a week for her favours. He was very generous in that respect too, especially if he was in a good mood, and he wasn't a bad performer, either. He had the vigour and stamina of a young man. She knew him to be a tea leaf, sometimes in clover, sometimes a bit skint, but that was none of her business.

Curly Harris, that was what he called himself. For her part, she wouldn't have asked questions if he'd called himself Bill Sikes. A wise woman didn't ask questions providing a bloke paid his dues like a gent. But he ought to do something about his short temper, because it had recently landed him in serious trouble. The silly boy had knifed some barman for not being respectful, so he'd said. It meant he was on the run from the cops. Once those bluebottles laid their lousy mitts on him, they'd have him up before the snotty-nosed Camberwell magistrates, who'd arrange a reserved seat for him at the Old Bailey. Magistrates. She knew something about them all right. Talk about the grief they could hand out to a woman jumped on by the Old Bill just for mixing pleasure with business in a Soho doorway.

She'd like to hand out a bit of grief herself. To the kind of people who were in favour of magistrates.

Like shopkeepers. Spiteful they were if you happened to forget to pay for what you fancied.

Close to the Elephant and Castle was the Adams clothing store, run very efficiently by Freddy Brown, younger brother of Susie, Sammy's wife. Freddy liked meeting customers, and he particularly liked meeting the people of Walworth. He was one of them. Apart from his soldiering days, he had never left the area, never wanted to. He still lived in Wansey Street with his wife Cassie, as lively now at forty-three as she'd been when a tomboy of eleven. He was also blessed with a son and daughter. Son Lewis, eighteen, was a bright lad working for a shipping company. Daughter Maureen, twenty, had one foot in the world of glamour, being a pin-up model. Freddy, forty-four himself, had no complaints about his lot as a husband, father and a fortunate survivor of the war in Burma. Too many mates had been buried out there for him not to appreciate his blessings. Cassie had once said that the reason why Boots hardly ever complained about life or people was because he had survived the Great War while a million other men hadn't.

Freddy had received a phone call from brother-in-law Sammy last night, and at this moment he was listening to him in the little staff room at the back of the store. And what was making his ears tingle were words concerning the possibility of expanding the size of the store. There were natural ifs and buts, of course, such as was the location right for an increase in customers? Freddy and Sammy answered that one together by stating their known faith in the natural enthusiasm of Walworth people for quality items at bargain prices. That had always been one of Sammy's pet principles. Don't sell rubbish, however cheap, because the customer won't come back again. Freddy would always go along with that.

'A larger store with a more varied selection of wares and a definite separation of ladies' and men's departments, each with its own cubicles, well, I'll eat my Sunday suit if that wouldn't increase custom considerable,' said Sammy.

'Well, you're the engine-driver, you always have been,' said Freddy, 'and I reckon if you'd had doubts, you wouldn't have listened to old Eli Greenberg for more than a couple of minutes. You'd have told him no go. Myself, I'd say the locals would go for it more than they're going for the Elephant and Castle development. It's too over-powering for a lot of people.'

'There we are, then,' said Sammy. 'Of course, you'd need more staff and a manager.'

'A manager? What happens to me, then?' asked Freddy.

'You run things from a position where you'd command the whole shooting match,' said Sammy. 'With a minimum salary increase of forty per cent, even if it gives the wages bill a painful headache.' Freddy had not only run the store at a healthy profit, he was also Susie's brother and accordingly very much one of the family, which, along with his abilities, made him notably worthy of his hire.

They talked on, while the store was busy attending to the wants of Saturday morning customers. Freddy's established assistant was Mrs Ruby Turner, a round-faced jolly

201

woman very much fancied by her milkman, but protected from being carried off on his float by his awareness that her husband, a muscular postman, would certainly come after him. And he couldn't get much speed out of his float.

Ruby had Saturday help in the shape of a bright young feller, Peregrine Peters. Peregrine regarded his baptismal as more of a mishap than a name, but he'd arrived in the world when some parents, including his own, had long been sold off Arthurs, Berts, Charlies and Willies, and were looking for inspiration in newspaper announcements of engagements. Peregrine, from Camberwell, was doing his best to live with what his mum and dad had landed him. Well past eighteen, he was earning midweek wages helping market stallholders to clear up on early closing day, and Saturday wages here in the Adams store. Put aside, such wages would help him meet some of his expenses when he entered university in September.

While Ruby was attending to a young lady customer, he was in conference with an old codger who was after a woollen scarf providing 20 per cent was knocked off the price.

'Sorry, granddad,' said Peregrine, lively and outgoing, 'these scarves are already at rock-bottom prices.'

'I ain't yer granddad, sonny,' said the

whiskery old codger.

'But you could've been if you'd married my grandma,' said Peregrine, which piece of logic didn't altogether impress the old and knowing gent.

'Listen, I don't want none of yer sauce,' he said, 'I just want one of them woolly scarves – that navy blue one – with a decent bit of discount. Well, I ain't Rockefeller, yer know, I'm a pensioner with holes in me socks. You got holes in yourn?'

'Well, no–'

'There y'ar, then.'

'All right, granddad, let you have the scarf for three and six.' The marked price for the chunky neck and chest warmer was three and sevenpence-ha'penny, but Mr Brown, the manager, would encourage knocking a bit off rather than allow the customer to escape. It was something initiated long ago by Sammy when he opened his first shop. 'That suit you, three and six?'

'How much discount is that?'

'Oh, pretty fair, I'll tell you that. Would you like it wrapped?'

'No, put it round me neck, it's cold outside, and me Saturday vest's a bit worn.'

The result was a satisfied old codger and a ring-up by Peregrine of three and six in the till. While he was attending to this, and while Ruby was attending to a housewife, a woman came in who began a survey of what was on offer to female customers on the left-hand side of the store. The right-hand side was for male customers. She was followed in almost at once by a tall, rangy man accompanied by a girl. Saturday mornings were always busy. Saturday afternoons even more so.

Peregrine offered his assistance to the solitary woman. Of course, if she was after something highly personal, he'd have to refer her to Ruby.

'Can I help you, madam?'

'I'm just looking,' said the woman, a bit of a flashy bird. All done up in a fox fur, mustard-coloured costume, saucy titfer and yards of make-up, she was admiring some very nice embroidered blouses. 'I'll let you know if I need your help.'

'I'm around all day,' said Peregrine.

'Well, fancy that,' said the tarted-up female, and moved on.

With Ruby still engaged, Peregrine advanced on the other newcomers, the long-legged man and his young female companion. Father and daughter, he reckoned. They were looking around.

'Can I help?'

'You could if you'll point me at your manager,' said Boots.

'Mr Brown, you mean, sir?' said Peregrine.

'That's the gentleman,' smiled Boots.

'There's someone with him at the moment,'

said Peregrine.

Boots, guessing it was Sammy, said, 'My brother, I think.'

'Oh, right,' said Peregrine, and took the duo through to the door of the staff room.

'You go in, Daddy,' said the girl, 'I'll look around.'

Boots knocked, received an invitation to enter, and went in to join Sammy in the discussion with Freddy. Peregrine spoke to the girl.

'Excuse me,' he said. He was a cheerful and obliging young man, with a liking for old ladies and a willingness to apply the boot to louts given to upsetting them. 'D'you want any help?'

'Help in looking around?' said Gemma, turning to him, and Peregrine was suddenly aware of beholding a gem. She was dressed in a sweater, skirt and little jacket. A beret crowned her dark, burnished hair. Her looks were enchanting, her eyes bright with the light of a smile. Peregrine blinked. Not so long ago, one of Sammy's bookkeepers, George Porter, had looked into the melting eyes of office girl Queenie Richards, and virtually fallen into them. Much the same thing now happened to Peregrine Peters. He looked into the smiling eyes of Gemma Adams and fell into a trance. 'Well, it's very nice of you,' he heard her say, 'but I think I can manage.' What a poppet, he thought, what a dreamboat. About seventeen? Yes. That was the age, he told himself, when Nature's true dreamboats were well on the ladder that led to the giddy heights of wondrous beatitude. (His trance was responsible for that piece of delirium.) More words floated into his ears. 'Are you awake?'

'Awake? What? Pardon?' It was difficult to come to. 'Oh, sorry, what was it you were saying?'

'Nothing important,' said Gemma, wondering what was making the young man look as if he wasn't all there, which was a pity, really, because he was otherwise quite dishy. Still, he couldn't be completely daft or he wouldn't be serving in one of Uncle Sammy's shops. She began to move around. This was the first time she had been in this particular branch, and she thought the family firm could really make something of it if permission to expand was granted, especially if the men's and women's departments could be fully separated.

With Ruby taking care of two more lady customers, Peregrine staggered up to his newfound dreamboat.

'You – er – sure I can't help?' he offered. Much to his mortification, he realized he was in failing command of his tonsils.

Gemma, a caring girl, looked at him and said, 'Excuse me, are you unwell?'

'Unwell?'

'Have you got a suffering chest?'

'A suffering chest?'

'Well, you do sound hoarse, and you do look unwell.'

'Well, I – well, I admit I'm not quite myself.'

'D'you need a doctor?'

'A whatter?'

'You're getting really hoarse.'

'It's my dry throat – er, what's your name?'

'Pardon?'

'I – um–'

'Your eyes look all funny. D'you have a kind of dizzy myopia?'

'Well, no, it's more a kind of disbelief.'

'Oh, d'you mean you're an atheist?'

'No. Er, did you say what your name was?'

'No, and it's a cheek to ask – oh, look at that woman!'

The tarty lady was just completing a snatch, a snatch that she stuffed inside her costume jacket. She then made quick tracks for the door. Peregrine, despite the drawback of his trance, realized at once what was happening. He went after the woman, catching up with her just outside the store.

'Sorry and all that,' he said, not a bit dry-throated now, 'but I think you've got stuff you haven't paid for.'

'Here, mind yer business,' said Elvira Figgins, who'd just done some shoplifting in her determination to start getting even with

207

shopkeepers for being on the side of the spiteful law. 'And let go of me arm or I'll sue you for assault.'

'I'm not holding your arm,' said Peregrine.

'Lucky for you, you saucy young bugger,' said Elvira. 'Now, do yerself a favour and push off before I call the cops.'

'No need to call 'em,' said Peregrine, 'there's one coming.'

Elvira panicked.

'Well, shoot,' she hissed, 'they're always where they ain't wanted. Here, help yerself.' So saying, she opened up her jacket and out fell a very nice selection of embroidered blouses. Peregrine caught them before they hit the ground, and then Elvira was away like a gaudy female cockatoo with a cat on its tail, disappearing into a shop at the Elephant and Castle. Whether or not she liked it, and most of the old residents of the area hated it for its lack of atmosphere, she nevertheless disappeared into it.

Out came the intrigued Gemma.

'Is that what she had under her jacket?' she asked, indicating the blouses. Buses trundled by and people passed by, and Peregrine almost fell into another trance. He was saved by the tingling effects of the clear cold fresh air. Even so, he was still hooked, for the young lady looked a picture of glowing health, the kind seen in French artists' impressions of skaters gliding round an open-air ice rink.

'You were saying?' he offered.

'Goodness, you're still a bit hoarse,' said Gemma. 'That woman was a shoplifter, wasn't she? Hadn't you better take the goods back into the store?'

Peregrine, the goods clutched to his chest, said, 'Oh, yes, I think I should.' Re-entering the store, Gemma with him, he asked off the top of his head, 'Excuse me, are you married?'

It was Gemma's turn to blink.

'What a daft question,' she said. 'I could ask you one. Are you a bit dotty?'

'I was all right when I left home this morning,' said Peregrine. His attention was then caught by Ruby, who indicated there were customers in menswear waiting for service. 'Oh, right,' he called.

'I'll put those blouses back on the hangers for you,' said Gemma, and did him a kindness by taking the purloined blouses out of his arms. He then set about seeing to the wants of a couple of hefty working men who were both after woollies.

Freddy was now out of the staff room and moving around in company with Sammy and Boots, the trio discussing the prospect-ive conversion in murmurs. Gemma, having put the blouses back in place after ensuring that none had been damaged by the swift stealthy hands of the painted shoplifter, watched the young man who had been suffering a sore throat and wonky eyes. He seemed all right now, he was dealing quite brightly with his customers.

The woman assistant was still attending to the two ladies, while promising attention to a new arrival. From all Gemma knew about the store, she was aware that Freddy was usually in the forefront of seeing to the wants of customers. At the moment, however, he was engrossed with Uncle Sammy and her dad. As if on cue he suddenly detached himself, gave her a smile of acknowledgement and then offered his services to the new arrival.

Gemma glanced again at the young man. Imagine him asking her if she was married. He had to be a bit dotty, except there he was, getting on fine with the two strapping working men. He didn't sound at all hoarse now, more as if he was cracking jokes with them. Having wrapped up their purchases, he saw them to the door, thanked them for their custom and said goodbye.

'Ta-ta, see you again sometime, Charlie,' said one, to which the young man responded with a laugh.

Since he was free for the moment, Gemma walked up to him.

'Is your throat better?' she asked.

'Pardon?' Peregrine found her delightfully piquant looks and bright enquiring eyes making mincemeat of his resolve to be his normal self, which he considered to be very normal. His impression that she was more of a young lady than a mere girl was no delusion. Gemma had grown up in the easy and civilized atmosphere created by her parents. She and James had both been encouraged to ask questions, offer opinions and make many of their own decisions. Result, she and James were very grown-up at seventeen.

'I asked if your throat was better,' she smiled.

'Pardon?' said Peregrine again, fighting his weakness.

'Oh, man, now you sound deaf,' said Gemma, whose life was free of the kind of distractions a girl could suffer when head over heels. She was entirely committed to college life, some park tennis now and again, and the prospect of becoming a fashion designer. 'Are you deaf? Well, a bit deaf?'

'Never heard of it,' said Peregrine. 'And if I had a frog in my throat, it's gone now.'

'But your eyes still look a bit funny.'

'My eyes?'

'Yes. Sort of twitchy.'

'Twitchy?'

'Yes.'

'Do I look as if I'm not seeing straight?'

'Yes, that's it. Perhaps you need glasses.'

'What I really need is help.'

'Help? What sort of help? Oh, look, you've

got more customers.'

A husband and wife team had entered, and the husband was being led to a display of men's ties. Peregrine alerted himself.

'Oh, yes,' he said. 'Well, nice talking to you – um, what's your name?'

'If we ever get to know each other,' said Gemma, 'I'll tell you.'

Peregrine perforce went to attend to the customers and Gemma rejoined her dad, who was still conferring with Uncle Sammy.

'Hello, angel,' said Sammy, 'how's your young self?'

'Oh, it's been getting a lot older since I last saw you, Uncle Sammy,' said Gemma.

'That wasn't more than a week ago, was it?' said Sammy.

'At my time of life you grow phenomenally older in a week,' said Gemma amid the bustling sounds of the store and an increasing inflow of customers.

'Phe-what?' said Sammy. 'Are you getting as educated as your dad?'

'I'm just getting some useful kind,' said Gemma.

'Yes, so did your dad,' said Sammy, 'and look what it did for him. Turned him into Lord-I-Am and made him a general.'

'Oh, I give you Lord-I-Am, Uncle Sammy, but not general,' said Gemma. 'Colonel, actually. Daddy, are we ready to go now?'

'Yes, we won't wait for Tim,' said Boots.

Tim was due to arrive and to take a look at the place before arranging any consultation with the firm's architects. 'You haven't been bored, I hope.'

'Not a bit,' said Gemma, 'I've been talking to Charlie.'

'The young male assistant?' said Boots.

'Yes, and he's quite nice, but a bit round the twist,' said Gemma.

'That's a fact?' said Boots, and glanced across the store at the young man in question. He seemed a healthy and personable representative of his kind, and was making easy headway with a woman who'd come in with her husband to help him buy a tie. Well, if Gemma had found him a little eccentric, that wasn't an uncommon complaint among the unconventional young people of today. 'Time we were on our way, poppet,' he murmured.

He and Gemma said goodbye to Sammy and then to Freddy. And on their way out Gemma gave the dotty young man a friendly wave, little realizing she was leaving him with a knockout impression of her as a ravishing young goddess, to say nothing of a sad acceptance that after their brief time together she had departed from his life for ever.

It made life hardly worth living.

Chapter Sixteen

Tim had driven to Walworth Road via Camberwell Green, turned right into Browning Street (named after the poet, Robert Browning, born in the area), and then left into Caulfield Place. Along the way, Jennifer had noted the hustle and bustle of the main road, a mixture of shops and dwellings. The East Street market had looked crowded. In entering Caulfield Place, a cul-de-sac, the hustle and bustle suddenly gave way to comparative quiet.

Tim pulled up outside the house in which Chinese Lady had started her married life with Corporal Daniel Adams of the West Kents. There it was, standing as solidly square to the world as ever, along with the rest of the terraced dwellings. Bombs had devastated the other side of the cul-de-sac, and development was rearing its concrete head. Residents were suffering it. Councils all over Inner London had for years been taking advantage of widespread bomb damage to rearrange the geography and residential nature of their boroughs. This hadn't proved to the liking of everyone. Many would have preferred the rebuilding of

214

their terraced rows of houses to the erection of concrete blocks of high-rise flats.

The right side of Caulfield Place offered Jennifer a clear picture of how Victorian planners had dealt with the problem of providing housing for London's ever-increasing population.

'So this is the famous abode where Grandma Finch brought up her family?' she said, noting the stone-pillared bay window and the sturdy-looking front door, painted a dark green.

'This is it, chicken,' said Tim, and Felicity sat in silent reflection of what she saw as the birthplace of the family she had married into. The Victorian-built house, in emerging whole from the Second World War, was a symbol of how the family had fought and survived. The only one to die had been Emily, Boots's first wife, acknowledged as the family's godsend before and after the First World War. How sad to have been taken from life when only forty-two. She had missed so much.

'It looks ever so old-fashioned but very solid, Daddy,' said Jennifer, 'like a lot of the houses in Brixton and Camberwell.'

'Well, the Victorians never used cardboard and glue for their building materials,' said Tim.

Street kids appeared and edged up towards the car. Tim, his window down, asked a question. 'Who's the eldest?'

'Me!' That from a girl of about nine.

'Me!' A challenge from a boy about the same age.

'Who likes chocolate bars?'

'We do!' That was from the whole group of six, all of whom had the look of Walworth's racy street kids but wore better clothes than those of past generations. Certainly, all had shoes on their feet.

'All right,' said Tim, 'if the eldest can tell me something I'll treat all of you. So, listen, eldest, who used to live in that house in the Twenties and Thirties?' He pointed.

'The Adamses!' shouted the two eldest in triumph and glee.

'How d'you know?' asked Tim, who already had half a crown in his hand.

'Mister, everyone knows!' That from the eldest girl.

'They're millionaires now!' That from the eldest boy.

'Are they?' smiled Tim. 'Who says so?'

'Me mum, of course.'

'Fair do's,' said Tim, 'so here you are, go and buy yourselves some chocolate.' He handed over the half-crown. He knew that Walworth street kids of whatever era and whatever circumstances all loved receiving a bonanza from a well-wisher.

'Mister, ain't you a toff?' said the eldest girl, who had taken charge of the half-crown.

'Who lives there now?' asked Tim.

'The Samuels.'

'A nice family?'

'Yes, there's eight of 'em, mister, and they're all from the West Indies.'

'Eight?' said Felicity.

'Well, it might be nine, I ain't sure, except I know it's a lot.'

At which point the dark green door opened and a plump young black girl appeared in the aperture. She had an armful of empty milk bottles.

'Watcher, Henrietta,' called eldest boy.

''Lo,' responded Henrietta, stooping to place the bottles on the ground in front of the doorstep.

She cast a glance at the car and its driver. 'Who's that?' she asked.

'A gent,' said eldest boy.

'A toff,' said eldest girl, hand firmly in control of the large silver coin.

Tim caught Henrietta's attention and asked a question.

'D'you like your house?'

'I suppose,' said Henrietta, ''cept it don't have no bath nor shower.' That admission seemed to embarrass her, for she suddenly shut herself off by closing the door.

'Ask a silly question and you get an awkward answer,' said Tim. Then, 'So long, kids.' And he turned the car and drove away. Jennifer waved goodbye. The six kids went haring off to the nearest sweet shop, hoping to find chocolate bars in unlimited supply.

'The house,' said Jennifer as Tim turned into Browning Street. 'Really no bathroom, Daddy?'

'They're all compact three-up, three-down dwellings,' said Tim. 'Built in Queen Victoria's time, when families used a galvanized tin bath to soak themselves on Friday nights. Grandma Finch will tell you so.'

'Crikey, did Grandpa Boots actually have to use a tin bath?' asked Jennifer, finding it difficult to imagine him doing so. 'And Aunt Lizzy and Uncle Sammy and Uncle Tommy?'

'Yep, all of them,' said Tim, re-entering Walworth Road.

'Three-up, three-down must mean it's short of space for any family upwards of four,' said Felicity.

'Well, if I know anything about our lot,' said Jennifer, 'I bet they all had a go at raising the roof.' Tim smiled and Felicity laughed. When they reached the family store, Sammy was still there, still conferring with Freddy when the latter wasn't attending to customers. Tim and Felicity joined them. Jennifer wandered around, and Peregrine, after dealing with a customer, asked if he could help her. No, she was only looking, she said, and had a little chat with him before he had to serve another customer. She had no idea, of course, that he had come to know Cousin Gemma, and that Gemma had found him quite barmy. But then at fourteen Jennifer didn't have the knockout effect on him that Gemma at seventeen had had.

Tim phoned Boots later.

'Pa, old sport,' he said, 'thought I'd tell you that your old house in Walworth is now home to a large West Indian family of about eight or nine. The street kids weren't sure of the exact number.'

'Well, in a happy family of eight, what's one more?' said Boots.

'No problem,' said Tim. 'Thought I'd also tell you that one of them, a girl name of Henrietta, made a point of informing us that there was no bathroom or shower.'

'Was it a complaint?' asked Boots.

'More of a good-natured statement, I thought,' said Tim.

'Well, next time you run into Henrietta,' said Boots, 'give her my regards and tell her I know how she feels about having to bath in a tin tub.'

'Noted,' said Tim. 'By the way, having had a good look at the shop and the adjoining cafe, I'm pretty sure our architects could go to work on designing what would be a bountiful department store.'

'Bountiful?' said Boots.

'Sammy's word,' said Tim.

'Well, in respect of business ventures,' said Boots, 'Sammy's vocabulary rarely trips up.'

Along with cousins and friends, Gemma and James were at the Brixton gig as usual that evening, James partnering Cathy. The band was great, guitar strings plonking away, the packed dance hall vibrating to the rockers and rollers. The number strumming out at the moment was Bill Haley's world-wide hit, 'Rock Around the Clock'.

Somehow in the swirl of skirts and legs and bodies, James lost contact with Cathy. That kind of happening, however, wasn't unusual when one was swinging at a distance from one's partner. Ceaseless quick movement seemed to create different patterns of who was with whom. No-one worried. Partners gravitated to link up again.

Cathy, unfortunately, found herself being gathered up by a tall streak of a young man who was decidedly opposed to letting her go. In fact, he was at no rock 'n' roll distance from her. He had her with his hands gobbling up her hips and his active pelvis far too close.

'No, excuse me, break it up,' said Cathy.

'Come on, let's go, baby, you're a sweet move, so let's hit the grooves,' he responded, a yard-wide grin splitting his long face in half.

'Just let me go, please,' said Cathy, pulling

away but without managing to break his hold. His arms slid around her waist and his fidgety pelvis became a burning embarrassment. And he actually tried to kiss her. She turned her face, avoiding his eager north-and-south. At the same time a hand appeared from behind his neck. It gathered up his chin and yanked his head backwards, dislodging him from Cathy.

'Who let you out of your pigsty?' said a voice close to his ear, and James completed his punitive action by yanking harder. The offensive bloke hit the floor with a thud, and nearby couples hastily retreated from the arena of a threatened punch-up. Whatever ideas the bloke had about fighting his corner disappeared when he took in James's tall, firm-bodied figure and the look on his face. He scrambled to his feet, mouthed the kind of language he hadn't known during his brief time as an innocent child and lost himself in the crowd.

Cathy's eyes shone like those of a maiden delivered from evil by a white knight. Even in this day and age, many centuries distant from the heroics of King Arthur's gallant band, a girl delivered from a lout could experience a moment of dreamlike fantasy.

'James, oh, thanks,' she said as he took her arm and led her to the refreshment bar where coffee and soft drinks could be bought.

'Well, I couldn't take you back to your Aunt Marie looking as if you'd lost a fight for the honour of your bodice,' said James.

'My what?' said Cathy.

'It happens a lot in modern novels,' said James. 'Old Aunt Victoria devours them, but says they shouldn't be allowed.'

Cathy laughed, gave him an impulsive hug of gratitude for his act of delivery, and said, 'Yes, they're called bodice-rippers. Aunt Marie also enjoys them.'

'Good reading on a wet day, I should think,' said James as the band swung into a new number and the dancing feet of a few hundred teenagers gave the floor another drumming. 'Have a banana.'

'Banana?'

'I meant coffee or Coke.'

'Coffee, please,' said Cathy. 'I'm more in the mood for that than a banana.'

James glanced at her. Her eyes were bright, her looks much more than merely pretty, and he realized that this girl he had known for years was turning into a stunner, the kind to make him revise his ideas of remaining uncommitted until he was older and wiser. This reflection was a bit of a laugh, of course. How had he come to think in terms as stuffy as that?

'You're a great girl, Cathy,' he said, and ordered two coffees.

Out from the throng slipped Emily and her

222

Teddy-boy friend, Bradley Thompson. Emily, in her sixteenth year, was still a pert and precocious young minx with ideas of becoming a celebrity and the wife of someone like a Monte Carlo yacht-owner. Conversely, Brad, real name Albert, was at twenty a man of sound habits and sound principles, despite his liking for fancy clobber.

'Oh, you two having coffee?' said Emily, a delectable eyeful wearing a ponytail, a fashionable jet-black top and flared skirt. 'I'm dying for a Coke.'

'Me too, baby,' said Brad, and eased his way into the crowd around the refreshments bar, while Emily chatted with James and Cathy. Up came a highly personable bloke looking like the epitome of the fashionable young male in a red and white check shirt and cuffed blue jeans.

'Fancy a stroll, cookie?' he said to Emily.

'Who's asking?' said Emily.

'Chippy Valentine.'

'All right, Chippy, just for a minute or so while someone's getting me a Coke,' said Emily, and paired off with him. Soon they were swinging amid the moving, swirling multitude of rockers and rollers.

'Well,' said Cathy to James, 'I don't think much of that, even if she is your cousin.'

'Well, one odd cousin out of many can't be helped, I guess,' said James philosophically.

'Hello, where's she gone?' Brad materialized with two Cokes. James, with a pointed finger, indicated the present whereabouts of Emily. Brad picked her out, rocking around with a young bloke who looked like a cowhand minus his horse. 'Man, that's hurting my peepers,' he said.

'Emily being over there instead of over here?' said Cathy.

'Well, no,' said Brad. 'With Em, no use trying to put a bridle on her, a guy's got to let her go walkies at times. No, I strictly mean the guy's shirt, it's louder than the band.' Brad never saw his own kit as a bit overcolourful. It was part of the fashion scene for young men who'd dumped conventional suits. He spent time drinking his Coke and guarding the one he'd bought for Emily, but when she finally returned she complained the drink was lukewarm. Had James still been there he might have said something fairly cutting, but he was back on the floor with Cathy, she a million miles away from emulating Emily's act of desertion. Well, a girl didn't go walkies with a cowboy or even his millionaire ranch boss when jiving with a white knight.

Later, Boots again collected the young people to drive them home, much to their pleasure. Cindy Stevens, Giles, Emily, Cathy, James and Gemma all managed to dovetail into place in the back and front of the car, and from the pavement Brad waved them all goodnight as Boots drove off. 'What's up with you, Emily?' said Giles, rather cross with his sister. 'You didn't even bother to say good night to Brad.'

'Oh, sorry, I'm sure,' said Emily. 'He's all right, but nothing special.'

'What's great about you, then?' retorted Giles.

'You're boring, d'you know that?' said Emily.

Boots, driving homewards through the lamp-lit streets, cut in to suggest that everyone should be friendly with everyone else.

'Fair comment, Uncle Boots,' said Giles, 'but I get a feeling sometimes that Emily's a bit of a weight on my shoulders. I'll get a bowed-down look before I'm even twenty.'

'Oh, dear, what a shame,' said Emily.

Cindy felt for Giles's hand and gave it an understanding squeeze. A collector of boy-friends in an attempt to find the one who suited her best, her favourites were Giles and James, although a young man who lived next door was making the kind of running that could well put him in the lead.

'Cathy,' said Boots, 'how are you and Gemma finding your friend from Finland now?' He had a definite idea that although Irena might have come to London from Finland, she wasn't a native of that little country. 'Is she settling in?'

'Oh, yes, and next Saturday I'm taking her home to meet my Aunt Marie,' said Cathy.

'Yes,' said Gemma, 'Cathy and I are taking her for another stroll and finishing up there. Miss Stanton's given permission, and I don't think we'll let her get lost. She likes being out and about. I expect because Dulwich is a monumental change from snowy Finland.'

'Monumental?' said James.

'Yes, kind of high and mighty,' said Gemma.

'Dulwich?' said James.

'Yes, a right royal picture compared to a frozen Finnish marsh,' said Gemma.

'Dad, your daughter's gone bonkers,' said James.

'Give her time,' said Boots, the wintry night and the overcoated figures of people going homewards making him hope for the early arrival of a warm spring. That, he thought, amid the unrestrained chatter of the teenagers, is a sign I'm getting old.

Damn it, I am old.

'Daddy,' said Gemma, 'what're you smiling about?'

'Thoughts,' said Boots.

'Share them, Mr Adams,' said Cathy.

'I'm thinking,' said Boots, making for Denmark Hill, 'of the day I was born.'

'Oh, historic day,' sang Gemma.

'I'm remembering,' said Boots, 'that I had prunes and custard for afters.'

Yells of laughter, and a comment from James to the effect that not everyone had a father whose memory was unbelievable.

Boots dropped the young people off in turn, arriving back home with Gemma and James. One more Saturday evening had come and gone. How many altogether in his lifetime? A quick piece of mental arithmetic told him more than three thousand. Good Lord, that many? He little knew that in a recent dream, Polly had attempted to count the number of times she had slept with him since their marriage. She had arrived at a million before the dream went haywire.

'Gemma, who informed me earlier that she thinks about such things, will tell you that you and I are a few hours older since supper,' he said a little later to Polly when slipping into bed beside her.

'Brilliant,' said Polly, 'but if being told the grim truth keeps me awake, you'll get burnt toast for your Sunday breakfast.'

'Again?' said Boots.

'What a rotter,' murmured Polly, and was asleep within another minute. Comments about her performances in the kitchen when Flossie wasn't around never bothered her. Everybody had one failing, however gifted they were.

Chapter Seventeen

Sunday's weather was again sharp but bright. In the afternoon hardy players were using the public tennis courts in Ruskin Park at the foot of Denmark Hill. During the war, Goering's bombers had come close to obliterating the park and turning nearby King's College Hospital into a mountain of rubble. Fortunately, both the park and the hospital had escaped, for which the people of Camberwell and Walworth were grateful.

There were two lithe young girls using one of the courts. Both chased about, fleet of foot, in their pursuit of the ball, whacking at it with swinging rackets. Their play was erratic but enthusiastic, errors accompanied by cries of disgust, winning shots by yells of triumph. They obviously didn't believe in a grim approach to the game.

Peregrine Peters, enjoying a brisk walk around the park, was heading for the cosy cafe just a little way out of it. He intended to drink a cup of tea and browse over a book on the life of Isambard Brunel, the engineering genius of Victorian times. Engineering was to be his subject at university. He chose to reach the cafe by way of the tennis courts, where he made a temporary halt to find out if any of the players had a real talent for the game. He had some modest ability himself.

He watched four young men playing doubles and thought them pretty good. And on the adjacent court two girls were playing with a lot more energy than finesse. That hardly mattered when it was obvious they were enjoying themselves so much, the skirts of their white dresses whipping around their running legs. From the far end, one girl thumped the ball with her racket. It sailed high over the net, high over the head of the other girl and landed close to the wire perimeter, against which it bounced and flopped. About to move on, Peregrine checked. The other young lady came running from the baseline to bend and collect the ball, which was bit grey from wear. She looked up through the wire, Peregrine looked down. He blinked. The young lady smiled as she straightened up.

'Hello, Charlie,' she said, 'fancy seeing you.'

Peregrine, mesmerized by her laughing eyes, her aura of exuberance and vitality, fell into a now familiar trance and said, 'I – er – yes, hello.'

'Help,' said Gemma, 'I think you're a bit hoarse again. What a shame. Never mind, take some cough mixture.' And she returned to the baseline to deliver a thumping serve. Alas that it hit the net. She served again, and the ball, landing correctly, was attacked by the receiver. A rally began, a competitive one that excited both players.

Peregrine, engineering degree a sudden irrelevance, looked on. The object of his attention was a delight, a bright, running athlete in the sharp sunshine of the afternoon, her long dark hair shackled by a red ribbon. He had a highly fanciful moment then, imagining that somewhere along its endless journey of creation, Nature had gifted the twentieth century with a young Elysian goddess.

No, be your age, he told himself firmly, you're going barmy. Elysian goddess my eye, she's just another girl. Well, perhaps a little more than that, but there's still no reason to let your head run a temperature. He wondered if she lived anywhere near the park. He lived fairly near himself, in Daneville Road, with his parents and sister.

He lingered at the perimeter wire, hypnotized by the grace, athleticism and enthusiasm of both girls, and the eye-catching sex appeal of one in particular. But he had to leave in the end, he had to take himself off before he turned into an earthbound lump. Seeing him go, Gemma gave him a friendly little wave. He returned it and went on his way, determined to put his head in order and re-establish himself as a normal, everyday bloke experiencing normal pleasant reactions to an attractive girl instead of going off his chump.

Enjoying his cup of hot tea in the self-service cafe, he browsed over his book on Brunel and was managing to reach a quite studious frame of mind when a voice, now familiar to him, floated into his ear.

'Hello again, got a good book there?' said Gemma.

He lifted his head. There she was, glowing from her exercise, in company with her tennis partner. They were both wearing coats over their tennis dresses, and carrying their tennis holdalls. He cleared his throat.

'Oh, hello, finished your game?' he said, and immediately put on a figurative hair shirt for stating the obvious.

'Yes, we've come for a spot of tea and fruit buns,' said Gemma who, of all outdoor pursuits, enjoyed tennis in the park more than anything else. Winter it might be, but a bright crisp day could always draw her out. 'Might we leave our holdalls with you while we go to the counter?'

'Of course, why not?' said Peregrine, enraptured but manfully striving to sound like a normal, everyday bloke. 'I'll keep an eye on them.'

'Thanks, Charlie,' said Gemma.

'You're welcome,' said Peregrine, and both girls placed their holdalls down beside the table.

231

'Come on, Jane,' said Gemma.

Jane smiled at Peregrine and then accompanied Gemma to the counter, where she said, 'Who's the feller?'

'Oh, I met him yesterday,' said Gemma. 'He works in one of my Uncle Sammy's shops. He's quite nice, but a bit barmy, and I think he's got some kind of myopia as well.'

'Well, he looks quite a dish,' said Jane. 'Let's sit with him and then I can find out what makes him a bit barmy.'

Peregrine watched as they ordered tea and buns, then picked up his book in a sudden fit of new determination. He was interrupted, however, by the return of the girls, his young Elysian goddess carrying the tray on which stood two cups of tea and a plate containing two fruit buns.

'D'you mind if we join you?' said Gemma, showing a friendly smile, two bright eyes and moist pink lips that had never been kissed. Not by any young man with designs on her as his rosy future, that is. Peregrine's determination went up the spout without any kind of struggle. But he did instinctively clear his throat again.

'Pardon?' he said. 'Oh, yes. Right, yes. Yes, help yourselves.'

'Thanks, Charlie,' said Gemma, and set the tray down. 'Meet my friend Jane.' Jane Symington was the daughter of a neighbour and also keen on tennis in the park.

'Hi,' said Peregrine as the girls seated themselves.

'Hi,' said Jane, a young blonde. She tidied her fair locks and passed a tongue over her lips. She liked the look of Charlie, no pimply adolescent but manly and good-looking. She liked his thick winter sweater and his crisp jet-black hair. Crikey, he could be first cousin to Frankie Laine. At seventeen, Jane was the same age as Gemma, but whereas Gemma lived mostly for her career prospects, Jane combined only a lukewarm interest in commercial prospects with an active interest in manly young blokes. Impulsively, she asked, 'D'you play?'

'Pardon?' said Peregrine, who was searching for something interesting to talk about. Not engineering, of course. Or steamships. Pop stars? Yes, both girls were probably hot on pop. Coming to, he said, 'Oh, you mean do I play tennis? Yes, now and again.'

'Jane's pretty lively with a racket,' said Gemma, sipping tea.

'So's Gemma,' said Jane, eating a fruit bun.

'Fascinating,' said Peregrine, meaning everything in general at the moment. 'By the way–'

'My racket's my best friend at times,' said Jane, eyeing him with growing interest. 'Do you have one?'

233

'One what?' Peregrine was flummoxed for a moment. 'Oh, a best friend, you mean? Our family dog, I suppose.' That was an attempt to be light-hearted. He hoped brilliance would come in a minute or so.

'Your family dog, Charlie?' said Gemma, looking up and catching his eye. By way of a change, he kept his head. 'Really your dog?'

'Well, it's favourite with family and friends.'

'If it's fond of roast pork I'll come and talk to it sometime,' said Gemma, and laughed, which induced both girls to treat their happily captive audience to the story of a dog belonging to a Mrs Blissett. Apparently, the animal had made off with her family's Sunday joint of roast pork before she'd had a chance to put it on the table for carving. And when she rushed out into the garden to try to rescue it, her dog had already invited the hound from next door to share it with him. The recounting of the incident was a laugh all the way over tea and buns, after which Jane put a friendly question to Peregrine.

'What's your novel like?' she asked, looking at his book.

'It's not a novel, it's a biography,' said Peregrine. 'About Brunel the famous engineer who designed and built the world's first steamship.'

'Ugh,' said Jane.

234

'No, haven't you heard of him, he really was a genius,' said Gemma.

Jane pointed out that at her time of life she wasn't much interested in geniuses, not even Broomwell. Brunel, said Gemma. Yes, him as well, said Jane, and let Peregrine know she was much keener on modern music, something that was going to make history, didn't he think so?

'Yes, don't you?' smiled Gemma.

'Well, it's my kind of history,' said Peregrine, and told himself he was normal at last in the fair face of divinity. The fair face of divinity? What the hell was up with him that his first feelings of normality should be instantly followed by a total collapse of his head? Couldn't he really see Gemma as just another girl? Well, no, he couldn't. She had too much going for her, gorgeous looks, big eyes, flying legs and oceans of happy vitality. Striving to repair his head while Jane was saying something to him, he heard her interrupt herself.

'Gosh, the time, Gemma, I've got to fly.'

'All right, let's put our wings on,' said Gemma, and both girls came to their feet.

'You're going?' said Peregrine, and put the hair shirt back on for again stating the obvious.

'Yes, got to,' said Jane. She and Gemma picked up their holdalls.

'Bye, Charlie,' said Gemma. 'Glad your

sore throat's better, and that your eyes haven't been a bit twitchy today.'

'Normally, they're fine for looking.'

'Good,' smiled Gemma, 'that's what they're for. So keep them open in case that shoplifter pops in again.'

'Eh? Oh, yes, right, I will,' said Peregrine.

'So long, Charlie,' said Jane, 'thrill to have met you – see you again sometime, perhaps. Come on, Gemma.'

So that's her name, thought Peregrine. Gemma. It occurred to him then that she still only knew him as Charlie, and always would unless he had the luck to see her again. He watched both girls leave the place.

He was left feeling magic had gone from the afternoon.

Tuesday morning.

In company with Mr Greenberg, Sammy came out of the Italian cafe owned and run by Joe Robinson (formerly Stanislaw Das-zynski), once a fighting soldier with General Sikorski's Free Polish Army.

'Very decent bloke,' said Sammy, 'even if his English is a bit Polish. I wish him luck when his missus carts him off to Glasgow. I had to listen to him with both ears meself, because in business, Eli, you have to make sure you know what the other bloke's saying.'

'Ah, vell,' said Mr Greenberg, 'it's a fact,

236

ain't it, Sammy, that some people don't speak English so good, not like you and me. But it don't mean Joe's a fly bird, he'll give you first refusal on the sale of his premises, like he's just promised. Now all you need is happy vords from the council about planning permission.'

'Well, no good buying the place unless we're sure we'll get a change of usage, and I'm leaving it to Tim and Daniel to make the right contact,' said Sammy, halting as he and his old friend reached the corner of the New Kent Road to look around. He shook his head and muttered.

'Something ain't pleasing you?' said Mr Greenberg. 'Something ain't to your liking, Sammy?'

'It's lost its soul,' muttered Sammy, contemplating what prolonged post-war development was doing to the Elephant and Castle, the junction at which six thoroughfares met, including the old and familiar Walworth Road, as well as St George's Road, wherein still stood the school at which Boots had received his superior education. Then the junction had been a bustling, picturesque and thriving meeting place alive with people, clanging trams, trundling buses and horse-drawn carts. Now, with development far advanced, Sammy suspected it was going to end up as a vast open arena bounded by concrete. No soul, no heart. 'I tell you, Eli, I ain't against change, but this kind seriously grieves me. What's in it for Walworth's old ladies except aching feet?'

'It's a pain to my old eyes, Sammy, a pain, ain't it? Don't it make the people look as if they ain't here?'

'You're bang on,' said Sammy. Yes, that was it. The new junction was so huge it made shoppers and pedestrians look few and far between. Fortunately, the store run by Freddy was distant enough to avoid being swallowed up. It drew a good proportion of its customers from Walworth Road shoppers, and consequently was a healthy part of the immediate area. 'Come on, old cock, it's nearly lunchtime, so let's drive to that pub opposite the old East Street market and treat ourselves to a Guinness and a kosher sandwich before we go back to Camberwell.'

'Vhich vill be my shout, von't it?' said Mr Greenberg, as they walked to Sammy's parked car.

'Not this time, Eli, I owe you for introducing me to Polish Joe,' said Sammy.

They enjoyed their time in the pub, much favoured by the market's costermongers. Sammy plonked two tenners and a fiver in Mr Greenberg's lap for making Polish Joe known to him.

'Ah, ain't it a pleasure, Sammy, vhen business is also friendship?' said the happy Eli.

'I concur, Eli, don't I?' said Sammy.

238

He then drove to his offices, dropping Mr Greenberg off at the old lad's Camberwell yard. No sooner was he back at his desk than he invited Tim and Daniel to come and see him. It was his pleasure to let them know the property company had been promised first consideration if it decided to purchase the Italian cafe, so would they like to let him know what had come about from their phone calls to the council? Had the planning department encouraged applying for change of usage?

'Glad you asked,' said Tim. 'We hit a blank wall.'

'Eh?' said Sammy.

'Fact,' said Daniel. 'We got no further than being told no prior discussion could take place. Rachel also had a go, but was told only that an application must first be made for consideration by the committee.'

'Hold on,' said Sammy, 'I know how long that might take, and I don't think Polish Joe's going to sit on it till Christmas. I don't think Mrs Polish Joe will let him. She's in a hurry to help him set up a haggis factory in Glasgow. You two bright boys have worked round sticky council buns several times in the past, so why not this time?'

'Well, Pa,' said Daniel, 'it seems someone has instructed all persons in the planning department to stick strictly to regulations on pain of death, or at least on pain of not being awarded a good service medal by the mayor.'

'Who's someone?' asked Sammy.

'A lady,' said Tim, 'lately promoted to head of the department. A regular do-it-by-the-book character.'

'What's her name?' asked Sammy.

'Jardine,' said Tim. 'Teresa Jardine, so I was told.'

'Jardine?' said Sammy. 'Jardine? Is a bell ringing?'

'Is it?' asked Daniel.

'It's an old bell, but it's ringing all right,' said Sammy. 'Tim, ask your dad if he'd do me a favour and come and join us.'

Tim did a brisk foray into his dad's office. Boots had no objections to joining the discussion and arrived in company with his son.

'What's on board?' he asked.

'Well, according to Tim and Daniel,' said Sammy, 'the council's planning committee is working strictly by the book, and won't offer any advice about our chances of a change of usage until they receive an official application form. And filled out in triplicate, probably.'

'We're talking, are we, about our possible purchase of the cafe by the Elephant and Castle?' said Boots.

'So we are,' said Tim.

'And drumming up a lot more business by

creating a regular department store for Walworth wage-earners,' said Sammy.

'I think you mentioned that when I was there with you on Saturday,' said Boots.

'And did I also mention I mean a store that'll sell 'em quality stuff but won't make 'em think West End prices have landed on their doorsteps?' said Sammy.

'Quality goods at an affordable price are something we've been specializing in since we began garment-manufacturing ourselves,' said Boots.

'Glad your brainbox is still working, old soldier,' said Sammy. 'On account of same you might recall talking your way round a female planning officer name of Jardine several years ago.'

'Jardine?' said Boots. A brief smile flickered. Miss Jardine, yes, he remembered her. Deputy to the chief planning officer at the time. He'd secured an appointment with her over thirteen years ago concerning planning permission for the first development scheme of the Adams Property Company Ltd. He'd enjoyed a very agreeable conversation with her – she'd seemed a little off balance but not in the least obstructive. Very helpful, in fact. 'Yes, I remember the lady, Sammy.'

'Well, do us all a favour,' said Sammy, 'talk your way round her again. Tell her we know all about the small print, and that what we're after is providing the working people of Walworth with extra facilities for fitting themselves out in style without it costing them their life savings. Don't try talking about fashionable wear or she'll think we're after middle-class custom, and you know what most Labour-run councils think of the middle classes. They'd like it if there weren't any. Talk her into telling you what our chances are for getting change of usage of Polish Joe's cafe. Tell her we can't hang about. Right, Boots?'

'That's the end of the first lesson, is it?' smiled Boots.

'Leave it to you now,' said Sammy.

'I'll see what I can do if I'm all we've got left,' said Boots. 'Live in hope, Sammy, you're a deserving ray of sunshine.' And he went back to his office.

'You heard that, did you?' said Sammy to Tim and Daniel, both of whom were wearing sly grins. 'He's just given me one more pat on the head. One day I'll bite.'

'You're still a deserving case, Pa,' said Daniel.

Chapter Eighteen

'Miss Jardine,' said the switchboard girl at the council offices, 'there's a Mr Adams on the line. He'd like to speak to you.'

'Mr Adams?'

'Yes. Mr Robert Adams.'

'Do I know him?'

'He's phoning on behalf of the Adams Property Company Ltd.'

'Adams?'

'Yes, Miss Jardine.'

Something clicked in the alert mind of Miss Jardine, something that took her memory back to a man who had once turned her head into what felt like a rice pudding. She quivered, drew herself up and spoke firmly.

'Put him through,' she said. Then, 'Hello?'

'Good afternoon, Miss Jardine,' said Boots, 'it's Mr Robert Adams here.'

'Oh, yes.' Miss Jardine attempted a casual response. 'Do we know each other, Mr Adams?'

'I had the pleasure of meeting you in connection with a planning application not long after the war,' said Boots, his mellow tones creating the kind of vibrations pleasant to any lady's ear. 'On behalf of the

Adams Property Company.'

'Oh, really?' Miss Jardine played for time. 'Do I remember that?'

'Probably not,' said Boots. 'Much water under the bridge since then, Miss Jardine. However, I remember myself how helpful you were, and I wonder if you could be helpful again.'

'Well, I'm extremely busy,' said Miss Jardine, 'but I can give you a minute or two to put me in the picture, Mr Adams.' That offer was a triumph for her fighting qualities, since she had been impulsively tempted to say half an hour.

'You're very kind,' said Boots, and explained why he was calling. He wished to find out what his firm's prospects were in regard to securing planning permission for change of usage of the Italian cafe near the Elephant and Castle. 'Obviously, there's no point in purchasing the premises unless we feel we'll get that permission.'

'I see,' said Miss Jardine. 'Yes, I see. Well, of course, we don't usually discuss such matters until an application has been received and considered, but there are always exceptions. Would you care to come and see me, when we can have a full discussion?'

'I'd be more than happy,' said Boots.

'Thank you, Mr Adams,' said Miss Jardine, and at once asked herself why she was thanking him. She was the one who was offering a favour, not the other way about.

'Would you like to name a time?' asked Boots.

'Ten tomorrow morning?' said Miss Jardine. 'I'll have had time to look into the matter by then.' And to come to my senses, she thought. She and a young man called Peregrine Peters had never met, and were never likely to, but were currently sharing common ground. Peregrine was still starry-eyed about a girl he had met in a store, and Miss Jardine was in a state of uncertainty over a man she had seen only once, and that had been quite some years ago. 'Well, until tomorrow then, Mr Adams.'

'I'll look forward to it,' said Boots. 'Thanks for being so co-operative. Goodbye now.'

'Goodbye, Mr Adams,' said Miss Jardine and hung up.

Sammy, Tim and Daniel were more than happy to hear that Boots was now on favourable terms with the chief planning officer, and would be seeing her tomorrow. Sammy said he could now live in genuine hope, since he was beginning to remember that the last time Boots saw Miss Jardine over a planning application, the council lady threw a wobbly. Daniel said that as Tim's dad still had something going for him, she might throw another one, and definitely in their favour. Boots said read your comics.

It was the following morning when Miss Teresa Jardine rose up from her desk, stiffened her back and spoke to her secretary.

'Show him in, Miss Bowyer.'

Boots, entering, recognized the lady immediately, for she was still much as before, a trim figure attired in a smart dark grey costume and pristine white blouse, her burnished blue-black hair neatly parted down the middle. He had thought her in her early thirties then. Now she must be in her mid-forties. Her smooth features made her look younger.

'Good morning, Miss Jardine, very decent of you to spare time for me,' he said with a light smile.

'Oh, yes, good morning, Mr Adams,' said the lady, and extended a hand across her desk in greeting. Boots took it and shook it, his clasp pleasantly firm. Now she was face to face with him. Their eyes met. Hers were a clear hazel, his were a deep grey, one deeper than the other. How strange that this should be, she thought. He smiled, she wavered.

'How well you look, Miss Jardine.'

'Yes?'

'Believe me.'

'Please sit down, Mr Adams.' She reseated herself, glad to have the firm security of the chair beneath her. He sat opposite. Again

246

they were face to face, he at ease, she a little reflective. She had chosen to devote her life to a career and to the care of her widowed and crippled mother. She usually made a point of avoiding men whose mere presence caused her to think of indulgences outside her career and her home. 'Now,' she said with what Boots considered refreshing directness, 'what was it we agreed to discuss?'

Boots referred to the Italian cafe, his company's wish to purchase and so to considerably enlarge the clothing store. It could, he suggested, be seen as no more than part of the widespread development that had taken place in that particular location since the end of the war. Miss Jardine gave lengthy thought to this.

'Are you with me?' smiled Boots.

'Oh, indeed I am, Mr Adams.' Miss Jardine consulted a file that lay on her desk. 'I've been looking at the possibilities of making a quick decision on behalf of your firm once you apply officially for change of use.'

'Frankly,' said Boots, 'we'd like to know if a quick decision can be made, and we'd like to know early, and whether or not it would be in our favour. We can't offer the cafe owner merely a prospect of delay, or he'll sell to someone else.'

Miss Jardine, a resolute woman in the main, offered the hint of a smile.

'Mr Adams,' she said, 'a clothing store of the size your company is envisaging could be an excellent development.'

'Glad you think so,' said Boots.

'Of course, you would be up against competition from the Elephant and Castle shopping complex.'

'I can tell you that my brother Sammy, who founded the business–'

'Oh, you have a brother? Is he like you?'

'Only if a self-powered generator is like an old carthorse,' said Boots. 'Competitively, Sammy in his time has seen off sharks.'

'Sharks?' Miss Jardine seemed spellbound.

'Yes, by getting in the first bite,' said Boots.

'The first bite?'

'That's an analogy, of course,' said Boots. 'But please don't think we cope unfairly with competition. No, simply by offering quality merchandise at the lowest possible prices. And we can do that because we manufacture almost all that we sell. There's no middleman.'

'Yes, I see,' said Miss Jardine. 'Well, of course the kind of store you envisage could be an excellent development.'

'I think we've passed that point,' said Boots gently.

'Oh, have we? Oh, yes. Well, now.' Miss Jardine leafed through her notes. 'Yes, well now, Mr Adams, as you need an early decision, I'll call a meeting of the planning committee tomorrow.'

'Tomorrow?' said Boots, more than happy.

'Did I say tomorrow? Yes, I think I could manage that. Then I'll let you know when you can come and see me again so that I can give you our decision on the spot. Perhaps before the end of the week?'

As quickly as that? That's in Sammy's dreams, thought Boots.

'I'm touched by your gesture, Miss Jardine,' he said. 'Would you be able to say which way you think the decision will go?'

'Oh, I can see no reason for anyone to oppose your application,' said Miss Jardine, giving Boots the impression she was certainly not going to oppose it herself. He came to his feet. She rose with him.

'Miss Jardine,' he said, smiling, 'you should be London's Lord Mayor. Or is it Lord Lady Mayor?'

Miss Jardine, just slightly tinted with colour, said, 'I can't see myself as either.'

'Believe me, you'd be a welcome change from some old City buffer, and the outfit would suit you.'

'I think you're joking, Mr Adams.'

'Not a bit of it. It's been a pleasure to consult with you.'

'I'll see you again, then, in a few days,' said Miss Jardine, setting aside what that might do to her usually well-ordered routine.

Today's had been under control, but only just.

Boots shook her hand again.

'Goodbye, Miss Jardine, and many thanks,' he said.

'Oh, goodbye, Mr Adams.'

'Well, old soldier?' said Sammy on his brother's return.

'The lady's a charmer,' said Boots.

'Had a cosy time with her, then, did you?' said Sammy.

'Well, she refrained from quoting regulations,' said Boots. 'She suggested there'd be no opposition to our application, and will make another appointment to see me soon after she's consulted with her committee. I've a definite feeling the news will be good.'

'Listen, mate, how d'you do it?' asked Sammy.

'It?' said Boots.

'Bring the birds down from the tree at your age,' said Sammy.

'Watch your imagination, Sammy, it's flying a bit high,' said Boots. He mused and a little smile flickered. 'There was one thing that kept me in my place.'

'Which was?' said Sammy.

'She didn't ask me to stay for coffee.'

'Well, dearie me,' said Sammy, 'ruddy hard luck, chum.'

Miss Jardine phoned Boots the following afternoon, telling him that her committee would not oppose the application for change of usage. The application, therefore, could be forwarded immediately.

'I'm delighted,' said Boots. 'There's no need for me to come and see you again?'

'No, no need,' said Miss Jardine. If she had secured the thanks and appreciation of Mr Robert Adams for doing away with all red tape on behalf of his company, she had also achieved a little triumph for herself. A triumph in that she had resisted all temptation to see him again – and again – and thereby had retained her self-respect. And kept her head. In any case, she could think of nothing more mortifying than losing it at the advanced age of forty-five. 'Mr Adams, I wish you the best of luck with your firm's plans.'

'I can't thank you enough,' said Boots. 'Truly, it's a pleasure to know you, Miss Jardine. Goodbye.'

'Goodbye,' said the council lady.

That evening, having acquainted Polly and the twins with the tale of a council officer who chucked rules and regulations aside to be helpful, Boots asked if anyone thought she should be rewarded.

'Rewarded, Pa?' said James.

'Rewarded?' said Gemma, the unknowing

star that had flashed into the life of Peregrine Peters and flashed out again, good as.
'What does Daddy mean, Mama?'

'Yes, I'd like to ask that question myself,'
said Polly. 'Boots, what do you mean?'

'A candlelit supper?' suggested Boots.

'Here, Pa?' asked James.

'No, at a table made for two,' said Boots.

'And in some high-life West End restaurant? Over my dead body,' said Polly.

'One can't take her a bouquet of lilies at
her office,' said Boots. 'Her colleagues would
notice, and as you all probably know, council
officials are strictly forbidden to accept what
could be construed as a bribe. So I thought
of taking her to a little out-of-the-way
restaurant and treating her to–'

'I forbid it,' said Polly, 'absolutely. And I
definitely forbid candlelight.'

'Yes, I'm afraid I have to forbid it too,' said
Gemma. 'It's simply not on, Daddy, and
boo to you for even thinking of it. Have you
forgotten you're a married man and a
father?'

'The lady's very deserving,' said Boots.

'Apart from that, what's she like?' asked
James. 'If she's a bit of a sexpot, Pa, I'll
stand in for you, as long as you finance it.
I'm not a husband and father myself, just a
hard-up volunteer.'

'Heavens, what a cretin the lad is,' said
Gemma.

'James, you too are forbidden,' said Polly. 'No woman, whether she's a jiving hopcat–'

'Hepcat, Mama, hepcat!' cried Gemma.

'Or,' said Polly, 'a slinky vamp–'

'Vamp?' said James. 'What's a vamp?'

'Dear boy,' said Polly, 'in my day a vamp was a Hollywood term for a tarty minx.'

'Well, pardon me, Dad,' said James, 'but is your council lady a tarty minx?'

'Far from it,' said Boots, 'and she's not mine, in any case.'

'I've been trying to say that she is never going to be,' said Polly. 'Candlelit suppers are out. Gemma, you and I must stand together on this and tie your father to the apple tree if necessary.'

'Not half,' said Gemma.

'Keep him away from the telephone,' said Polly.

'You bet,' said Gemma.

'Great heavens,' said Polly, 'the trouble we have in saving him from some woman or another.'

'I'm grateful, of course,' said Boots.

'Dinner's ready, everyone,' sang Flossie from without.

'Coming, Flossie,' sang the family from within.

Over the meal, the conversation turned on America's far-reaching plan to send a rocket to the moon, possibly even with a crew aboard. James said the idea was fantastically brilliant, as long as they could bring the crew back. Gemma asked what was the point of going there, anyway, it was dead, wasn't it? Boots said humankind was always obsessed with the challenge of the impossible, although for his part he was content with keeping the lawn mower in working order. His own interest in science had come to a crushing end, he said, when he caused a Bunsen burner to blow up in class during his time at school. Polly said she really wouldn't mind going along for the ride herself as long as she didn't have to wear something hideous. One can get away with anything hideous at the age of eighteen, she said, but not at forty.

'Forty, Mama?' said Gemma.

'Or thereabouts,' said Polly.

In this way the imagined enemy, Miss Jardine, sank without trace.

Chapter Nineteen

Saturday morning in the heart of Dulwich.

'Ah, this is where your dear aunt lives?' said Irena Leino, stopping, along with Cathy and Gemma, outside the house owned by Cathy's Aunt Marie. The house itself was as grand and handsome as a mansion. It was seen through the tall wrought-iron gates set between high brick walls. Its cluster of chimneys soared skywards, and its latticed windows, caught by the morning light, blinked and winked at the viewer. The wide oak door was framed by stone pillars. 'Such a magnificent house,' said Irena in total admiration.

Gemma, about to ask if it was anything like the Leino family house in Helsinki, bit the words back. Irena, she remembered, had lost her parents in 1944, during the war against Russia.

The young woman stood looking, her gaze caught by the brass figure 8, mounted on one of the gates. The brass shone like gold, bringing the house number gleamingly to the eye of the beholder. Irena Leino issued the faintest of sighs. One might have said it was a sigh of regret.

'Well, don't let's stand here,' said Cathy, 'let's go in and say hello to Aunt Marie.' She opened the gates and the three girls walked up the drive to the front door. Cathy used her key to open it. The butler, Charles Rogers, materialized so quickly to welcome the girls that Gemma thought he must have heard their footsteps. He led the way to the sitting room. Irena, deeply interested, took note of everything around her and murmured little words of admiration.

In the sitting room, Aunt Marie was found to be immersed in a novel by the internationally famous author Rebecca West. She was so absorbed in the narrative that not until her butler announced the arrival of Cathy and her friends did she look up and realize the girls were actually there. Then she at once placed the book aside and came to her feet. Dressed in pale flowing lilac, she was, as always, the epitome of grace and charm.

'Cathy, my dear girl, hello. And Gemma, I see. And is the other young lady your new friend? Irena, is it?'

'Yes, this is Irena, Aunt,' said Cathy.

'How nice,' smiled Aunt Marie, and regarded the young lady from Finland with studied interest. There might have been a sudden clash of emotions, for Finns did not regard Russians as the most likeable of people, due to the war Moscow had waged against them from 1939 to 1940 and again from 1941 to 1945. But, of course, Aunt Marie was an old-style and courteous Czarist Russian and Irena was a young lady of fine manners. So there was no clash, only an exchange of smiles.

'I am happy to meet you, madame,' said Irena.

'Here, we are all happy,' said Aunt Marie, then spoke to her butler. 'Charles, would you serve coffee, please?'

'Of course, madam,' said Rogers, and slipped quietly out.

Aunt Marie invited the girls to divest themselves of their coats and to enjoy coffee with her. When they were all comfortably seated, the butler served coffee with little iced buns. The sitting room, tastefully furnished, drew Irena's interest. Looking around, she asked if madame spent much time here.

'Yes, many restful hours every day,' said Aunt Marie.

'Ah, why not?' said Irena. 'It is such a nice room, isn't it?'

'I think so, yes,' said Aunt Marie. 'Now, tell me about your home in Finland.'

Irena said it was only a small apartment in Helsinki, where she lived with her un-married aunt, who had taken care of her since she lost her parents. But it was a very nice apartment in an exclusive part of

Helsinki, close to St Nicholas Cathedral and many fine shops.

'But it's a shame, isn't it, that fine shops for the rich stop us thinking about ugly shops for the poor,' she said.

'Grief,' said Gemma, 'what brought that up?'

'Fine shops are the mark of every civilized city,' said Aunt Marie. 'And one cannot help the fact that the shiftless, the work-shy and the unfortunates are always with us.'

'My cousin Paul's wife is an ardent socialist,' said Gemma, 'and is sold on the idea of transferring the royal family to a council house in Bermondsey and using Buckingham Palace as a residence for London's unfortunates.'

'Utter nonsense,' said Aunt Marie.

'Well, just look here, everyone,' said Cathy, 'I always promised myself not to talk about politics until I was ninety. I mean, it hardly matters if you're boring at that age – oh, sorry, Aunt Marie, I'm not pointing a finger at you.'

'Only at the subject,' smiled Aunt Marie.

'Ah, yes, politics,' said Irena, 'that is something for when we are old, not for when we are young and life is exciting to us.'

'Are you finding your time in England exciting?' asked Aunt Marie.

Irena said yes, every minute was new and exciting, and that she was looking forward to the famous boat race between Oxford and Cambridge. She was, she said, much excited about seeing it on television.

'Well, I never,' said Gemma, 'who'd have thought it, a native of Finland going wonky over the boat race? No wonder my father says there's always something new to learn, even if it's only to find out that it's unlucky for a chicken to lay a square egg.'

'Unlucky for your father?' smiled Aunt Marie.

'No, for the chicken,' said Gemma. 'Well, it's painful, you see.'

That prompted laughter, and politics were forgotten. The young ladies, articulate Cathy, bubbly Gemma and poised Irena, made their individual contributions to a shared conversation with Aunt Marie for the pleasantest kind of coffee hour. Aunt Marie was all smiles throughout, for Cathy and her friends were never less than entertaining. At the end, Irena thanked her hospitable hostess for being so kind, and left in company with Gemma, who took on the responsibility of walking her back to Maiden Hall and back into the care of Miss Stanton.

'Well, what did you think of Irena?' asked Cathy of her aunt when they were alone together.

'Oh, very civilized and interesting,' said Aunt Marie, 'and with very fine eyes. Looking eyes.'

'Looking?' Cathy laughed. 'Well, isn't that what eyes are for, Auntie?'

'Cathy my dear, eyes that look are not quite the same as eyes that merely see.'

'With Irena, it's always a sign of how interested she is in everything English,' said Cathy.

'Well, I repeat, she's interesting herself,' said Aunt Marie. 'This evening, will you be going dancing with James as usual?'

'Yes, he's dating me again,' said Cathy.

'What, I wonder, will all this lead to, dear child?'

'My friendship with James?'

'He's very attached to you, isn't he?'

'Oh, but he's very relaxed about it.'

'James has a relaxed relationship with you?'

'It's mutual.'

Aunt Marie smiled.

'Is it the same thing as a friendly friendship?' she asked.

'We like it that way,' said Cathy. 'Well, it's kind of civilized.'

'Heavens,' said Aunt Marie, 'I've always thought a civilized relationship was exclusive to two people who didn't really like each other. You like James, don't you?'

Cathy gave thought to the answer, then said, 'Yes, I do, Aunt, very much, but it's best not to go in for sighs and sobs like the maiden who sat by the seashore waiting for her shipwrecked lover to rise from the waves.'

Aunt Marie indulged in a fit of laughter. After a moment or two Cathy joined in. In a little while, Aunt Marie found voice.

'Sighs and sobs? Oh, Cathy.'

'There, you see, Aunt, much better to be like James.'

'Yes, much better, sweet girl, to find fun in a friendship. Fun promises far more than sighs and sobs.'

Her phone rang. She picked it up.

'Yes, who's that?'

'It's me, Figgy.'

'Who's me?'

'Yours truly.'

'My missing lodger?'

'You bet,' said Curly Harris, speaking from a public call box.

'Where are you?' asked Elvira Figgins, thinking of an afternoon trip to Oxford Street and aggravating some of its emporium managers with a slippery piece of shoplifting. In any case, she could do with some fancy new lingerie, the kind that was a bit on the wild side and would cause a punter to breathe a touch heavy and forget there was something a bit younger round the corner.

'Ramsgate.'

'Ramsgate? What for, cockles and winkles?'

'No, I'm after a bloke that sold me whereabouts to the Old Bill,' said Curly. 'I been after the bleeder for a while now, and I don't fancy his chances when I catch up with 'im. He's around here somewhere, I had that from a bloke who knows it ain't good for his health to lie to me. Listen, Figgy, I ain't liking it 'ere a lot, it's like all seaside places in winter, it's too bleedin' draughty.'

'Well, you'd be sitting here with me in front of me fire if you hadn't lost yer temper with some barman.'

'Bleedin' saucy, he was,' said Curly. 'Listen, are the rozzers still watching yer front door?'

'They are, the buggers,' said Elvira. 'They might think I ain't noticed, but I have, so stay away. I'm missing you as me paying lodger and me occasional comfort, but stay away, I tell yer, or they'll jump you. Mind, if you want to show some decent appreciation for me past kindnesses and considerations, send me a postal order. Where you staying in Ramsgate?'

'Out of the way of the fuzz, and if I don't lay me mitts on a certain copper's nark by tomorrer, I'm coming back,' said Curly. 'I thought if the fuzz had given up watching yer front door, I could chance joining you night-times.'

'Leave off, you daft donkey, ain't I just told you to keep away?' said Elvira.

'Listen, I'm not offering meself to some other landlady in south London,' said Curly. 'Too risky.'

'Yes, well, see what you did for yerself when you put that barman in hospital,' said Elvira irritably. 'Try the Salvation Army in Whitechapel. The cops won't be looking for you there. Now I've got to go. I've got to see someone in Oxford Street.' And she rang off.

In Ramsgate, Curly Harris came out of the call box, saw a bobby on his beat and made tracks for the shopping centre, a place in which to lose himself while still keeping an eye open for Dodgy Dan.

Dodgy Dan was in Camberwell. At Camberwell Green to be exact. For the time being he'd given up trying to get to Blackpool, since all the railway officials seemed to be lining up to victimize him unless he could produce a ticket that entitled him to a seat, which didn't mean a platform ticket. He'd done his best to let them know he was a war hero who'd fallen on hard times and had had to sell his medals to keep himself alive. But they couldn't have cared less, even though he'd offered to show one of their bossy number where he'd been wounded several times during the Normandy landings and twice at Stalingrad.

'Stalingrad? Listen, sniffy, that's in Russia,

not France.'

'Yus, well, I lost me way a bit, didn't I? It was bleedin' dark at night, I can tell yer, and I didn't always know where I was, did I?'

It made no difference. No free ride to Blackpool.

What with all that and his suffering nerves on account of the police still not having Curly Harris locked up in the clink, Dodgy Dan was feeling pretty upset. Mind, he'd found he could tuck himself down on a bench in the little oasis of Camberwell Green at night, with no-one bothering him. He couldn't go back to the Bermondsey dosshouse, not while Curly Harris was still out and about. However, he'd been down East Street market a couple of times and relieved one woman of her purse and another of her set-aside gloves while she dipped into her handbag. Fine, wafer-thin suede gloves they were, and he'd pawned them for five bob. And the contents of the purse enriched him by a pound and ten-pence. But the total earnings of one pound, five shillings and tenpence didn't make his nerves feel much better. And no-one could have said they amounted to a decent return for his labours.

On this breezy March afternoon he was wandering about, thinking of spending a couple of hours with a cup of tea in a warm cafe where they didn't ask a bloke to sit outside. His suitcase he'd left at Euston station several days ago. He knew it would now be in the station's left-luggage store and safe as houses. Once he was well britched, say with about five quid in his pocket, he'd give in to unchristian authority and actually buy a train ticket to Blackpool. He wasn't safe anywhere in London while Curly Harris was still on the loose.

He turned about on the busy pavement by the junction and set off for the cafe, a little way down Camberwell Road. Shambling along amid pedestrians and shoppers, he could hardly believe his eyes at what he was suddenly seeing. There she was again, that dangerous female capable of putting a bloke in hospital for a week. Large as life in her black fur hat and her fawn coat with the black fur collar. Only this time she'd got company. A tall cove and two kids, a boy and a girl. They were all looking at a window display, and she was gassing away to the bloke. Husband, probably.

Dodgy Dan slowed in his approach. That is, his shamble turned into a cautious shuffle. If she turned her head and saw him, she might just point him out to her husband, who looked as if he was capable of even more tough stuff than her. Blimey, I could be dead any minute. About to do the wise thing and beat a retreat, he saw the female enter the shop, in company with the young girl. Daughter, probably. The bloke remained outside, talking to the small boy. A brainwave struck Dodgy Dan, which was a bit of a miracle, and he lost no time in shuffling up to the father and son.

'Here, excuse me, guy, but could yer spare a tanner or so for a cuppa tea? I'm fair skint. Well, to be honest, I been down on me luck ever since the day me ship was torpedoed and I spent Gawd knows how many days in a lifeboat. I grant yer might not believe me, but I could show yer an 'orrible scar where I got bit by a shark, and—'

'You're right, granddad, I don't believe a word,' said Daniel Adams, an amiable grin showing. 'But it might break some woman's heart, so here's a couple of bob, enough for two cups of tea and an hour of soap and hot water at Manor Place baths. Your friends will like you a lot better after that.' So saying, he produced a florin and flipped it into the smelly old tramp's ready mitt. 'Now do me a favour and disappear.'

'Well, thank yer kindly, guy, you're a toff,' said Dodgy Dan, and went on his way at a fair old lick before the fighting female came out of the shop and bumped into him. As it was, she had no idea he'd got his own back and done her in the eye by touching her better half for a useful piece of silver. Blimey, wouldn't she hit the ceiling if she found out?

Patsy emerged from the shop with Ara-bella, her purchase that of various coloured wools for tapestry work.

'Mum,' said Andrew, 'Dad gave some man two shillings.'

'Did you?' asked Patsy of Daniel. 'What for?'

'A bath,' said Daniel as they all resumed the shopping stroll.

'Fill me in,' said Patsy, and Daniel recounted the tale of the smelly down-and-out with a hard luck story no-one would believe, not even a blind nun.

'So he earned himself two shillings for a cup of tea and a bath?' said Patsy.

'Forget the bath,' said Daniel, 'he'll give it a miss. My offering was a way of getting rid of him and his smell.'

'Yes, he wasn't half whiffy,' said Andrew.

'I've come across that kind of dubious guy myself,' said Patsy, little realizing that it was her old tramp who had touched her fun guy for two bob, and that he'd done so just to pay her back for walloping him.

Dodgy Dan enjoyed his tea and a hot sausage roll and a long sit-down. Me luck's changing, he thought. I might just wake up in the morning and find out Curly's been copped and taken out of me life for a few years.

I dunno why that bloke talked about a bath. I had a wash in the public toilets this morning, didn't I? And I might treat meself to a shave sometime next week. And what's more, I think I'll take meself off to a cinema tonight, just when the customers are coming out, and do a quick flip through the place to see who's left what behind. It happens.

Chapter Twenty

March had a bad night. It poured cold, ill-tempered and heavy showers down on London and the Home Counties. Shakespeare's reference to the dropping of gentle rain from heaven didn't quite fit. Gutters and drains gushed with water, and when people woke up they rather expected the day to be a wet and depressing continuation of the night. But, as a Knightsbridge vicar might have said to his wife seeing it was Sunday, lo and behold, the sun is shining.

It was. Brightly. And the sky was a clear blue. No-one quite knew how long the improvement would last, and people turning up for church were taking the precaution of wearing raincoats or sporting brollies.

By mid-afternoon, however, there was still no sign of returning showers, and Peregrine Peters set out from his home in Daneville Road for another recreational wander around Ruskin Park. He carried the biography of Brunel with him, although it has to be said his mind was not so much on that engineering genius as on a young Elysian goddess.

No, no, you fool, he said to himself as he

entered the park, don't start thinking in those terms again. If she's here, if she's playing tennis again, just regard her as a – well, as a bit of all right. A bit of all right? That's brilliant, I don't think. It's probably what King Charles II called Nell Gwynn when he first clapped eyes on her and her basket of fruit in Drury Lane. Well, she was a bit common, wasn't she? You can't call this girl common, not when she has eyes shining with the light of an angel.

Light of an angel? Give over, or you'll end up twittering.

The sharp sunlight danced on moist green grass, and the first shoots of daffodils peeped from beds of dark, enriched soil. Should he go straight to the tennis courts to see if she was there again? No, that would be the act of an adolescent, he told himself firmly, and I'm in my nineteenth year, with university coming up.

So he went on a walk-around, keeping to the slow pace of a citizen deep in thought, while other young males strode briskly, mostly in the direction of unattached young females. Despite startling social changes, due to young people boldly knocking the stuffing out of conventional do's and don'ts, Sunday afternoons in London's parks still saw a lot of old-style boy-meets-girl stuff, except that contact was quicker and franker.

Peregrine held himself in check for a good

twenty minutes before his feet carried him to the path that ran alongside the tennis courts. And there she was, dashing this way and that, as quick and lithe as one would expect of a young goddess. Her dark, ribboned hair was flying about as she ran and chased, and, just as last week, connected either brilliantly or erratically with the ball. And although she was on the far side of the court on this occasion, she still came to his eyes as a rare gift from heaven – no, give it a miss, you dope, a rare gift from heaven is a hallucination, are you going screwy again? Just look at her as a girl who's a little bit special, that's all.

Still, it was true to say she and her friend Jane were both worth far more than a brief glance. Both contributed to the appeal of the sunny afternoon, with their well-shaped legs and lively cries of triumph or disaster from time to time. On the next court a quite accomplished mixed doubles was taking place. There was gusto there too, much as if the crisp March sunshine was activating limbs and spirits.

Jane, picking up a ball close to the wire fence, essayed a glance, recognized Peregrine among the several onlookers, and spoke.

'Hi there, Charlie, fancy seeing you.' This greeting was accompanied by a cheeky wink.

'Hello, you two are here again, then,' said Peregrine.

'Yes, and so are you, what a lark,' said Jane, and biffed the ball back to Gemma, who caught it and prepared to serve. She checked as Jane called, 'Charlie's here.'

Gemma looked, waved her racket in friendly acknowledgement, then served, and the two girls were in action again, running, jumping, darting and flailing. Peregrine, helplessly engrossed in the quicksilver movements of Gemma, felt as if his feet were glued to the ground. But he had to move, he couldn't just stay there like a gawping dummy without her thinking his clockwork had run down, poor bloke.

It still took him time to get started, however. Catching Gemma's eye, he gave her a little wave of hello and, he supposed, of goodbye. But it was Jane who called to him.

'Hey, Charlie, wait for us.'

In fact, their time on the hired court was up, a young couple approaching with rackets at the ready. The two girls put on their coats, stowed rackets and balls into holdalls, and came off the courts through the perimeter gate. Peregrine met them. Gemma was glowing from her activity, and looked like a colourful advertisement for what a hot Bovril could do for a girl on a cold day.

'Hi,' she said.

'Hi,' said Peregrine.

'Are you going for a cup of tea?' she asked.

'Well, I did have that in mind.'

272

'Oh, super,' said Jane, 'we can share a pot for three with toasted teacakes, Charlie.'

'My treat,' said Peregrine. 'By the way–'

'You'll have to excuse Jane for her cheeky hint,' said Gemma. They were on the move, the three of them, heading towards refreshments. 'She's not as backward in coming forward as she ought to be.'

'No, I'd like to stand treat,' said Peregrine. 'It's a feller's privilege. Otherwise some of us wouldn't amount to much in a cafeteria.'

Jane giggled, Gemma laughed. Peregrine caught a glimpse of shining white teeth, and the sparkle of vivid life in sunlit eyes. He fell into one more trance. He couldn't help himself. There she was next to him, a living gift from God. A living gift from God? Go home, you lump of porridge. Anything else like that and you'll qualify as a third-rate nutcase before the afternoon's out. That'll be a sight for sore eyes, that will, you being carried gibbering out of the park by a couple of blokes in white coats.

'...and I wouldn't dream of saying no.' That was from Jane, but what had preceded it had passed him by.

'Yes, all right, Charlie, your treat if it's going to be a privilege,' said Gemma.

'Fine. Yes. Fine. A pleasure, in fact.' Peregrine had come to. Gemma, however, was eyeing him with a half-smile, as if she knew he still had problems.

They reached the cafe just outside the park, and Jane said, 'Here we are, out of the cold into the warm.'

Inside, Peregrine somehow managed to organize himself, getting the girls to sit down while he went to the counter to state their combined wants, which amounted to a pot of tea and toasted teacakes for three.

At the table, Jane said, 'I think Charlie's a bit shy.'

'He does have lapses, isn't that a shame?' said Gemma.

'Lapses?'

'Yes, every so often he doesn't seem to know where he is or what he's doing,' said Gemma.

'Yes, because he's shy,' said Jane. 'I like him, though, don't you?'

'Yes, but I do feel sorry for him,' said Gemma. Thoughtfully, she added, 'I suppose he could have moments when he's wondering if the end of the world is coming.'

'End of the world?' said Jane. 'Who's a cuckoo?'

'Well, some people are like that, not just funny old professors,' said Gemma. 'If Charlie thought deeply enough about when the end of the world was coming, or about something equally calamitous, like the UK suddenly disappearing into a hole in the ground, it could – well, kind of paralyse his mind for a couple of minutes.'

'You and your imagination,' said Jane, 'you're trying to tell me that when Charlie's acting a bit absent-minded it's because he's paralysed. Now tell me about Goldilocks and the three bears, and who ate up the porridge.'

'Well, something makes him a bit twitchy,' said Gemma, 'and I just hope it's nothing serious – no, never mind, here he comes.'

Peregrine made something positive of his return by placing the tray firmly down on the table and asking, 'Who's going to be mum?'

'I will,' said Jane, who, despite the possibility that Charlie's head might need looking at, liked the thought of him taking more notice of her than of Gemma. Mind, that shouldn't be difficult because Gemma was more interested in her career than in fellers. 'I'll be glad to, Charlie.'

'By the way–'

'Sit down,' said Gemma, patting the chair on her left, and looking up at him with a kind of melting sympathy in her eyes. Peregrine, of course, with no idea that she was concerned about his mental state, thought she was signalling a kind of encouragement, and he fell happily into the chair. A cup of tea appeared in front of him, placed there by Jane.

'And have a teacake, Charlie,' she said, offering the dish of three. He helped himself to one, with a plate, the while preparing to take a brilliant part in the conversation.

'By the way,' he said, 'my name's not Charlie, it's Perry.'

'Perry?' said Gemma.

'Yes.' That was what his sister and friends called him. Everyone, except his parents, seemed to consider his full name totally forgettable. 'Yes, Perry.'

'But the men in the shop called you Charlie,' said Gemma.

Peregrine laughed.

'Oh, that kind call everyone Charlie,' he said, 'the same as bus conductors call every woman "love".'

'Perry, though,' said Jane. 'Oh, yes, I see, like Perry Como, the American singer. But I think I still like you best as Charlie.'

'Yes, it's kind of chummy,' said Gemma.

'It's still not mine, but I'm not dying to argue about it,' said Peregrine, and the three of them then established friendly terms with their tea and toasted teacakes. Healthy appetites demolished the latter, after which Peregrine addressed himself to She-of-the-Starry-Eyes. 'Let's see, you're Gemma.'

'Well, among friends, it's no secret,' said Gemma, feeling happy for him. Right now his eyes weren't twitchy and he seemed all there. His family, she thought, must be grateful that he is all there sometimes. I wonder, did Uncle Freddy know about his lapses when he gave him the job as Saturday assistant? I mean, how does he manage to see to customers whenever he's a bit twitchy? 'You're feeling fine today, Charlie?' she asked.

'He seems fine to me,' said Jane, who hadn't so far found anything barmy about this dishy young man.

'Actually, I haven't been ill,' said Peregrine, 'I've just had one or two absent-minded moments.' Gemma's starry eyes again seemed to offer him sympathy. His struggle not to fall into their depths was valiant, but not successful. His senses went haywire and he heard himself say, 'Listen, you girls aren't engaged to some super blokes, are you?'

'Engaged?' said Gemma, and she and Jane fell about amid the clatter of cups and saucers.

'Crikey, Charlie, what a question,' said Jane, and glanced covertly at Gemma. Gemma smiled, and Jane responded with a little nod to indicate she now recognized that Charlie really was a bit round the twist at times. 'What made you ask?'

'Pardon?' Peregrine was all at sea. 'What did I say, then?'

'Don't you know?' asked Gemma gently.

'I think I said something,' conceded Peregrine, 'but I can't quite remember what it was.'

'You asked us if we were engaged to super

beings,' said Jane.

'Did I?' Peregrine slapped his forehead. 'What a pillock. I'm losing my mind. Can't think why. I'll get over it.' He gathered himself. 'Um, any more tea in the pot, Jane?'

'Pass your cup, Charlie,' said Jane, thinking not for the first time that he was so dishy she wouldn't mind having him as her boyfriend, as long as she could cure him of his lapses. He passed his cup and saucer, she gave him a refill from the pot and asked, 'D'you go dancing sometimes?'

'Frequently,' said Peregrine, still trying to work out what it was that kept happening to his head.

'D'you want to invite me?' asked Jane, her smile encouraging.

'I'll give that some thought,' said Peregrine.

'Take care, Jane,' said Gemma, who knew her friend's dad would throw a big question mark at any feller who seriously interested his daughter. He thought her worthy of someone notable, like the son of a duke, and certainly not a bloke she'd met in a park. 'Watch your step.'

'Nothing's happened yet,' said Jane, and looked at her watch. 'Oh, blow, time to go.'

'Come on, then,' said Gemma, and the girls rose lithely, presenting themselves momentarily as a photogenic duo to Peregrine. He thought Jane undeniably appealing, but it was still Gemma who put him in mind of a heavenly young body gracing the sylvan glades of Eden. Her aura of rich, colourful vitality made him feel that for once his flight of fancy could stand.

'Bye, Charlie,' said Jane, giving him a come-on smile.

'See you again sometime,' said Gemma.

'Yes, come again next Sunday,' said Jane, and departed along with Gemma.

Peregrine was left wondering if infatuation such as his could possibly be cured. He could try an aspirin, of course, or hitting his head against a wall. On the other hand, it was possible that his condition could happen to the strongest-minded man if the girl in question happened to be a dream of divinity.

A dream of divinity? No, that can't stand. I'm definitely round the bend, and definitely on the way to being certified.

'Apart from that, he's really rather nice,' said Gemma. She was home, showered and changed, and talking to her mum and dad.

'But, darling,' said Polly, 'if, as you say, he's something of a half-wit—'

'Oh, I didn't mean that,' said Gemma, 'just that he loses touch from time to time.'

'Even so,' said Polly, 'your Uncle Freddy would hardly have taken him on if he was truly like that.'

'Yes, isn't it odd that he did?' said Gemma. 'But, of course, we all know he's soft-hearted, and I daresay he found Charlie kind of agreeable. Shop assistants need to be agreeable, don't they?'

'You've personally found him agreeable?' said Polly.

'Yes, I've just said he's really rather nice. Jane quite fancies him.'

'I don't think Jane's dad will let that develop,' said Boots. 'He'll want to know everything about Charlie before letting him anywhere near Jane.'

'Well, I can tell you Charlie's not making any running,' said Gemma, 'and I should think he has a girlfriend, anyway.'

'The kind to keep an eye on his odd moments?' smiled Polly.

'Well, I think that's the kind of girlfriend he needs,' said Gemma with a touch of Christian understanding.

'What's up with you, Perry?' asked Penelope Peters of her brother. Penelope, twenty, had chestnut hair, a healthy complexion and a noticeable figure. She worked as a dentist's receptionist and was accordingly well acquainted with the visibility of nervous symptoms. But it wasn't nervous symptoms her brother was exhibiting. It was an air of being out of touch with life. 'Good grief, you're not going broody, are you?'

'Broody?' said Peregrine, who had just arrived back from his excursion to the park and his encounter with divinity.

'Well, you're about as lively as a wet sack,' said Penelope, 'and you've been like it on and off for a fortnight.'

'It's my social life,' said Peregrine, 'it's all over the place.'

'Why?'

'If I could answer that and make sense, I would,' said Peregrine.

'Well, give Lisa Docherty a ring, she'll cure your blues,' said Penelope.

'I went off Lisa months ago,' gloomed Peregrine, unable to confess he'd been hit for six by the handiwork of God.

'Well, she was a bit loud, I'll admit,' said Penelope. 'Try Amy Onslow, then.'

'Amy went off me when she met that glamorous theatre bloke who moves stage furniture about,' said Peregrine, frankly sure his social life wasn't worth living unless he could rely on the flower of Eden to be close by.

'Take an aspirin, then, lovey, or help yourself to a bottle of Dad's beer,' said Penelope. 'When he and Mum get back from Aunt Mary's in about ten minutes, let them know I've gone out to meet Wilfred.' Wilfred was her young man. 'Come on, buck up, mate, don't let the responsibilities of forthcoming university get you down, if that's what it is. Ta-ta.'

'Enjoy yourself,' said Peregrine, who wasn't the kind of bloke to wish suffering on others because he was on the rack himself. Somehow he had to persuade Gemma that she was the light of his life, not Jane, and that something mutually ardent should come about.

Chapter Twenty-one

'Cassie?' It was Wednesday evening, and Freddy Brown was home from his day at the store.

'I'm here, Freddy.' Cassie was in the kitchen of their old but sturdy house in Wansey Street, their home since the day they were married over twenty years ago. They owned it and had enlarged the upstairs loo to fit in a bath and shower. At this moment, Cassie was preparing the evening meal, which she and Freddy, their daughter Maureen and son Lewis, and her old dad, would enjoy together around the kitchen table, as always. Lewis had begun to talk about having his in an armchair in front of the telly. Cassie was against that, full stop. It's antisocial, she said. Worse, she said, it's anti-family. And lazy behaviour as well. Lewis ventured a but or two. No buts, said Cassie, everyone in this family sits up at the table for every meal or they'll get nothing to eat, not even a dry crust. So Lewis stopped 'butting' and confined himself to murmuring under his breath. He was a bit of a goggle-box buff.

Entering the kitchen, Freddy plonked a

kiss on Cassie's fair face and regarded her with a saucy twinkle. She was still a bit of all right, and he himself hadn't lost the better part of his manly vigour, despite his wartime experiences. It was a fact, as analysts of the nation's health and fitness were beginning to find out, that the generations who had existed on strict civilian or military rationing all through the war and afterwards were now in excellent shape. Overweight men and female fatties were, relatively, few and far between, while most contemporaries of Cassie and Freddy were as fit and personable as they were.

'Greetings, Cassie me love,' said Freddy, 'we can start thinking about moving to Ascot now.'

'Ascot?' said Cassie, brushing back a loose lock of her dark hair. 'Ascot? Where the nobs live, and the Queen keeps her parasols?'

'Well, perhaps not Ascot exactly, just somewhere a bit more countrified than Walworth,' said Freddy. 'Sammy let me know today that planning permission's been officially received for the conversion job and the firm's going ahead with it. I'll be in full charge of the store with a forty per cent salary rise. So we can look for a house with a garden, buy a car and treat your old dad to a new bowler hat and a hundredweight of his favourite tobacco. How about that, eh, Cassie?'

'Oh, I'm so pleased for you, Freddy love, I

really am,' said Cassie, 'but we don't have to move, not unless we have to. We've lived here all our married days, and in Walworth from the day we were born. I'm a Walworth girl and you're a Walworth feller. It's where I've always been happy, except when Hitler's rotten lot were dropping bombs all over during the war. As for Dad, we could buy him a new armchair as well as a new bowler.'

'It's your say-so, Cassie,' said Freddy. 'Just think about it for a week or so, and then make up your mind. I'll go along with what you decide.'

Cassie pointed out that Maureen and Lewis wouldn't be living at home for ever, that they'd probably both be married and building their own nests in a few years' time. She and Freddy could then think again about whether or not they'd like to move. Freddy said that made sense, which was a pleasure to his ears, because when Cassie was young she never made sense at all.

'I don't take any notice of that kind of soppy remark, Freddy Brown, because – oh, never mind that, there's something I want to tell you. I went shopping down the market this afternoon and heard that dear old Ma Earnshaw died on Sunday.'

'Old Ma's gone at last?' said Freddy, sobering up. He thought of the days when Ma, owning a fruit and veg stall in the East

Street market, would hand him and Cassie some specked apples from under the stall. Her grandson had taken over from her two years ago, when Ma finally retired at the ripe old age of eighty-six. And now she'd gone. She'd been a kind of landmark, one of the many characters who had made the market what it was, a place that drew the hard-up and resilient cockneys of Walworth to its variety of offerings at bargain prices. 'Well, I'm bloody sad about that, Cassie, you bet I am.'

'Yes, I know, Freddy, so am I,' said Cassie, testing boiling potatoes to find out if they were soft enough to be mashed. 'Listen, the funeral's on Friday and I wonder, d'you think we ought to let the Adams family know? Only Boots and his brothers and Lizzy all grew up around people like Ma Earnshaw. They all had a soft spot for her, and so did Boots's mother.'

Freddy looked at his watch.

'I'll just treat meself to half a bottle of light ale,' he said, 'then I'll phone Boots.'

When he'd poured himself the beer, he silently drank to Ma Earnshaw, remembering she'd liked a milk stout herself. He remembered too that during the tense moments of uneasy quiet in the war against the Japs, his thoughts always turned to home. And home embraced Cassie and the kids, and the magical days of his youth. Ma

286

Earnshaw had been part of those days.

Then, while waiting for Maureen and Lewis to arrive home, he used the phone to call Boots.

Friday afternoon, the weather cloudy but quite mild.

Scores of people had attended the funeral service for Ma Earnshaw at St John's Church in Larcom Street. This familiar Walworth landmark had escaped the bombs and was still standing square to the world of saints and sinners. The vicar ensured the service was one that gave Ma Earnshaw her due, finishing up with that fine old hymn 'We Plough the Fields and Scatter'. That was a reference to the fact that her stall always offered the produce that was harvested from much of the scattered seed.

A great many people, including market stall-holders, also made the journey to Southwark Cemetery to say a final goodbye to Ma. Some stalls in the market were temporarily closed or in the care of stand-ins.

Boots, Tommy, Sammy and Lizzy had attended the church service and were now at the graveside. With them were Chinese Lady and Sir Edwin, as well as Susie and Vi. All had known Ma Earnshaw since the trying days before and during the First World War. Ma had almost been one of the family. It had been impossible not to come and say goodbye to her, impossible not to remember her, plump, jolly, customer-wise, and proud that she never sold anything but the best to all who patronized her.

'Bloody shame, y'know, Boots,' whispered Tommy as the vicar prepared to intone the burial service in the presence of the black-clad mourners.

'I know, Tommy, but she had a good innings, and enjoyed every day she spent behind her stall.'

'In snow and hail and all?'

'There were one or two days, Tommy, when I daresay she'd have preferred to be sitting by her fireside,' murmured Boots and glanced at Chinese Lady, a few feet away in company with Sir Edwin. There she was in her eighty-third year and, incredibly, still upright, still firm and neat of bosom. Her coat, a dark grey, was, he knew, worn over a black dress that had attended more than one funeral. There was silver now in her hair that showed beneath her hat, but no signs of physical frailty. And her mind was as sharp as ever. Every member of the family, of course, wanted her to live for ever.

'Ashes to ashes, dust to dust...'

Ned had gone. Uncle Tom, Vi's dad, had gone. So had Polly's father, one of life's true military gentlemen. Families would slowly crumble if new lives did not sustain them.

288

It was over for dear old Ma Earnshaw. Her coffin rested deep in the earth with that of her husband, he always as bony as she was well-rounded, and having departed five years before.

'Boots?' Lizzy was beside him, whispering.

'Lizzy?'

'They're far behind us now, Boots, the good old days.'

He knew she was thinking of Ned and the magic of being in love when she was a mere fourteen and Ned no more than seventeen.

'Good old days, Lizzy, don't actually leave us, since no amount of time can take away our memories.'

'No, but on occasions like this I worry about Mum and Dad sometimes, they're both in their eighties.'

They were there then, Chinese Lady and Sir Edwin, and damn me, thought Boots, if they both don't look as sprightly as spring chickens. Allowing for a touch of silver in their feathers.

'Well, it was a nice service, Boots, and a tidy burial,' said Chinese Lady, 'and I'm glad to see all of you here.' Yes, Boots and Lizzy, Sammy, Susie, Tommy and Vi were all present, and that pleased her. 'It was right for us to come and say goodbye to Mrs Earnshaw, a good friend to us in our Walworth days.' It was true, the dear departed had often slipped an extra apple or an extra onion into

289

Chinese Lady's shopping bag during the latter's most penurious times. 'Now me and your dad would like all of you to come home and have tea with us.'

'Well, kind of you, Ma,' said Sammy, anxious to get back to the office, 'but–' He winced. Boots had trodden on his foot. 'Fair enough, Ma, me and Susie, we'll come.'

'We'll all come, of course we will,' said Lizzy, knowing that Chinese Lady wanted her immediate family around her at a time like this, when an old friend had gone. She would make a large pot of tea and talk to everyone about all the changes she'd seen over the years, and declare that none of them had done any real good. And she'd be sure to mention something to the effect that Kaiser Bill and Adolf Hitler had been invented by Satan when God turned His back one day.

The Adams family, having placed their floral tributes in position, left the cemetery and headed for the parked cars. On the way they encountered Cassie and Freddy, and Chinese Lady at once invited them home, much to their pleasure. Freddy's assistant, Ruby, had found a friend to stand in for him at the store.

Chinese Lady then asked a question of Boots.

'Boots, where's Polly? Why didn't she come with you?'

'Polly never knew Ma Earnshaw, old lady,' said Boots, 'but as a gesture to our kind of day, she's gone with her stepmother to visit her father's grave in Dulwich.'

'Oh, I see,' said Chinese Lady.

'I still miss Sir Henry,' said Sir Edwin.

'So does Polly,' said Boots.

Polly at this moment was leaving the grave in Dulwich with her stepmother, both having indulged in a little spiritual reunion with Sir Henry. They had left colourful floral sprays in the metal containers.

'Stepmama,' said Polly, as elegant as ever in a stylish coat and fur hat, 'how many people do you know who would attend the funeral of a market stallholder?'

'Why, the stallholder's family and friends, of course, although I might not know them personally, Polly dear,' said Lady Dorothy Simms, at seventy-eight no less upright than Chinese Lady. Her never-ending charity work kept her active and healthy. 'You're thinking of Boots and his unchanging friendship with the people of his youth, whether or not they were dustmen, street cleaners or stallholders.'

'Stepmama, I'm always thinking of that man of mine,' said Polly. 'It's absurd, of course.'

'Absurd? Not at all,' said Lady Simms, as they passed through the cemetery. 'When absent, your father was rarely out of my mind, especially during both wars. In thinking of our men, Polly, we know we're always ready to stand with them, whatever their failings. Of course–' Lady Simms smiled. 'Of course, there are times when we're tempted to deliver a blow or two.'

'Believe me,' said Polly, 'if I landed an old-fashioned wallop on Boots, he'd simply ask if the house was on fire, and if so ring for the fire brigade. That man is so relaxed it's like living with a peace treaty.'

'You'd prefer the warrior type?'

'Spare me brass and cymbals,' said Polly, as they reached her stepmother's vintage Rolls with butler-chauffeur Thomas waiting at the wheel. 'Having lived through two wars, I favour peace treaties, especially my own, even though I suspect that at this moment, if he's still at Southwark Cemetery, he's more likely to be thinking of Emily than of me.'

'You must allow him that, Polly,' said Lady Simms. 'Emily, I believe, was his tower of strength during his blind years.'

Polly accepted that with a wry smile, then followed her stepmother into the car, Thomas holding the door open for them.

Subsequently, while Polly enjoyed a leisurely tea interval with her stepmother, Boots relaxed at his mother's home on Red Post Hill. There, he and her other immediate

292

family members, along with Cassie and Freddy, were able to enjoy unlimited cups of tea and home-made fruit cake. Chinese Lady still indulged her gift for baking, doing so in unrushed fashion, for her daily help, Mrs Plumstead, did the bulk of the housework.

While the atmosphere at the home of Lady Simms was quietly civilized, with occasional outbreaks of laughter offering proof that stepmother and stepdaughter both owned a sense of humour, the air at Chinese Lady's gathering was charged with the ability of all present, including Cassie and Freddy, never to be short of something to say. Indeed, there were frequent moments when everyone, apart from Sir Edwin and Boots, seemed to be talking across everyone else. However, Chinese Lady was listened to in fairly respectful silence when, as expected, she touched critically on social changes and then reminded the family, as they had known she would, that Kaiser Bill and Adolf Hitler had been born of the Devil himself.

That gave Sammy the cue to point out that Ma Earnshaw had somehow kept her stall going all through the war, and that he hoped the good lady was now resting in peace.

'Yes,' said Vi impulsively, 'like Emily and–' She stopped before Ned's name slipped out.

Chinese Lady, guessing which name Vi had had in mind, said casually, 'Lizzy, you sure you're still all right living alone?'

'Quite all right, Mum, I don't have any problems,' said Lizzy, 'and I've always got my family close by if I need help. Bobby and Helene still do most of my gardening for me.'

'You don't have any worries at night?' asked Chinese Lady.

'That's no problem, either,' said Lizzy, keeping to herself any mention of the occasions when she woke up in the middle of the night and suffered wrenching moments of loneliness.

'There we are, Maisie, we need not worry about our Lizzy,' smiled Sir Edwin.

'Well, if you say so,' said Chinese Lady, which brought the gathering to an end, and saw the departure of her guests.

She spoke to Boots, the last to leave, letting him know the funeral had paid proper respect to Mrs Earnshaw.

'I'd only say,' murmured Boots, 'that after all her years in the hustle and bustle of the market, the old lady might find things a little too quiet where she is now.'

'There you go, making fun of the dead,' said Chinese Lady, but her firm lips twitched.

Boots, who had picked Lizzy up in his car to drive her to the church and the cemetery, drove her home. On the way she said it was about time the police made an arrest of that disgusting thug who'd done his evil best to murder the barman right in front of the eyes of Polly and Boots. Boots said it was obviously going to take time to nail the social misfit, but he'd bet on the police doing so in the end.

'Well, I just think they ought to get a move on,' said Lizzy. 'While there are horrible specimens like him around, none of us are safe in our beds.'

At this moment, Curly Harris was back from Ramsgate, having found no clue to suggest Dodgy Dan had ever arrived there. He was now convinced that that wily old tramp, in mentioning Ramsgate to Spongy, had deliberately laid a red herring. Wait till I finger the smelly old varmint, he'll wish he'd never been born. He's cost me a cosy lodging with Figgy, thought Curly.

Chapter Twenty-two

Saturday morning, and the weather was lousy.

'Where the hell is he?' asked Chief Inspector Walters of Sergeant Bootle at the Camberwell police station. His temper was lousy too.

'You're referring, guv, to Curly Harris?' said Sergeant Bootle.

'Who else?'

'Well, guv, have you thought about the fact that his description probably needs rearranging?'

'I'm thinking about it all the time and it's damaging my appetite. I've gone off my food since last night, and why? Because I realized as soon as I ducked into my pit that I've missed the obvious. He's had a haircut, of course he bloody well has. And probably grown a moustache into the bargain.'

'All the same, guv, we were right to show him as a hairy head in the first place.'

'Yes, in the first place, but now the description we've been circulating has got to be rearranged. I'm certain the bugger's going around looking like an advertisement for a self-respecting barber. See to it, see that

Jarvis comes up with a new artist's impression. See he gives Curly Harris a haircut. And a moustache on an alternative impression.'

'Right you are, guv.'

Curly Harris, back to sniffing around in search of Dodgy Dan in the wilds of southeast London, did a house over during an afternoon excursion. Well, he was almost skint and accordingly in need. The house was in the best part of Norbury. He'd seen the family go off in a car on some outing, and it hadn't taken him long to force an entry into the rear of the property. All done quietly, with the back garden's high hedges preventing him from being seen by neighbours. He'd picked up some very nice saleable items, mostly silver with a bit of jewellery, and had parted with the loot to a Soho fence early in the evening. Then he treated himself to a posh seat at the Windmill Theatre, which was staging its usual fare for tired businessmen, a saucy revue. That is, the comedians were bawdy and the stage maidens not only wore very little, but nothing at all in the closing tableau. The Windmill was famous for never having closed all through the war, despite the bombing raids and what the V1s and V2s had done to London. It had provided on-leave GIs with some morale-boosting performances by the United Kingdom's wartime sex kittens. Its post-war popularity was constant.

Curly Harris, having had a real eyeful by the time the final curtain rang down, took himself off to an address in Soho, an address that represented an apartment above a shop. He asked to see Figgy, as Elvira Figgins was known to her intimates. All done up in a filmy see-through wrap covering skimpy corset and black stockings, she received him in a room set aside for a certain kind of private goings-on.

'Now listen, Curly, what've you come 'ere for?' she said quite sharply. 'This is me busiest time, with the punters turning out of theatres and looking for a bit of what they fancy before going home.'

'Well, I ain't here to waste yer time, Figgy,' said Curly, himself all done up in his classy raincoat and a well-fitting bowler hat. 'I'm fairly flush right now, and I'd like to treat you to a late-night supper at Darkeys.' Darkeys was a restaurant with an inner pink glow that served suppers with cabaret until two in the morning. 'So put yer dress and coat on and–'

'You're flush?' said Elvira suspiciously. 'What with?'

'Backed a winner at fifteen to one, didn't I?' said Curly.

'I can believe that?' said Elvira, not because she was law-abiding, but because it wouldn't do her any good to be seen with

Curly if he was just hot from a break-in and still wanted for GBH.

'Now would I tell yer a porkie?' he said plaintively. 'Course I wouldn't, not you, sweetheart.' He was fond of Elvira. She'd never offer him up to the Old Bill, and although she was knocking on a bit and had lost some of her bloom, she still had a good body and had taught him all he needed to know about how to be inventive at bedtime. Mind, the lessons hadn't been for free, nor had he expected them to be. Well, she had to make a living, he'd understood that. 'So come on, let's hit the pavement and head for Darkeys,' he urged. 'After which, I'll take you home and keep you company all night.'

'All night?' said Elvira, irked by knowing that some of her young competitors were already earning welcome lolly this evening. 'If that's what you'd like, I'm game, but only if the coppers and their big boots don't 'appen to be hanging about. By the way, ducky, all night will cost yer more than a bob or two.'

'Fair enough,' said Curly, and Elvira slipped off her wrap and slid herself into a slinky dress.

'Like I've mentioned before, that was a silly mistake you made, cutting up that barman,' she said, reaching for her coat. 'The coppers won't never stop looking for you.'

'What I'd like most,' growled Curly, 'is to

meet the tomtit that chased after me. Ten to bleedin' one he gave the police more verbal abuse than anyone else about me and me description. Yes, I bleedin' would like to meet him again. In the dark.'

They left, heading for a late supper and a bit of low life.

It was well after midnight when Lizzy woke up. It wasn't one of those moments that were all to do with thoughts of Ned, it was a moment when she knew she'd been brought to startled wakefulness by an unexpected noise. She lay there, listening, her body stiff. Another little noise. And it came from down below. And there was something else. The suspicion of a cold draught coming through her bedroom door, ajar.

She knew what that meant.

The front door was open.

She should never have told Chinese Lady there was no problem about being alone at night. She'd tempted Providence, and now look, there was someone in the house.

She made no risky attempt to investigate, she kept her head and used a finger to make contact with a buzz button beside her bed. Bobby and Helene, with their wartime knowledge, had fixed up an alarm buzzer. There were three buttons for it, one beside her bed, one in the kitchen and one in the living room.

She pressed the bedside button.

A low but sharp buzzing noise lasting a few seconds hit the ears of Bobby and Helene in the bedroom of their Thurlow Park Road home, not far from Lizzy. They came instantly awake, and Bobby was out of bed almost at once, Helene following.

'She's in trouble,' said Bobby, pulling trousers on over his pyjamas. Trouble meant real trouble, otherwise his mother would have phoned, not buzzed.

'Hurry, then,' breathed Helene, seizing a thick winter coat from her wardrobe and slipping it on over her nightdress. Her feet sought her shoes. Neither Estelle nor Robert, their children, had woken up. Helene seized a few seconds to dash off a note telling Estelle that she and Bobby were at Grandma's. In the event of the girl waking up, she placed the note on Estelle's bedside table. Then, with Bobby in a thick sweater over his trousers, and herself in her coat, they rushed silently down the stairs and out of the house to their car, parked in the drive. Helene carried a torch. They were in the car and away in seconds.

Lizzy's house in Sunrise Avenue off Denmark Hill was dark and shadowy, its open front door a yawning void. Bobby and Helene, their car lights switched off, parked some way from the house to avoid giving any intruders notice of their coming. They got out and made a quick but silent approach. Helene checked, nudged Bobby's arm and pointed. There, a little way beyond his mother's house, was a small dark blue van just touched by the light of a distant street lamp. At that moment a man emerged from the house. He was a dim figure, but with eyes now used to the night, Bobby and Helene could see that he was carrying a television set, his arms wrapped around its square bulk.

Bending, they pressed themselves close to the five-feet front hedge of a house and became quite still, watching. The burly nefarious bloke approached the van, then stooped and placed the television set carefully down on the pavement. Straightening up, he opened the van's rear doors, then bent to pick up the set. At which point Bobby put his mouth close to Helene's ear and whispered.

'If he goes back into the house, get up to the van, note its number and then remove the rotor arm.'

With the burglar carefully placing the television set into the van, Helene whispered back.

'Quick, you must get to Mama and let her know we're here.'

'At the right moment.'

The burly cove silently closed the van doors, then walked rapidly back to the open gate of Lizzy's house, made his way up the front path and disappeared into the yawning void. Helene and Bobby straightened up. Helene, about to make a dash for the van, held back, for out of the house came another man, carrying a canvas holdall. Bobby drew a breath. He knew that his father, during his many years with the wine trade, had accumulated souvenirs and gifts with much more than an intrinsic value. There was a bounty of silverware for the taking, and he surmised that a lot of it was now in that holdall. He and Helene stayed watching. They saw the second man, a thinner version of the first, put the holdall in the van and return to the house.

'Now,' whispered Bobby.

The years since they had carried out hair-raising missions for SOE in aid of the French resistance movement seemed to roll away as they made their move to deal with the despoilers of Lizzy's house and belongings. Helene effected her lightning dash to the van, and Bobby sped to the front gate and up the path to the open door. He knew why it was open. To allow the men easy coming and going with their loot, and to provide them with an unimpeded getaway in the event of being disturbed.

Bobby didn't intend to disturb them, or to set about them and create the kind of uproar that would really alarm his mother.

So, at the open door, he listened. He heard them. The sounds were mere murmurs, but still he heard them, coming from the room that had been his dear old dad's study, the place where he attended to paperwork brought home from his office. A little metallic chink broke through the murmurs.

More silver, thought Bobby, and moved again, speeding silently through the hall and up the carpeted stairs to his mother's bedroom. Soundlessly, he pushed the door open. He needed no torch, nor any light, for his eyes were now thoroughly used to the darkness. Quite clearly, he made out the shadowy figure of his mother sitting up in bed. He whispered, 'It's Bobby, Ma, don't worry, don't say anything, stay quiet.'

There was a palpable indrawn breath of relief from Lizzy. Going to the landing, Bobby made out two figures flitting through the still open front door of the house. They left it open, avoiding the noise of closing it. He went down the stairs and into the kitchen. There he crossed to the phone and by touch alone, dialled 999.

The two villains, notably Black Jake and Slim Gibbs, in ransacking the ground floor, had acquired a television set and various prize valuables. And they had done so, they assumed, without waking the lady of the house. Now they were cursing and spitting in their inability to get their van engine to fire. Everything was as dead as the dodo. Deader, in fact, and they spared the bird nothing in their cursing references to it, which was more than a little spiteful considering the dodo had never been known to do harm to any man.

Helene was standing off, waiting in deep shadow, impatient rather than anxious. She knew enough about Bobby's flair for improvisation to feel confident the next act would see the burglars bagged.

She kept a watching brief on the two men as they investigated the engine under the raised bonnet. It wasn't all that long before a police car came racing into the avenue, and she knew then exactly how Bobby had dealt with the situation.

The guilty duo were, in effect, caught with their braces dangling, their detention witnessed by Bobby. Helene had dashed into the house to comfort and reassure Lizzy.

'Well, well, Blackie, and you, Slim,' said the police sergeant, while a constable handcuffed the pair, 'only a couple of months out of the Scrubs, and you can't wait to get back. Tck, tck.'

''Ere, what bleedin' 'appened?' asked Black Jake, one of the old and rough brigade.

'Yes, exactly what happened?' asked Slim Gibbs, who'd been educated. 'We did a nice clean and quiet job, taking care not to alarm the lady of the house or tread on her cats, and now look. It's not a fair cop, Sergeant.'

'Yus, if some interfering git hadn't done a lousy job on our motor, we'd of been far gone by now,' said Black Jake.

'Hard luck, I don't think,' said the sergeant, thankful that no harm had come to Mrs Somers, the householder. Black Jake was capable of swinging a heavy fist if interrupted during a break-in. 'Now, the pair of you coming quietly?'

'If you insist,' said Slim Gibbs, and he and his heavy half entered the police car without more ado. The sergeant and constable said good night to Bobby and let him know they'd be in touch. Then away they went, with the frustrated wrongdoers and the swag.

Bobby found his wife and mother in the kitchen. Lizzy, in a dressing gown, was seated at the table, drinking tea, Helene standing beside her.

'Oh, there you are, Bobby,' said Lizzy, who looked and sounded calm. 'Thanks ever so much for acting so quick, you and Helene. Helene's just made a pot of tea to help me steady my nerves.' Actually, she seemed remarkably short of nervous tremors. 'Would you like a cup?'

'Not here,' said Bobby. 'I'll get back home, just in case the kids have woken up.'

'Bobby, I'll go,' said Helene, 'you stay with Mama and talk to her. We must decide if it's wise for her to continue living alone.'

'I hope no-one's going to fuss,' said Lizzy.

'Your mother will, once she gets to know about tonight,' said Bobby.

'So sorry, Mama, that this happened,' said Helene, 'but see, everything will be returned to you when the men have been convicted.' She stooped and kissed Lizzy's cheek. 'I must go now.'

Bobby saw her out and watched her hasten to the car. As soon as she was on her way, the car headlamps lighting her going, he returned to his mother. He helped himself to a cup of tea, then sat down to have a ten-minute talk with her before seeing her back to her bed, and settling down for the rest of the night in his old room. No further disturbance happened. All was peace and quiet, although there was an unhappy absence of a number of valuables.

As for Helene, she was relieved to discover that neither Estelle nor Robert had awoken. She found them still wrapped up in the sleep of the innocent.

If the Herne Hill police were happy at having caught a couple of old sweats red-handed, the Norbury police were fuming that investigation of a daylight burglary had offered no fingerprints except those of the burgled family.

On an incidental note, Chief Inspector Walters of Camberwell was dreaming fitfully of the elusive Curly Harris. That bad-tempered, antisocial young lout, who had a dangerous affinity with a knife, was spending the night snug in the bed of Elvira Figgins.

On Sunday morning, Bobby phoned Boots and told him of events.

'Good God,' said Boots, 'that happened, did it, so soon after Grandma Finch had asked your mother if she was all right living alone?'

'It happened right enough,' said Bobby. 'I'm still here with her, but thought I'd get on the blower and let you know about it before I make tracks for home. The point is, can we expect everyone in the family to sound off about whether it's unwise for Ma to continue to live alone? I can tell you, last night's happening hasn't put her off.'

'She isn't frightened, shaken up or worried?' said Boots.

'Believe me, old sport,' said Bobby, 'now that she's had time to think about it, she's only angry, angry that two shifty numbers broke into her house and dared to lay their dirty mitts on things that didn't belong to them.'

'Cast your mind back, Bobby, and you'll be reminded that was exactly how Grandma Finch felt, and how she reacted,' said Boots, remembering the way Chinese Lady had dealt with a burglar a few years ago. She had struck him a blow in fury. 'As I've mentioned before, your mother will never leave that house until she's carried out feet first. And since the buzzer system worked to perfection, I suggest everyone goes along with that. In other words, allow her to keep her independence, even at the risk of being burgled again.'

'Fair enough,' said Bobby, 'although I suspect the outside world might regard that as being a pretty casual attitude towards the welfare of our old folk.'

'The outside world isn't closely acquainted with your particular old folk, or her blithe spirit,' said Boots.

'Good point,' said Bobby. 'I'll talk to my side of the family.'

'Bobby, I've offered my advice,' said Boots, 'but the last word naturally belongs to you and Helene.'

'Well, you've come up with the first word,' said Bobby, 'and any last word from Helene and me is sure to agree, old chap.'

'I leave it with you,' said Boots. 'By the way, give your mother my love, and let her know my feelings about uninvited uglies coincide with hers.'

Lizzy did indeed feel incensed that anyone should enter her house uninvited and make off with belongings precious to all that appertained to the many years she had shared with Ned. That was the worst thing about burglars, she told Annabelle and

Emma as soon as her daughters hurried round to see her. The villains took items that meant so much to people, irrespective of what they were worth money-wise.

By mid-morning a minor uproar had travelled around the Adams families. By midday it had been reduced to no more than another talking point. Bobby had quietened his brother, sisters and in-laws, Boots had exercised a soothing effect on Chinese Lady and other family members, and Lizzy had told anxious enquirers over the phone not to worry because she herself didn't intend to, especially as Bobby was arranging for the alarm system to be connected to the local police station as well as to his bedside.

As for Curly Harris, he was up and away from 21A Blackfriars Road well before anyone representing the Old Bill turned up. He left Elvira Figgins feeling that although other customers didn't have his quick temper, they didn't have his generosity, either. Or his rating as a performer.

Dodgy Dan, meanwhile, was preparing to do an honest job of work around the markets of the East End. That meant nicking anything that nobody seemed to want. He was still intent on losing himself up in Blackpool, even if he had to pay to get there.

Unless glad tidings arrived to the effect that Curly Harris had been copped.

Chapter Twenty-three

Sunday afternoon's weather was just right for athletic people who liked to get out of doors and exercise their limbs. If the temperature was not exactly of the kind that graced the tropics, being what was known as bracing, the sky itself was an unbroken ice blue, the sunlight untrammelled.

'Tennis again?' said Boots to Gemma an hour or so after Sunday dinner. 'Jane's been in touch?'

'You bet,' said Gemma.

Boots smiled. There she was, his daughter, more of a young lady now than a girl, and keen to enjoy some healthy activity with one of her many friends. He knew Cathy was top of that list, but Cathy had no yearning for tennis, whereas Gemma liked a regular game once the spring arrived. Her supple limbs made it easy for her to fly about the court.

'Enjoy yourself, sweetie,' said Polly. She and Boots, having spent most of the morning gardening, were content to relax this afternoon, and to let time travel leisurely by. When one was over sixty, there was no desire to help it rush. Gemma, coat over her tennis dress, red ribbon tying back her hair, was about to depart for the park.

'Oh, by the way, dear ones,' she said, 'you remember my mentioning the young man who works for Uncle Freddy in the store on Saturdays?'

'The one you said was quite nice, but a bit barmy?' said Boots.

'Yes, he kept having funny moments,' said Gemma. 'Well, he seems to be a regular visitor to the park on Sunday afternoons. I think he likes watching Jane and me trying to make a name for ourselves at Wimbledon one day. I also think Jane's a bit gone on him.'

'Yes, you've hinted at that,' said Boots, 'but does her father know? And are you saying Jane's a bit gone on a young bloke seen only through the wire surround of the courts?'

'Oh, didn't I tell you we meet him for refreshments after we come off the court?' said Gemma.

'I don't think so, ducky,' said Polly.

'Well, we do,' said Gemma. 'Charlie seems to like our company, although–'

'Charlie?' said Polly.

'Oh, his real name is Perry,' said Gemma, 'and if Jane is really smitten, she'll have to let her dad know. Oh, well, can't stop now, must go – see you when I get back – so long, folks.'

'Aren't you taking your book?' Mrs Gladys

312

Peters, meeting her son in the little hall of the family house in Daneville Road, Camberwell, put the question to him.

'My book?' Peregrine looked puzzled for a moment. 'Oh, the book on Brunel. Well, no, I've finished it and made all the notes I want to.'

'That's good,' said Mrs Peters, wife of Joe Peters. 'Your dad says after all the hard work you did leading up to your exams, you ought to give yourself a rest from studying. Then you'll have a fresh mind, he says, when you start university.'

'It's OK, Ma, I enjoy studying, it keeps my brain alive,' said Peregrine, thinking, of course, that the reverse happened whenever he did a kind of study of a certain young vision of grace and beauty. Then his brain fell apart.

'Well, have a nice walk, dear, I'll be doing a high Sunday tea this evening,' said Mrs Peters. 'You and your dad will like that.'

'Thankfully for your efforts, Ma, so will you and Penny,' said Peregrine, and went on his way determined to be his age in the event of seeing his flight of fancy again.

He was at the tennis courts later than usual, but they were there, the two girls. However, they weren't alone. A broad-shouldered, healthy-looking man in a thick sweater and trousers stood at one of the net posts, calling encouragement to Jane.

'That's it, sweetheart, always try to get the ball back – always try to make Gemma play one more stroke – don't whack at it every time – now look, you ran into that one – never mind, try again, and keep your eye on the ball.' And so on.

Peregrine had eyes only for Gemma, of course. Glowing from her exercise, she came up to the wire to retrieve a ball. She saw him, came closer and spoke confidentially, for his ears alone.

'Hello, Charlie – Jane's dad is here – don't let him know you and Jane are matey. He's against her having boyfriends he knows nothing about. He's old-fashioned – his favourite pin-up is Queen Victoria. Can you believe it? Just thought I'd tell you.'

For a brief second her bright starry eyes held his, then she turned and hit the ball back to Jane. Jane's protective dad spoke up.

'Who's that?'

'Oh, a friend of mine,' said Gemma, and Jane served. Gemma hit a fine forehand return, and another rally was under way, with Jane doing her best to perform to her dad's coaching. The game went on, both girls chasing everything reachable, but never once did Jane acknowledge Peregrine's presence. There was no hint that she knew him. He supposed, from what Gemma had said, that the father figure had reason to suspect some pimply pipsqueak was after his daughter. Even with the changing Fifties well on the way to the Sixties, there were still a hell of a lot of dads sticking to the outdated belief that their daughters shouldn't date fellers who picked them up in a dance hall. Or a park. Their motto was 'Dad knows best'.

Peregrine couldn't quite work out how it was that he'd been bracketed with Jane, when he was heart and soul attached to his radiant young princess.

Heart and soul? Radiant princess?

I'm not getting any better.

But look at her, running, flying, dancing, laughing, yelling – what a delight. There's a girl who radiates a sheer love of life.

Thinking of going on his way, he heard the father figure saying so long to both girls, with an injunction to Jane to keep her eye on the ball and not on anything in trousers. He then watched the man depart. A minute later, with the girls back into the swing of their game, he departed himself, feeling it was time he did.

Jane called to him.

'Hi, Charlie, be seeing you in a tick.' It was the happy call of a girl suddenly free of the awesome shadow of a Victorian-minded dad.

Peregrine made a casual gesture of acknowledgement and went on his way.

'So that was your dad,' he said to Jane over tea and buns a little later. She and Gemma had joined him in the cafe.

'Yes, that was him,' said Jane.

'He wants to save Jane for someone like a bank manager, which she thinks is a bit off,' said Gemma. 'Could you be in line for that kind of job?'

'Me?' said Peregrine, relieved that so far he was keeping his head. 'No, not much. I'm in the middle of my year waiting for university. In between studying I'm earning myself some pocket money working on Saturdays at your family's store and down the Walworth market on Wednesday afternoons.'

'Oh, yes, of course, Saturdays at the store, so you are,' said Gemma. 'Silly me. So it's university for you, is it, Charlie?' She began to think his dotty moments had to be recent and only temporary, otherwise he could never have passed a university entrance exam or dealt efficiently with customers on busy Saturdays at the store. Her eyes bright and teasing, she said, 'You're not after a degree in banking, I suppose? Only if you were, Jane's dad might–'

'Never mind my dad,' interrupted Jane, 'he'll grow up one day. Lots of dads do. They don't all stay stodgy and old-fashioned. Would you believe it, Gemma,

Mary Meredith's dad is drummer with a skiffle group. What's your dad like, Charlie?'

Peregrine, still relieved that he hadn't yet fallen off his horse, as it were, informed the girls that his good old dad was in insurance, that he'd been in it all his working life, and had joined a bowls club two years ago.

'Probably in lieu of joining a group, seeing he's never been great on music except for "Land of Hope and Glory".'

'Oh, poor bloke,' said Jane. 'Charlie, you did say you went dancing.'

'Yes, fairly often on Saturday nights,' said Peregrine, wondering how to let her know, without hurting her feelings, that Gemma was his preference.

'I go most Saturdays to the Denmark Hill Youth Club,' said Jane. 'Only it's a bit tame compared with what I've heard about the Brixton gigs. But my dad won't let me get anywhere near Brixton on a Saturday evening. Honest, he's my cross. He's lucky that I'm fond of him or I'd be his thorny crown. Still, if you came to the youth club some Saturday, you'd see me there.'

'I think I'd better meet your dad first,' said Peregrine, 'and let him know I'm harmless.'

'Are you harmless, Charlie?' asked Gemma playfully. 'My Aunt Susie once told me that boys are harmless only up to the age of five, and that from then on they're a danger to everyone, themselves included.'

'Oh, my Aunt Flo cured me long ago, when I was six,' said Peregrine.

'How?' asked Jane.

'Dropped me on my head,' said Peregrine.

Jane giggled, Gemma laughed.

'That accounts for you losing your way sometimes,' she said.

Peregrine glanced, saw mirth reflected in the dancing light of her eyes, thought about heavenly young maidens swanning through the marble halls of pearly Olympus, and nearly had a relapse.

'Believe me, it's only lately I've had one or two absent-minded moments,' he mumbled.

'The point now is how do we get you to meet Jane's dad kind of formally?' mused Gemma. 'I mean, you'd like to, Charlie, wouldn't you? Then there'd be no bother about dating her. Unless you've already got a girlfriend.'

'Here, d'you mind?' said Jane. 'I can look after my own private life, and I'm sure Charlie can look after his.'

'Oh, just offering a little help,' said Gemma.

'Isn't she a cuckoo, Charlie?' said Jane, with a bit of a giggle.

'Pardon?' said Peregrine.

'Gemma, isn't she a cuckoo?' said Jane, not in the least put out by what she thought was Charlie playing hard to get.

Peregrine wasn't sure how his dreamboat

could be related in any way to a cuckoo without turning fact into fiction.

'I think I'd better pass on that one,' he said.

'Well, let's talk again next week because I'd better start getting back home now,' said Jane. She jumped up.

'Yes, time we left,' said Gemma, and came to her feet gracefully. 'So long, Charlie, see you.' She gave him a happy smile. 'Ta for the tea and buns, you're a sport.'

'So long,' said Peregrine. He received a wink from Jane, then watched as the girls, carrying their holdalls, walked out of his life once more, although they did turn at the door to give him a little wave. On his feet, he returned the gesture, one of friendliness on their part, one of hope on his.

He shook his head at himself for being so useless. It wasn't actually impossible, was it, to let a young goddess know he fancied her? What a disaster, being useless at his age. Who'd have thought it? His sister would shriek with laughter if she knew his head fell off every time he was eye to eye with a girl called Gemma.

Not long after she'd dropped off to sleep that night, Gemma woke up for no reason at all, except that she found she was thinking of Charlie, the young man who spent Sunday afternoons in Ruskin Park and had made a hit with Jane. What a nice young man he was, even if he still had moments when he seemed confused. And he was definitely a bit shy about making headway with Jane, despite her encouragement. He needed help, first of all with Jane's dad, one of what Uncle Tommy called the old brigade, meaning his word was law where sons and daughters were concerned. Imagine, there were parents still like that ... and lots of them...

Gemma went back to sleep.

Chapter Twenty-four

Tuesday evening, and Miss Marjorie Alsop was doing her nut again, in the vernacular of the locality. Addressing a meeting of Brixton's Young Socialists on the question of how to persuade the Minister of Trade to encourage workers in the fur trade to demand a change from the skinning of animals to the shearing of sheep, she had suddenly spotted a traitor in the audience. A traitor in the shape of a young woman clad in a fur jacket and a fur hat.

Now she was tempestuously calling, in effect, for the young woman to be bundled off to the Tower and executed. All kinds of accusations sprang from her. Uproar ensued, with some members of the audience shouting support for a lynching, while a free-thinking johnny tried to point out that all individuals had a right to dress how they liked, even if it did make them look as if they inhabited nancified Mayfair drawing rooms. And the young woman herself, trying to let everyone know she'd bought the hat and jacket at a charity jumble sale last Christmas, stood on a chair to make her point and promptly fell off it into the arms of a bloke whom she immediately and loudly accused of molesting her.

The meeting ended in disorder, and the audience expelled itself from the hall in noisy and argumentative bits and pieces. That left the speaker, Miss Alsop, alone on the stage, except for her mentor and support, Lulu Adams.

Lulu, disgusted, spoke her piece.

'You've done it again, you idiot woman. How many times do I have to tell you that in the long run it's sensible argument and discussion that win the day, not verbal violence? Yes, all right, I know that look of yours, I know I still get my own knickers in a twist sometimes, but not as much as I did in my unmarried days.'

'Is being unmarried significant?' asked Marjorie.

'Frankly, yes,' said Lulu. 'In that state, you're a bit heady and undisciplined. Of course, there's the satisfaction of standing on your own as a woman and showing men, by your achievements, that you can do without them. That gets up their noses, believe me.'

'So why did you opt for a married state, then?' asked Marj.

'If I knew I'd tell you,' said Lulu. 'All I can remember is going through a time when my priorities were all over the place and, like you, I was preaching violence as the solution to the problems of the working classes. Then one morning I woke up wearing just a wedding ring, and Paul was next to me in the bed. That's it, roughly. Still, things could be worse than marriage. It's probably just what you need.'

'Marriage?' said Marj dubiously.

'Do it with the right kind of bloke, of course,' said Lulu, 'the kind who'll do what you tell him. The other kind are a waste of time. More of a nuisance, really, than an asset. Most women are born to run things, and most men are born to think the world needs them more than us. It took me a little while to cure Paul of that notion, but I succeeded eventually, since when he's stopped answering me back. So there you are, I'm pretty sure marriage to the right bloke will calm you down and stop you hollering for a revolution every time you spot a woman wearing fur gloves. I found out early on that even our suffering workers put out the Union Jack whenever royalty comes around to pat their babies' heads. Not that I've definitely given up campaigning for Buckingham Palace to be turned into a workers' hostel.'

'All very ducky, I must say,' said Marj, 'but tell me, where do I find the right kind of husband?' She'd have opted for someone like Mr Robert Adams or his brother Sammy, but wouldn't say so.

'We'll do some looking,' said Lulu. 'Meanwhile, stand up for the main priority, which is getting the Labour Party back into power. Once that happens, well, you and your comrades can press the relevant minister to consider an anti-fur Act. As it is, the sneaky Tories are trying to make themselves popular by implementing recommendations for the building of by-passes and motorways to help with the traffic problem. It's a perpetual thorn in Mr Gaitskell's side.' Mr Gaitskell, leader of the Labour Party, was doing his very best to provide mettlesome opposition. 'Now, have you calmed down, Marj?'

'Well, yes,' conceded Marj, 'but would you believe any young woman could attend one of our meetings all decked out in furs? What's that if it's not brainless provocation?'

'It happens,' said Lulu, 'and you've got to grin and bear it, to make a name for yourself as a cool type. Now I'm going home. I want to make sure Paul put little Sylvie safely to bed ages ago. He knows her bedtime, but you can't always rely on a man to remember a routine.'

Bless this one, she thought, when she arrived home. Paul had their daughter tucked up and sleeping soundly. Accordingly, Lulu treated him to a kiss and then to an account of how the meeting of the Young Socialists had broken up in disorder consequent on Mad Marj letting go of her marbles again. So she'd told Marj that what she seriously needed was something that would take her mind off suffering seals. Socialist politics had proved not to be enough, after all.

'Pity,' said Paul, who'd been enjoying a television comedy show in preference to a live interview with a prominent Labour MP who was making headlines. Had Lulu known, she'd have queried his loyalty as well as his IQ. 'Yes, pity,' he murmured.

'Yes, you'd think striving on behalf of socialism and the workers would be enough for most thinking people, wouldn't you?' said Lulu. 'But it isn't for Marj, so I suggested she took up with some eligible bachelor, the kind she can exercise her mind on.'

'Exercise her mind?' said Paul. 'What for?'

'To take it off animal humanity,' said Lulu, spectacles agleam with earnestness, 'and concentrate on training the chosen bloke.'

'For what?'

'For marriage, of course,' said Lulu, still earnest, 'and to make quite sure he won't boss her about.'

'Can't she make do with a performing monkey?' asked Paul.

'Not a brilliant comment, Paul,' said Lulu. 'Some women get that kind of husband without even trying. Listen now, any woman who gives up her independence for marriage needs to make sure she won't get mucked about. You know what men are like, you're

325

one yourself, but not the thick kind, thankfully. If we can help Marj to train her man, once she's found him, we'll automatically be helping her to change her priorities. At the moment, she's still stuck on the evils of skinning crocodiles.'

'A bit rough on the crocs, that's true,' said Paul, 'but as to your ideas about marriage, I think some of them need revising, so come here, you doll.'

Husband took hold of wife. Wife objected.

'Paul, don't you dare try that heavy Victorian stuff with me! Paul! Paul, let me go!'

Paul let her go. Lulu tumbled back onto her bottom.

'Well, I'm jiggered,' said Paul, 'it looks like your knickers are in a twist, Lulu.'

It was Lulu's opinion that some men were fresh out of a cave, and hairy with it.

'I'm not quite sure if Irena Leino is serious about qualifying for the entrance exam to Oxford,' said Gemma over supper on Thursday.

'What makes you say that?' asked Boots.

'Well, I keep getting the impression she's not bothering to concentrate, that her mind's on something else,' said Gemma. 'And sometimes when a lesson requires written answers, she takes a peek at mine. Not that I mind, if it's a help to her.'

'Is it a help?' said James.

'I shouldn't think so, not in the long run,' said Polly.

'Oh, but she's very sweet,' said Gemma, 'and always calm and collected. Also, even if she's a bit behind on some subjects, she's tops at European history, which we've been doing since last term. Yesterday, we had a list of questions to answer about the end of the Great War and how it led to the Russian Revolution, and when and where was Lenin born, and what was his real name. Your learned daughter, Mama, scratched around a bit hopelessly on Lenin, and so Irena slipped me the answers in a jiffy.'

'She's probably hot on Russian history because she lives in Finland, next door to the land of Lenin,' said James. 'Listen, Mama, I don't want to upset anyone, but there's not much beef in my casserole.'

'Dear boy,' said Polly, 'I'd be surprised if there were any, and so would Flossie. It's lamb casserole.'

'I think my school dinners are ruining my palate,' said James.

'Daddy, as a young man, you were around when Lenin was doing his stuff, so what do you know about him?' asked Gemma.

'Nothing intimate,' said Boots. 'We never met. Just as well. He'd have fed me politics and pamphlets, and pamphlets give me indigestion.'

'In any case,' said Polly, 'I absolutely

forbid any suppertime discussion of politics and politicians now and in the future. Suppertimes represent family get-togethers of a happy and civilized nature. Darlings, let us keep them that way.'

'Hearing you, Mama,' said Gemma, looking impressed.

'Got you, Ma,' said James, looking agreeable.

Boots said nothing. He simply looked thoughtful.

Curly Harris was now lying low in the wilds of Streatham. Well, he was an unknown quantity there, and he'd found new lodgings with an old dear near Streatham Common. To add to his new-found liking for the area, he'd just had another easy picking. After a late breakfast of tea and toast, supplied by the old dear, who talked into his lughole twenty to the dozen, and wouldn't have noticed if Crippen had been her lodger, he had sallied forth with a valise and a hope. He was in need again. He'd been a bit overgenerous with Figgy. So he strolled the streets and avenues until he saw a woman leave a house in Vale Road. She was carrying a shopping bag. It didn't take him more than a couple of seconds to decide she was a housewife going shopping, that her husband was at work and any children were at school. So he let himself in round the back way with the help of a glass-cutter, and sure enough there was no-one at home.

Undisturbed, and wearing thin rubber gloves, he looted the place of its silver, its French carriage clock and the lady's jewellery, what there was of it, stowing everything in the valise. To make sure the cops didn't relate the breakin to the one in Norbury, he smashed a few things up and chucked others about. The job in Norbury had been tidy, this one was rough. When the housewife returned, she'd probably faint, but so what, everyone had to put up with a bit of bad luck. He himself had to put up with Dodgy Dan, his own bad-luck story.

Now he was on a bus and on his way to Soho to do another trade with his favourite fence. Should he stop on the way, and chance a call on Figgy? No, better not, not in broad daylight. He was dead against taking the risk of being nicked and introduced to the inside of a cop shop. He didn't need that kind of intro, it could lead to a lousy lock-up like Wormwood Scrubs, where the company was known to be heavy, ugly and grizzled, and would make mincemeat of a newcomer only twenty-two.

Where, he wondered, was Dodgy Dan? He was ten times certain it was that old bleeder who'd pointed the fuzz at him on account of having his locker cleared of cash. Well, he didn't ought to have kept oof there, it was inviting a look from someone seriously short of the ready. Anyway, he'd catch up with him sometime and do for him, whether he was in Margate, Ramsgate or the flaming Tower of London.

Dodgy Dan was still doing his best to earn enough to actually pay for a ride to Blackpool. He had a growing feeling that Blackpool would prove nicely lucrative, especially with Easter and the summer coming on. So to do the earning, he'd returned to his old endeavours in the hustle and bustle of London's markets. Which meant picking pockets and looking out for lucky dips into handbags. Which also meant risking getting victimized by the fuzz, like times before. Still, a bloke had to make a living somehow, especially when he'd never had insurance stamps put on a card. No stamps and you didn't qualify for handouts. It was criminal the way a bloke was treated by his own government.

At night and part of each day, he was hiding himself in a Wapping hostel while hoping Curly Harris would either get nicked by the Old Bill or run over by a bus.

Sunday afternoon having arrived without rain, thunder or lightning, Gemma and Jane, as usual, were running, dashing and dancing about on one of Ruskin Park's hard tennis courts. Any moment they expected Charlie, their friendly acquaintance, to turn up. Such a moment didn't arrive. He was absent throughout their game, nor was he there when they left the court.

Jane was a bit miffed, Gemma a little surprised.

'Perhaps he's got flu,' said Jane.

'Well, I do hope he hasn't broken a leg or something like that,' said Gemma. 'Of course, he could be spending the afternoon with a girlfriend. I expect there is one in his life.'

'That's it, make me unsure of my chances,' said Jane. 'Anyway, he's never mentioned any girl.'

'That doesn't mean he doesn't have one,' said Gemma.

'Well, our Charlie would be a hot date,' said Jane.

Peregrine was being kept away by a visit of favourite relatives, Aunt Maud and Uncle Patrick. They'd come for lunch and were staying for tea, and were such a jolly and endearing couple that neither he nor Penelope would have dreamt of absenting themselves. Aunt Maud and Uncle Patrick were family in a very affectionate sense.

Peregrine, however, still had moments when his fertile imagination conjured up highly diverting pictures of his fleet-footed

Diana gracing the tennis court. On one such occasion his Uncle Patrick asked him what he was thinking about.

'Oh, angel cake,' said Peregrine off the top of his head.

'Angel cake?' said a puzzled Aunt Maud.

'Yes, isn't it curious what enters our minds sometimes?' said Peregrine. 'Without any reason?'

'That's when we start needing a doctor,' said Uncle Patrick and roared with laughter.

The Streatham police were as confounded by the ugly and messy burglary as their colleagues at Norbury had been by the neat and tidy break-in. There wasn't a single foreign fingerprint to be picked up at either house.

And the Camberwell police were no nearer laying their hands on Curly Harris than they'd been from the beginning. Boots and Polly were still waiting patiently for news of his arrest, while Joe the barman was convalescing from his grievous wound.

March seemed a happy month for burglars. Even the nation's wartime leader of worldwide repute, Sir Winston Churchill, suffered, for on the last day of March, while he and his enduring wife, Clementine, were away, his Chartwell home was rifled. They lost valuables amounting to £10,000.

That upset many of the country's people, especially those who had known the defeatist attitude of appeasers and the totally aggressive and uplifting attitude of the old boy. Chinese Lady was among the indignant.

'Well, I just don't know, Edwin,' she said to her receptive husband after listening to the radio announcement of the incident, 'that wireless of ours is still giving me aggravation and upsets. Is it true what it said about Mr Churchill?'

'I'm afraid so, Maisie dear,' said Sir Edwin, having taken the news more calmly than his wife, who was still quivering. 'And it's Sir Winston now.'

'Yes, I know,' said Chinese Lady, 'which makes it all the worse. I mean, those thieving wretches ought to have had more respect for him than to rob him and his wife like that. What's this country coming to when our Lizzy gets burglars one week and Mr Churchill the next? I hope burglary's not going to be catching, like a disease. It's honest hard work that makes a man, not taking what doesn't belong to him. Are you listening to me, Edwin?'

'With both ears, Maisie.'

'I don't like going on about things, but for Mr Churchill to have burglars, well, what next, I ask? I just hope our wireless comes up with better news next time we turn it on. I was only saying to Boots when he was last here...'

Chinese Lady carried on. Into Sir Edwin's

333

sympathetic ear.

Irena Leino was buckling down in earnest to the task of raising her academic standards, having recovered from a phase of apparent indifference to some lessons and some lectures. Gemma had offered a little warning at morning break one day.

'You are saying I am not paying attention, Gemma?'

'I'm saying I think our teachers will begin to notice you don't seem very committed,' said Gemma.

'But I am, I have to be,' said Irena, 'I wish to take the Oxford entry exam, yes.'

'Well, it's up to you, of course,' said Gemma. 'I just thought I'd make a point.'

'Ah, thank you, Gemma, you are such a good friend. I will make sure I pay very fine attention, you will see.'

So she was now concentrating very conscientiously. And no more at night did she creep down to the kitchen in search of biscuits. Miss Stanton was pleased to report to morning assembly that the petty pilfering had stopped.

Chapter Twenty-five

'Oh, bother,' said Gemma after taking a phone call on Saturday morning.

'Trouble?' said Boots, about to join Polly in the garden. They were continuing to prepare the vegetable plot for spring planting. If Polly lacked enthusiasm for cooking, she was completely sold on the joys of planting, nurturing and harvesting the family's own vegetables. 'Is oh bother on the serious side?'

'Not half,' said Gemma. 'Just as Jane and I are into the swing of the tennis season, she's sprained her ankle, so the game's off tomorrow.'

'Well, I'm sorry for both of you,' said Boots, 'but isn't there someone who could stand in for her? Heaven knows, your college alone must be overflowing with talent. What about Cathy?'

'Hot at netball, a dud at tennis,' said Gemma. 'I think you'll have to turn out, Daddy.'

'Must I?'

'No, I'll excuse you,' said Gemma, 'I know what I'll do.'

The phone rang in the house of Mr and Mrs Peters that evening. Peregrine answered it.

'Hello?'

'Oh, is that you, Charlie? It's me here.'

'Me?'

'No, me. Gemma. My Uncle Freddy, your Saturday boss, gave me your phone number a few minutes ago, so I thought I'd ring you.'

'You did?'

'Yes, and that's why it's me here.'

'Good grief.'

'Pardon? You're all right, are you?'

'Fine.'

'I didn't ring earlier, knowing you'd be working all day at the store. Look. Jane's sprained her ankle, so she's off tennis for a while. I think you said you played a bit. Do you?'

'Now and again.'

'Oh, jolly good, Charlie. Could you be a sport and stand in for Jane tomorrow afternoon at three?'

'Well, I – yes, I think–' Peregrine was chuffed, of course, if slightly disbelieving.

'I just love my Sunday afternoon tennis,' said Gemma, 'and next year, when I think I'll be up to a decent standard, I'm going to join a club. So say you'll be at the courts at three.'

'Believe me, I can't wait,' said Peregrine.

'Well, thanks,' said Gemma. 'I'm off to the

Brixton Palais for a gig with friends in about ten minutes. Will you be taking your girlfriend somewhere?'

'I would, yes, if I had a steady date, but I haven't,' said Peregrine, 'so I'll be going round to one of my more intellectual friends to try to beat him at chess.'

'Oh, classy stuff,' said Gemma, 'and the best of luck. I expect Jane is disappointed, knowing she won't be seeing you tomorrow, but I daresay she'll be hopping around by next week.'

'Well, it's not a serious disappointment, of course,' said Peregrine.

'Who knows?' said Gemma with a little laugh. 'See you, then, Charlie.'

'I'll be there,' said Peregrine, and they hung up.

Well, he thought, who'd have imagined my young Arcadian goddess would actually have invited me to partner her in the Elysian fields of Olympus?

All right, on the park tennis courts.

There's a future for me yet, as long as my loaf of bread doesn't fall off.

His sister came into the little hall.

'Who was that, Perry?' she asked.

'A friend I met in the store one Saturday,' said Peregrine. 'She's the niece of the manager.'

'She? Hello, hello,' said Penelope.

'Don't fall about,' said Peregrine, not

337

wanting to give his sister reason to make a meal of what might turn out in effect to be only a spoonful of cornflakes. 'She's just an acquaintance.'

'With talent?' murmured Penelope.

'Talent?' said Peregrine.

'Don't think I don't know what you fellers mean when you talk about female talent,' said Penelope. 'It's nothing to do with our bridge-building diplomas. Anyway, best of luck, brother. Are you dating your acquaintance this evening?'

'No, I'm playing chess with Monty.'

'Oh, well, good for keeping your brain in trim, but not my idea of a brilliant Saturday night,' said Penelope, and regarded him with curiosity. Peregrine stood up to her examination, but failed to convince her he was entirely his normal happy-go-lucky self. Lately, he'd had some odd reflective moments, as if he'd set himself an engineering problem he couldn't solve. 'All right, chum, might I ask the reason for the phone call?'

'Sure,' said Peregrine, 'the lady's keen on tennis. Her usual partner's sprained an ankle, so she asked if I'd give her an hour's practice.'

'Well, well,' said Penelope, 'what made her turn to you in her hour of need?'

'I'm a Christian,' said Peregrine. The front door knocker sounded. 'That's all, sis, can't talk any more, got to get round to Monty's,

338

and I fancy that knock means Wilfred's arrived to take you to a whist drive.'

'The Leicester Square Empire, actually,' said Penelope, and opened up to allow Wilfred to step in.

Peregrine lost his chess match. He couldn't concentrate.

Gemma, as ever, had a lively time at Brixton with the usual crowd of friends, while noting that Cousin Emily was treating boyfriend Brad like a hired help. Gemma hoped Brad would up and bite sometime, but then she supposed he was too enamoured to risk Emily giving him the push. One thing, nobody in the family suggested it wasn't on for Emily to be dating someone who was only a plumber's mate. The family might be collectively prosperous now, enjoying an affluent way of life, but its antecedents were all linked with the world of the working class, and hadn't Uncle Sammy, as a young man, run a market stall? Grandma Finch always said that being poor was a worrying thing, but no excuse for not behaving yourself and earning everyone's respect.

Sunday afternoon. Dry but cloudy.

Peregrine was there, waiting at the gate to the park tennis courts when Gemma arrived just before three. She thought he looked healthy and vigorous, much as if his peculiar moments were all well and truly behind him. She was wearing her college blazer over her tennis dress. Tennis holdalls were in evidence.

'Well, hello, Charlie, thanks for filling in,' she said, offering a warm smile.

'Hello yourself,' said Peregrine, noting the burnished gleam of her dark hair, the brightness of its red ribbon and her aura of vitality. If I were seeing her for the first time, he thought, I know I'd still place her as a heavenly being, and I can't help it if third parties would think that barmy.

'Come on, let's make a start,' she said, and they entered the courts, heading for the one Gemma always booked for three o'clock. She took off her blazer and Peregrine started to warm up. In his white shirt and shorts she thought he looked super-athletic. No wonder Jane was a bit gone on him.

They began the game, and Gemma suspected Charlie was keeping his muscles to himself, because there was nothing she couldn't cope with in his serves and returns.

'Your game,' he kept calling.

She walked to the net and beckoned him. Up he came until they were eye to eye over the net.

'You're playing dolly tennis,' she said.

'You're a dream,' said Peregrine.

'No, I'm not, there's an awful lot of room for improvement,' said Gemma, 'and I need to be stretched. Hit the ball at me, don't dolly it, or I'll bash you with my racket. You got that, Charlie?'

'Right, got it, Gemma. By the way, I'm Perry, not Charlie.'

'Never mind that, start playing tennis, or watch out for being kicked to death. I'm nobody's delicate flower. Right?'

'Right, Gemma, yes. Right.' And Peregrine, who hadn't wanted to make things difficult for his young goddess, took her threats to heart and began performing in a way that stretched her limbs and her expertise to the giddy limit. Gemma suddenly found herself up against an opponent far deadlier than Jane. His serves were filthy, his forehand foul, his backhand wicked. The ball rushed at her, raced at her, jumped at her. She was full of yells and shrieks.

'Charlie, oh, you beast!'

'Something wrong, Gemma?'

'You're showing off, you Hun.'

'Sorry – I'll calm down, shall I?'

'Just play tennis without showing off, d'you hear?'

'I hear, Gemma,' said Peregrine and moderated his game. Gemma, who still needed to be stretched, accepted the compromise of being made to run here, there and everywhere just that much more than with Jane.

Then he began to get her goat again. He began to run to the net after serving and to smash her returns into the yawning void of infinity, or something like that. She yelled.

'Charlie!'

'Yes, Gemma?'

'I'm going to kill you, d'you know that?'

'Well, no, I didn't know, Gemma, but I appreciate being given notice.'

'Carry on, anyway, you've still got ten minutes left of your life.'

'Thanks,' said Peregrine, waiting to serve. He saw her preparing to receive. She was flushed, vibrant, colourful and alive. A truly radiant being.

'Well, come on, Fred Perry,' called Gemma.

He came out of his trance and served, and these last ten minutes proved the best. He played to give her own game a boost, to help her to be more consistent and less erratic. At the end she was forgiving.

'Charlie, I'm sparing your life.'

'That's a promise, Gemma?'

'Believe me.'

'I'm grateful.' Gemma was putting on her blazer. He looked warm from activity, and she – in his dizzy eyes – looked as radiant as a young goddess who'd just succeeded in fleetly out-distancing a saucy son of Jupiter.

'You're a real player,' she said generously.

'You're a dream,' said Peregrine fervently.

'That's a lie.'

'No–'

'Yes, it is. You said it before, and it was a lie

then. A kind lie, I'm sure, but you know now I'm a bit of a duffer compared with you, and that my game needs to improve one hundred per cent.'

'I wasn't thinking of your game – look, can I have the pleasure of taking you to the cafe for tea and a bun?'

'Thanks, but no, I've a better idea.' Gemma walked from the courts with him. 'I owe you for standing in for Jane, and as you've missed seeing each other today, I'm going to make it up to you by taking you to see her. I've a good excuse for calling, it's to ask how she is. The fact that you'll be with me will only be kind of accidental. I'll introduce you to her parents, of course, especially her dad, and that'll help you get one foot in her door, if that's the right phrase.'

'Well, I appreciate all this,' said Peregrine, 'but–'

'No, don't thank me,' said Gemma, advancing blithely in the direction of the park gates. 'I know you two have been hitting it off, and this is a chance to let her dad see you're fairly civilized. Then he'll allow you to date her.'

'How about your dad,' said Peregrine, 'will he allow me to date you?'

'Now, Charlie,' said Gemma as they came out of the park, 'don't let's get confused – look, let's run for that bus coming up the hill. It's going my way, and will drop us quite near my home and Jane's. Come on, your time's your own, isn't it?'

Peregrine knew he had to get out of this one. He'd land in deep water if he didn't, and he'd bet there'd be no-one standing by with a lifebelt. And it was all happening because he hadn't ever been able to let Gemma have any idea of how he felt.

'So sorry,' he said, 'but I'm tied up for the rest of the day.' It was a lie, of course, but he could turn it into something like the truth by immersing himself in his studies as soon as he arrived home. 'Give my regards to Jane, and tell her I hope her ankle's coming on a treat. Oh, and thanks for the game, Gemma.'

'You'll be a disappointment to Jane, you know,' said Gemma. 'Oh, well, never mind, see you sometime. Bye now.' And away she went, hallowing for him the ground over which she fleetly sped. He still suffered highly imaginative moments.

He watched her board the bus, then began his walk home.

'What?' said Jane. She was seated in an armchair, her bandaged left ankle resting on a footstool.

'Yes, he couldn't make it,' said Gemma, 'he was all tied up. But he sent you his love.'

'His love?' said Jane, looking colourful in a bright sweater and blue jeans. 'You sure?'

'Well, good as,' said Gemma. 'Jane ducky, you should see the kind of tennis he plays. It's super stuff.'

'Blow his tennis,' said Jane, 'did he give you the impression he fancies me?'

'Of course he fancies you,' said Gemma, 'he's made that obvious each time he's seen you.'

'He hasn't fallen over himself,' said Jane.

'That's because he's on the shy side,' said Gemma.

'Not much, shy fellers are history these days,' said Jane. 'Anyway, I'm not sure Charlie doesn't fancy you as much as me. I mean, he does behave sometimes as if he can't make up his mind which of us he wants to date. Still, famous idea of yours, to bring him along so that you could introduce him to my dad. Just a pity he's tied up – hey, suppose it's with a regular girlfriend? Then where do I stand, or you for that matter?'

'Nowhere,' said Gemma, and laughed, then fell into a musing moment. 'He really can play tennis,' she said. 'Well, must get off home now, Jane, I'll be in touch.'

'Where are you going?' whispered the student who shared a small dormitory with Irena Leino. It was well past one in the morning, and she'd been woken up by the rustling sound of Irena slipping from her bed.

'I am going to the bathroom, that is all,'

whispered Irena.

'You aren't going to try for biscuits again? Only I've heard Miss Stanton has set a trap just in case.'

'No, I am not going to look for biscuits, just to the bathroom. Go to sleep.'

'Well, I like that when it was you who woke me.'

'So sorry,' said Irena, and disappeared.

By the time she returned, her fellow student was asleep again.

Chapter Twenty-six

'Hi there, Cathy.'

'Hello, James.'

It was Tuesday afternoon, the weather still cloudy and dull, and James had arrived at the gates of Maiden Hall to meet Cathy and walk her home. It was an established weekday ritual, but their handclasp was warm and immediate, thus disproving any suggestion that the ritual had become a mere routine. Other students, some from the girls' college and others from boys' establishments, watched them go on their way, sauntering hand in hand. One or two sniggers and one or two whispers followed them.

'I think we're getting talked about,' said Cathy.

'After all these months I'd be surprised if we weren't,' said James. 'What are they saying, d'you know?'

'Oh, something silly, I bet,' said Cathy, who, truth to tell, was frequently asked teasing questions about whether or not James was playing the game with her, as a Dulwich boy should, or was she having to fight him off? Her response to all such questions was to say do grow up, Angela. Or Debbie. Or

Jemima. Or whoever else it happened to be. She said nothing to James about such silliness.

'How's your Finnish friend getting on now?' asked James.

'Would you believe, she's brilliant,' said Cathy. 'This afternoon, during our music class, she danced.'

'That's brilliant, dancing?' said James.

'Well, you see, Mrs Tremont, our music teacher who's Italian and a wonderful pianist, played some excerpts from *Swan Lake*, and Irena performed just like a ballerina.'

'I'm not great on ballet,' said James as they strolled along Court Lane, its evergreen trees darkly green with winter's moisture. 'But I know about ballerinas, they wear tights and some kind of funny floating skirt, don't they?'

'Floating skirt?' Cathy pealed with laughter. She startled a blackbird, which expelled itself with a rush of wings from out of a tree. 'You mean a tutu.'

'Sounds like a Zulu maiden's hairdo,' said James.

'Well, it isn't,' said Cathy, 'it's a ballerina's frilly skirt.'

'Did Irena Leino wear one when she performed during your music class?' asked James.

'No, Mrs Tremont doesn't supply any kind of dance costumes, just music instruction,' said Cathy. 'This was a bit special and Irena really was brilliant. Aunt Marie loves ballet. Well, you know she's Russian-born, and Russians invented it. Their ballerinas are the tops.'

'How come that Irena's brilliant when she's Finnish?' asked James.

'Oh, every European country has its own ballet company now,' said Cathy. 'Don't you know that we've got our own Royal Ballet, and that a dancer called Margot Fonteyn is its prima ballerina?'

'I think I'm kind of vague,' said James, 'I think I'm better at Fred Astaire and Ginger Rogers stuff.'

'Stuff?' Cathy laughed again. 'James, you're a heathen.'

'Oh, well,' said James, 'it's accepted that blokes are hairy and birds are civilized, so you make up for my failings.'

'Oh, I'm a bird, am I?' said Cathy, and swung round to face him. There was more laughter on the brink, her lips slightly parted, her teeth a white glimmer. So James, the self-confessed less civilized vessel, naturally gave in to temptation and kissed her. Smack on her lips. And not lightly, either. He'd never kissed her quite like that before. Cathy quivered, but not indignantly. 'Oh, help,' she breathed when it was over. The grey of the wintry afternoon was tinted with faint purple on the far horizon. Red at night, shepherds' delight. 'James, did you kiss me?'

'Well, as a matter of fact, I did,' said James, resuming his stroll with her. 'I truly believe you should be kissed regularly, and that I should be the one to do it. I'm against leaving the privilege to your milkman.'

'Never mind the milkman,' said Cathy, 'how often is regularly?'

'I'll speak to your aunt,' said James. 'She's your present guardian, and she'll work out a reasonable allowance, I'm sure—'

'Allowance?' said Cathy. 'Allowance?'

'If she'll only allow once a month—'

Another peal of laughter put a stop to all that flannel, and they went on still hand in hand, but skipping along now in the intoxication of being young.

James saw her to her door, delivered her into the affectionate keeping of her aunt, and then went home, where his mother awaited him.

'Oh, there you are, James dear.'

'Yes, here I am, Mama. Glad to see you looking like next year's pin-up.'

'Thank you, darling.' Polly was wearing a Tricel dress based on a fashion known as the 'sack', a design Paris had introduced a couple of years ago. It hadn't proved very popular. One of Sammy's seamstresses had said a woman might as well put on a tarted-up flour sack. Nevertheless, Polly looked elegant, as always. Glancing up from her armchair, where she was clasping a book, she asked, 'To what do I owe this welcome compliment?'

'Total admiration, Mama, total,' said James. 'What's the book you're reading?'

'It's all about greenhouse cultivation,' said Polly, 'I borrowed it from the library.'

'Greenhouse what?' said James.

'Yes, quite so, darling, all about growing tomatoes, melons, peppers and lots of other goodies under glass,' said Polly. 'I shall ask your father to have a greenhouse installed and throw myself into producing exotic eatables for the family.'

'Mama, you're magic,' said James. 'Is Gemma home?'

'Yes, up in her room doing her homework,' said Polly.

'Any tea going?' asked James.

'Whizz off to the kitchen, dear boy, and Flossie will pour you a cup and also give you a slice of fruit cake.'

James took his tea and cake upstairs, where he had a chat with Gemma about the Finnish marvel, described by Cathy as a brilliant balley-mania.

'Balleymania? Grief,' said Gemma, 'is that supposed to be screamingly funny?'

'No, not much,' said James, 'just the best I can do.'

'I officially demote you to Wet Cabbage

Number One,' said Gemma.

'Ta, very decent of you,' said James.

Gemma, nibbling away at her biro in an attempt to find an inspired answer to a geography homework question, said, 'Where's Mount Everest exactly, and how high is it?'

'It's on the Nepal and Tibet border,' said James, 'and about thirty miles high.'

'Oh, you're useful sometimes,' said Gemma. 'Here, wait a minute, thirty miles? You sure?'

'About twenty-nine thousand feet and a bit, actually,' said James. 'It just feels like thirty miles to mountaineers. Listen, Cathy was really taken with Irena Leino's dancing. Were you?'

'Super,' said Gemma.

Over supper Gemma mentioned Irena Leino's performance to her parents, and how good it was, and James chimed in by saying Cathy thought it brilliant.

'Is that her speciality, then, ballet?' asked Polly.

'She's never said so,' said Gemma.

'If she's really brilliant,' said Polly, 'she could make a name for herself without worrying about a university degree in science or whatever. The appeal of ballet is going up by leaps and bounds, and prima ballerinas can live like royalty, with a palace in Monte Carlo and a butler to look after their fluffy

Pekinese. Perhaps one Saturday evening when your father feels a little slice of culture might be good for all of us, he'll take us to Covent Garden to see *Swan Lake*.'

'I can't say men leaping about in tights excites me too much,' said Boots. 'However, if–?'

'Yes, thanks, old love, we all accept,' said Polly, 'that's if Gemma and James can live without Elvis and his pelvis for a whole Saturday evening.'

'Now, Mama,' said Gemma, 'don't overdo the comic stuff.'

'When I was a girl,' said Polly, 'the prima ballerina of the time was Pavlova, quite a Russian sensation, my little one.'

'Little one?' said Gemma. 'Mama, now that's too much.'

'Pavlova eventually settled in London,' said Polly. 'I wonder if Cathy's Russian aunt knew her or saw her.'

'We're all breathless with curiosity,' said Boots, thinking that Irena Leino was almost certainly the defecting Russian gymnast. Dancing, ballet or otherwise, would be second nature to a female Russian gymnast.

Later that evening Gemma made a phone call to find out if Jane's sprained ankle was on the mend. Her mother answered and informed her that Jane still couldn't put her foot to the ground without feeling pain.

Gemma said she was sorry to hear that, but perhaps there'd be a welcome improvement by the weekend. We'll see, said Mrs Symington, and Gemma said she'd phone again on Friday.

Tuesday, mid-morning.

'I don't know where it's got to,' grumbled the cook in an undertone.

'Where what's got to?' asked her kitchen assistant.

'I thought it was missing yesterday, and there's not a sign of it today.'

'Not a sign of what?'

'If I don't find it by the time me day's finished, I'll have to report it to Miss Stanton, I suppose.'

'Report what?'

'It couldn't have been put in the dustbin accidental, I wonder?'

And so on like that for another minute or so.

Without being seen, a tall slim student, wearing a coat over her uniform, slipped out through the tradesmen's gate at the rear of the college at breaktime, and walked with quick purposeful strides in the direction of Court Lane.

Charles Rogers, Aunt Marie's efficient butler, was serving coffee to her when the gate bell buzzed.

'A caller?' He knew his mistress was expecting no-one, either tradesman or otherwise. It could be a parcel delivery, perhaps, or something of the kind. 'I'll see to it, madam,' he said, and went off to check from the hall window. Recognizing the caller at the gate, he pressed the button that electrically controlled it. Its lock clicked in release, and the caller was able to open the gate and walk up to the front door of the mansion-like residence.

It was opened by Rogers.

'Ah, good morning,' said Irena Leino, 'could I please to see madam?'

'You are the friend to Miss Catherine?' said the butler.

'Yes, and it is about Catherine I have to see her aunt.'

'Miss Catherine could not leave the college herself?' The butler was always careful about admitting callers into the presence of madam.

'No, that is why I wish to see madam myself, thank you.'

'Very well. Please take a seat for a moment while I let her know you're here.'

Irena seated herself on a hall chair and Rogers glided away to apprise his mistress of the caller and to find out if she could be admitted. He returned with the information that madam would be pleased to see Miss Leino, and he escorted her to the sitting room, where Aunt Marie, on her feet, welcomed the young lady from Finland.

'A charming surprise, Irena.'

'Yes, I am happy to see you, Aunt Marie.'

'Ah, you remembered I like to be called that by Cathy's friends?'

'But yes.'

Aunt Marie dismissed her butler with a little nod and a smile, and he silently disappeared.

'Take your coat off, my dear, and let's sit down,' said Aunt Marie. 'Then please let me know what it is you have to tell me about Cathy. Nothing unpleasant, I hope.'

Irena removed her coat and they sat down.

Rogers burst in only a minute later. He had been no further away than outside the door. Like his mistress, he trusted no-one who came calling without an invitation from madam. His clue to interrupt had come when he heard her call his name.

'Charles!' A cry, followed at once by a choking gasp.

And there she was, forced back in her armchair, Irena Leino's left hand violently clamped over her mouth, right knee in her stomach. In the right hand of the young lady from Finland the blade of a knife flashed. Its point would have been driven into Aunt Marie's heart if Rogers had not dealt Irena's hand a fierce, crippling blow.

The knife fell, Irena whirled about, spat a venomous word or two at the butler, and then sped for the door. He rushed after her and brought her down in the hall with a rugby tackle. He was a powerful man and exceptionally fit. While he held the scratching and spitting Irena, Aunt Marie telephoned the police and then the college.

An hour and a half later, a detective inspector and a detective sergeant of the local police had interrogated Irena Leino without getting a single word out of her. They were now in the grounds of the house, taking a break at the request of a gentleman from Whitehall, who had arrived ten minutes ago after an urgent phone call made by Miss Stanton. In Aunt Marie's sitting room, Irena Leino, handcuffed, was being addressed by the gentleman, with Miss Stanton and Aunt Marie standing by. Outside the door stood the butler, on guard.

Irena Leino suddenly broke her simmering silence and shed her catlike bristles to quietly and calmly explain herself.

She was, she said, the daughter of Alexis Czernin, the second son of Pyotyr Czernin, once the steward of a Prince Mikhail Yakanov. Pyotyr's first son had been cruelly done to death by being flogged with a knout, a punishment ordered by the prince for a minor infringement. Pyotyr had laid a curse on the prince and his family. It resulted in the death of the prince's son and wife, and of the prince himself. All these deaths were at the hands of Pyotyr Czernin, my grandfather, said Irena Leino, and added that her real name was Natasha Czernin. The prince's daughter Tanya, however, escaped vengeance by being sent to England, where she met and married an Englishman named David Tunnicliffe, later Sir David, although this was not discovered until 1932.

Pyotyr Czernin, who became a Bolshevik commissar and served both Lenin and Stalin well, died in 1939 at the age of 75, having spent much time trying to trace and destroy the last member of the prince's family, namely the daughter Tanya. He failed, although he sent agents to England looking for her. His younger son Alexis, also a loyal Party member, took over the responsibility of carrying out the last act of the curse, and did what he could when he could in an attempt to find the daughter and eliminate her. The war against Hitler interrupted his endeavours, but total vengeance for the brutal killing of his brother was never given up, merely postponed. He himself died in 1946 from the pernicious effects of wounds suffered during the battle of Stalingrad. He had not married until 1934, and it was in 1939 that his daughter Natasha was born.

'Myself,' said the calm young woman.

'Continue, please,' said the man from Whitehall.

Her father had spoken often of the brutal killing of his brother and of her grandfather's oath of complete vengeance. At his death her father left her a letter enjoining her never to forget her family responsibility. She was an only child and therefore the last direct descendant of her grandfather. So she began to plan how to carry out the mission of death. She meanwhile trained as a gymnast and eventually gained a place in the national team, by which time a member of the local soviet, in whom she had confided, had instituted fresh enquiries into the whereabouts of the prince's daughter Tanya, long the wife of one David Tunnicliffe. But Tanya had obviously known the Czernin family was hunting for her, and she had moved several times since the death of her husband. Soviet agents lost track of her until a clue pointed them in the direction of Dulwich, south-east London.

And so, said Natasha Czernin, alias Irena Leino, she decided on action. With the help of her Soviet friends she effected what was thought to be the act of a defector when the Russian gymnastic team arrived in London from Helsinki. She asked for asylum, and this was granted. The Soviet Embassy, aware of the real reasons for her so-called defection, cooperated, acting with hostility at first towards the British authorities, and subsequently declaring they had no further interest in her. They were ready, however, to take her into protective custody once she had accomplished her mission, which could be accounted a deserved final strike at a family of once powerful Czarist overlords. Natasha asked the British authorities if she could be found residence in Dulwich, because she had heard it was very nice there and not far from London and its famous theatreland. She was given a place as a boarder at a college for young ladies. Meanwhile, people in Moscow were doing what they could to help her find the prince's daughter, having discovered she had become Lady Tanya Tunnicliffe and then changed her name on the death of her husband to Mrs Marie Edwards, obviously in the hope of concealing her identity. Apart from the fact that Soviet agents knew she was living somewhere in Dulwich, her actual address was a mystery until a week or so ago.

'And that information was confirmed for me when Catherine Davidson, her niece, took me to visit her.' The granddaughter of Pyotyr Czernin turned her eyes on the genteel lady known to young people as Aunt Marie. 'Yes, you, madam.'

'Child,' said Aunt Marie quite gently, 'I am so sorry for you.'

Natasha Czernin shrugged.

'Thank God you failed in your misguided act,' said Miss Stanton. 'I know now why the cook reported a kitchen knife was missing.'

'I would not be here now, but on my way to the Soviet Embassy, if I had succeeded in my mission,' said Natasha.

'Heavens, don't you realize it was a mission of murder?' said Miss Stanton, shaking her head.

'You may call it that,' said Natasha, and the man from Whitehall regarded her with an expression of deep regret. 'What will happen to me?' she asked without, apparently, any great emotion. Gemma Adams had always thought her very cool, very composed. There had been only one moment of departure from that front, the moment when the butler frustrated her in her attempt to kill the last surviving member of Prince Mikhail Yakanov's family. 'Yes, what will happen to me?'

'I must tell you you will almost certainly be detained in a place of correction for every remaining year of Lady Tunnicliffe's life,' said the man from Whitehall.

'I thought so,' said Natasha. 'Well, I did not come to England to suffer that, or to live with failure.' Her lips parted in what seemed to be a mocking smile, and her white teeth gleamed before snapping shut. There was the tiniest of crunching sounds as her teeth bit on a cyanide capsule. The poison rushed down her throat, her face seemed to drain of blood and turn pallid in a split second. A brief spasm of movement brought her cuffed hands up to her heart, and then she crumpled and fell.

Half an hour before the end of classes Cathy was asked to go and see Miss Stanton in the principal's study. Miss Stanton had been absent for most of the day. She greeted Cathy with a kind smile.

'Sit down, Catherine, I have something to tell you about the lady you know as your Aunt Marie.'

'Ma'am?'

'Yes, sit down.'

With the girl seated, Miss Stanton proceeded to tell her everything that had affected her aunt's life since the time when she was sent to England to escape the consequences of the barbaric punishment inflicted on a servant boy, a punishment ordered by Aunt Marie's father, an autocratic Czarist landowner. It came to mean that Aunt Marie never felt entirely free of those consequences, that she and her husband had had to move several times and that, on his death, she had changed her name from Lady Tanya Tunnicliffe to Mrs Marie Edwards.

Cathy, spellbound and shocked, shook herself and said she now understood the real reason why her aunt discouraged visitors and kept her house securely fenced in and locked against intruders. It was not because she was reclusive by nature, after all.

Miss Stanton said something had just happened that had almost certainly secured a more settled existence for her aunt. She paused for a moment, then recounted the events of the morning in as calm and lucid a way as possible, though she could not avoid a dramatic note as she touched on the moment when the butler struck the knife from Natasha's hand and the moment when that misguided young lady swallowed poison and died. That action, however, at least freed Cathy's aunt from all further worries in respect of the strange and deadly Russian curse originating with Natasha's grandfather.

'Oh, how is she, how is my aunt?' asked Cathy, quite overwhelmed and not a little agitated.

'Amazingly well, wonderfully calm,' said Miss Stanton. 'Everything is being quietly settled, and there will be no publicity. You and your aunt will not have to run that gauntlet.' A bell rang in a corridor, the sound signalling the end of classes for the day. 'There, dear girl, you may go home to your aunt now without dreading to find a nervous wreck. She'll be delighted to see you and to let you know the front gate will no longer be kept locked against your friends.'

'Thank you, ma'am, thank you so much

for all you have meant to my aunt today,' said Cathy. 'And to me. But do you know,' she added impulsively, 'I can't help feeling sorry for Irena – I mean Natasha.'

'I think you'll find you share that feeling with your aunt,' said Miss Stanton. 'And I'm not judging Natasha Czernin too harshly myself.'

Cathy experienced a completely happy moment when she found James had arrived at the school gates and was waiting for her.

'Oh, lovely,' she said, slightly breathless.

'You can't mean me,' said James, 'I'm one of the hairy mob.'

'I mean your being here, I've got such a lot to talk about, I just need to tell someone, and I'm glad it's you. Come on, let's walk.'

They detached themselves from the usual crowd at the gates and, as ever, began their walk hand in hand. From that point onwards James received from his beguiling girlfriend a dramatic telling of all the events recounted by Miss Stanton. He was as shocked by her account as she had been by Miss Stanton's.

'Heavens,' he breathed at the end, when they were near her home, 'that's a bit much, Cathy, an attempted assassination and a successful suicide in your aunt's sitting room within a couple of hours of each other. Sensational – or is it April the first?'

'Not, it's not April the first, James, not yet, and coming from Miss Stanton I'm sure every word is true.'

'Unbelievable,' said James. 'Your head must be spinning. Well, I know mine's rolling a bit.'

When they reached the gates of the house, she said, 'Will you come in and say hello to Aunt Marie and see what she has to say herself?'

'I don't think so, Cathy,' said James. 'I think this is an occasion for just the two of you, and to work out if she's still going to be Aunt Marie to you and your friends. I'll be tickled to meet her some other time and find out how to survive Russian voodoo. A feller never knows when that kind of wrinkle might be useful to life and limb. Give her my best wishes, Cathy, see you tomorrow.'

He helped himself to a kiss, freely given, and departed. Cathy entered the drive. The gates weren't locked, and at the front door, the butler was there to receive her.

'Welcome home, Miss Cathy,' he said. 'Ah, you know?'

'Yes, everything, from Miss Stanton. How is my aunt?'

'Waiting to welcome you, Miss Cathy.'

Cathy ran to the sitting room.

James did not burst in on Gemma and Polly when he arrived home. He waited until the family were all gathered at the evening meal before delivering the startling news concerning Cathy's aunt. It took minds off much of what was on their plates, and caused interjections.

'What? What was that?' From Polly.

'I don't believe you, you're making it up.' From Gemma.

'I want to believe you, but I'm not sure I should.' From Boots.

'It's a fact, it has to be if it came from Miss Stanton,' said James. 'The girl actually drew a knife on Cathy's aunt, a knife she'd stolen from the college kitchen, and would have killed her with it if the butler hadn't been lying in wait. And that's not all.'

He carried on manfully, despite other interjections, and such was the sureness of his telling that eventually all scepticism fell away and his listeners ended up stunned but convinced.

'Holy ghosts,' said Boots.

'All these years, with the avengers never letting go,' said Polly.

'Crackpots,' said Gemma. 'Not that it wasn't a rotten business in the first place. Anyway, loud cheers for Cathy's Aunt Marie – oh, crikey, Lady Tunnicliffe, I mean.'

Chapter Twenty-seven

The following day, when James once more walked Cathy home, he received from her the assurance that her aunt had coped marvellously with the frightful events, and was making plans to come out of her shell and to enjoy a shopping expedition in Regent Street as soon as certain fussy matters had been settled with her solicitor. Would James like to come in and say hello to her this time? James said yes, and went into the house with Cathy to be greeted very affably by Charles the butler, and finding the lady of the hour as charming as ever in the welcome she gave him. A very happy conversation followed, during which James thought the reservations that had sometimes been evident behind the charm were now gone. And yes, she still wished to be known as Aunt Marie on all informal occasions, especially those that took in Cathy and her friends.

James suggested she and Cathy might like to come to tea one Sunday. Aunt Marie said she'd be delighted, so James said he'd talk to his mother and let Cathy know which Sunday would be suitable.

Cathy, seeing James out, said he was a

lovely bloke to think of such an invitation.

'That word lovely is beginning to shake me,' said James. 'I'm going to start feeling like a bunch of lilies if it goes on.'

'Not you,' said Cathy, 'not while your favourite sport is rugby.'

When asked by James if she'd like to entertain Cathy and her aunt to Sunday tea, Polly said that in the past she'd have fought tigers before allowing any Russian female to put one foot over her doorstep, but under present circumstances she really couldn't wait to meet the extraordinary lady who had escaped the fiends of darkest Africa.

'Not Africa, Mama,' said Gemma.

'Well, you know what I mean, dear child,' said Polly. 'As James said, it was all some kind of voodoo. Yes, tell Cathy Sunday week, James. Five o'clock for tea at five thirty. Informal dress, of course, unless your father decides to wear spats.'

'Spats, Mama, spats?' Gemma fell about.

'Mother dear,' said James, 'I think we're long past spats.'

'And you ought to know that Daddy would never have been seen dead in them,' said Gemma.

'Very well, darlings,' said Polly sweetly, 'informal dress quite definitely, then.'

James arranged the date with Cathy and her

aunt, and emphasized that formal dress wasn't necessary. It would be quite OK for Cathy and her aunt to wear something comfy and casual.

'Something comfy and casual?' said Aunt Marie. 'What can your young man mean, Cathy?'

'Oh, just a decent frock,' said James, 'and no coronet.'

It was Aunt Marie's turn to fall about.

Peregrine Peters, who had been trying to work out what to do about his precarious mental state, received another phone call from Gemma on Saturday evening. She wanted him to know that Jane was still out of action because of her wonky ankle. It was improving, but not enough to risk any tennis. So would Charlie be a sport and stand in again for her?

'I'd welcome another game, Gemma. By the way, I'm–'

'Once I start knocking a tennis ball about at the end of winter, I don't like to miss a Sunday unless the weather's simply too foul,' said Gemma, 'so I've got to tell you you're being a hero, especially as it means you still won't be seeing Jane. Never mind, I'll call in on her again, and you can come with me. See you at the courts about five to three, then?'

'Not half,' said Peregrine, 'and I'll work

out the rest of the afternoon for myself.'

'Pardon?'

'Bring your best form, Gemma.'

'Yes, I'll need to, you're hot stuff on a tennis court, Charlie.'

'Perry.'

'Perry?'

'Yes, not Charlie.'

'But Jane and I both like you as Charlie.'

'In this context, Charlie's a lemon.'

'Crikey, you're not turning funny, are you?' said Gemma.

'See you tomorrow,' said Peregrine, suddenly running out of steam. Gemma murmured a goodbye and hung up. As the phone went dead he wondered how he'd managed to talk sensibly with young and lustrous divinity for all of a minute. Somewhere in his head he must be improving.

The morrow, the weather bright, but tingling from the effects of overnight frost. 'Where are you off to with your tennis gear again?' asked Penelope.

'The park,' said Peregrine, dodging doorwards.

'Who with?'

'Gemma.'

'Is she new?'

'New-born, you mean? No, seventeen, I'd say.'

'Being comical, are we?'

'No, she's the girl I met at the store one Saturday, and I can't stay to answer any more questions or I'll be late.'

'I think you're–' The rest of what Penelope was going to say died a death, for the front door opened and closed quickly, and what had been visible before was now no longer in the frame. It was on its way to the park.

He was there several minutes early, while Gemma didn't arrive until right on the stroke of three. What a picture, though. Wrapped around in a blue coat, the crisp, tingling air of the late March day had given her colour and sparkle, and that, together with her red hair ribbon, put him in mind of Christmas.

'Hi there,' she said, smiling.

'Bit of a cold day,' said Peregrine.

'Yes, but don't let's talk about the weather, let's get started, shall we?' said Gemma, much unlike her perceptive self in that she still thought his preference was for Jane. 'The court's free – oh, and keep me on my toes but don't overdo it or I'll tell Jane you're a show-off.'

'Jane?' Peregrine was stripping off for the fray. 'Who's she?'

'Now, Charlie,' said Gemma, taking her coat off, 'you're not being funny again, are you?'

'Who's laughing?' said Peregrine, and took

up position on the baseline.

Well, thought Gemma, as they began a knockup, I must say he hasn't suffered any twitches lately. It must have been a temporary complaint, an allergy or something. But what's he mean by asking who's Jane?

They began a competitive game. It was brilliant, the sharp afternoon sun giving them light and energy, and Peregrine keeping Gemma very much on her toes while at the same time helping her to improve. However, there was an occasion when his killing instincts got the better of his chivalry and he executed an unreturnable smash. She yelled a warning to the effect that if he did it again he'd be found dead on his doorstep.

'With flowers?' called Peregrine.

'Flowers?'

'Well, a wreath, then.'

Gemma giggled.

'Charlie, I think you're trying to make a name for yourself,' she called. 'Come on, play up, it's your serve.'

On went the game. A girl, passing by, stopped on the path to observe the play, and to take note, it seemed, of Peregrine's manly frame. When he came to the wire to pick up a ball, she spoke to him.

'Is that your sister on the other side of the net?'

'No, I've left my sister at home,' said Peregrine, 'I think she's washing her smalls.'

'Oh, I do mine on Sunday evenings, and my mum irons them on Mondays. Listen, would you like my phone number?'

'Here, who let you out of your cage?' grinned Peregrine.

'Hi, Charlie!' Gemma was yelling. 'Are you keeping an appointment or something? I mean, shall I go home?'

'Coming,' called Charlie – no, Peregrine. He returned to the baseline and served. The lingering girl lingered a few minutes more and then went away. The game finished, Gemma said how much she'd enjoyed it, apart from one or two moments when things went a bit sideways, and would he now like to come with her to see Jane and perhaps meet her dad?

'Well, I don't think I'll have much in common with her dad,' said Peregrine, 'unless he's an expert engineer.' He coughed, trying not to let his mental faculties fall into Gemma's big dewy translucent eyes and drown. 'Um, if it's OK with you, Gemma, I'll see you home and then go home myself to see what my mother's putting on for Sunday tea.'

'Pardon?' said Gemma, blinking.

'She sometimes treats us to a really worthwhile Sunday tea.'

'Well, I'm thrilled, naturally,' said Gemma, as they left the courts, 'but you want to see Jane, don't you?'

'I don't mind waiting till Christmas, say,' said Peregrine, his resolve admirably firm, 'but in the meantime – well, you take a bus home, don't you? The least I can do is ride with you and see you to your door, and I won't necessarily ask to meet your dad. Unless you insist.'

Gemma stopped. She took a good look at him. Peregrine's head wavered a bit, then regained balance. He was fighting for a place in Gemma's life, and had to hang on to intent and resolution.

'Charlie, are you serious?'

'Yes, hope you don't mind.'

Gemma smiled.

'Well, you're an odd one,' she said, 'I was sure you'd taken a shine to Jane.'

'She's a very nice girl,' said Peregrine, 'but not quite a radiant divinity.'

'A what?'

'Did I say something?'

'It's all right, I'm used to your pickled moments.' Gemma laughed, and they moved on. Lawns opened up on either side of them, the trimmed grass lushly green, a sign of coming spring. 'OK, Charlie, if you'd like to be one of my regular friends, I'm flattered. But I'm not yet ready to be any bloke's one and only. There's too much else going on in my life right now, and I don't believe in early commitments, do you?'

'I just believe in keeping upright.'

'What does that mean?'

'It means that just lately I've felt that even a feather could knock me down,' said Peregrine, 'and I think it has once or twice.'

'Oh, when you were having your twitchy moments?' said Gemma, and laughed again. For some reason she was feeling unusually happy. 'But you don't look twitchy now, and no-one could say you look tottery, either. You look as if all your muscles are in fine form. Did you know that girl who spoke to you?'

'No, never seen her before,' said Peregrine, 'but she wanted me to know she washes her smalls on Sunday evenings and that her mother irons them on Mondays.'

There was one more laugh from Gemma. Almost a shriek, in fact. Park promenaders cast glances. She laughed some more.

'Charlie, if you think I believe that—'

'You're right, I could hardly believe it myself,' said Peregrine, 'but it happened.'

'I'm still suspicious,' said Gemma. 'But never mind, we're good and regular friends now, and once Jane is on her feet, we'll play some hectic mixed doubles. I'll get my father to make the fourth. He's still pretty useful with a racket himself. Now I'm going to see Jane for a few minutes. I promised I would. Then I'm not going home, I'm going to my grandma's. My parents are there for tea. I'll have a shower and there'll be a change of clothes waiting for me. Oh, and just to show you're thinking of me and our friendship, you can phone me in the week and we'll have a chat.'

'What's your phone number?' asked Peregrine, feeling he had cleared a hurdle without breaking a leg or losing his head.

Gemma quoted, Peregrine noted. They were out of the park then, Gemma looking for a bus. Peregrine walked her to the stop.

'Happy with arrangements, Charlie?' smiled Gemma.

'Chuffed,' said Peregrine, 'and I hope it won't bore you to be reminded I'm Perry, not Charlie.'

'Oh, yes, I'll try to remember,' said Gemma. Along came a number 68, and she boarded.

''Ello, miss, how's yer young self?' grinned the conductor, who knew her.

'I'm fine, how's your old self?' said Gemma, and turned to wave at Peregrine as the bus set off up the hill.

He watched her depart once more from his life. But he'd won. He'd stiffened his sinews, put his back to the wall, summoned up his courage and made his advance. And the young goddess from the Garden of Eden was now a pal.

A pal? Who wants a young goddess as a mere pal?

He'd have to improve on that, he'd have to

make another advance sometime.

Home he went. His mother welcomed him.

'Well, there you are, Perry love, you're back from tennis, I see, and looking ever so pleased with yourself.'

'Yes, I tilted at a windmill this afternoon, Ma, and didn't get knocked off my horse.'

'You and your funny sayings, I'll never get used to them,' said Mrs Peters fondly. 'Oh, I'm doing poached eggs on toast for tea, and then my own custard tarts.'

'Whacko,' said Peregrine.

Over a typically filling Sunday tea at the home of Grandma and Grandpa Finch, in company with her parents and brother, Gemma came up with the news that she had a new friend.

'Oh?' said Polly.

Boots asked if new meant the friend had only just seen the light of day, and Chinese Lady told him, of course, that if he spent any more years of his life being a comic he'd end up joining Harry Lauder and his like, wherever they were. James said probably up in the holy hall of jokers. Chinese Lady sighed for her son and grandson alike.

'I'm sorry to say so, Daddy,' said Gemma, 'but I'm afraid you're going off a bit, and James isn't a lot better. Do excuse them, Grandma. Mama and I do try to do our best with them, but I think it's a losing battle. Anyway, this new friend of mine, he's the young man who helps Uncle Freddy in the Walworth store on Saturdays, and is a super tennis player.'

Polly asked was this official and was it the same young man who was slightly barmy?

'Barmy?' said Chinese Lady in slight shock. 'I hope I didn't hear you right, Polly.'

At which Gemma said not to worry, Grandma, Charlie had turned out to be quite sane.

James took a healthy bite at a slice of his grandma's home-made Victoria sponge lavishly filled with blackberry jam, thereby showing he wasn't fazed about his sister's friendly acquisition of Uncle Freddy's hired Saturday help.

Gemma said Jane had taken a fancy to him, but she'd had to tell her only a little while ago that she herself was Charlie's fancy, did Jane mind? And Jane said she knew then what a mistake it had been to sprain her ankle.

'I felt a bit mean,' said Gemma, 'but I couldn't point Charlie at Jane if he didn't have any meaningful feelings for her. Of course, I did tell him that ours was only going to be an easygoing friendship, that I'm not committing myself to any serious relationship at this stage of my life. But of course, Grandma, if someone utterly wonderful came calling, I'd probably think about changing my mind.'

Grandma blinked, and Polly spoke up.

'Can we take it, then, Gemma, that your new friend Charlie is definitely not in the utterly wonderful class?' she said. 'That we aren't expecting to wake up one morning and find you've eloped?'

'Well, of course not, Mama,' said Gemma, and if the subject had thrown Chinese Lady into a little confusion, she was at least saved from having recourse to her smelling salts by everyone's tactful decision to still keep her ignorant of the fact that Polly and Boots had been present on the occasion when barman Joe was nearly done to death in the Camberwell pub, and that Boots had attempted to catch the assailant. The whole incident would have appalled her. She was only aware that her wireless had reported the assault without mentioning names. It also informed her and Sir Edwin every so often that the police were still hunting the hooligan. If she had known the full story in the beginning, she'd have tottered in immediate search of her smelling salts and then instructed Sir Edwin to ring up Scotland Yard and the Flying Squad, while she herself delivered a severe lecture into the ear of her only oldest son not only for being in a public house that entertained hooligans, but also for reckless charging about at his age.

Boots had the last word on the subject of Gemma's new friend.

'I'm not sure he's a Charlie,' he said.

Nobody commented. Everybody accepted Chinese Lady's invitation to refill their tea-cups.

Tuesday, with April knocking at the door.

Dodgy Dan had had a bad fright and a stroke of luck all on the same day. Leaving a Hackney dosshouse on Sunday morning, he'd bumped into a fellow unfortunate who informed him that someone had been asking after him. The description told him that Curly Harris had crossed the water to look for him in the East End. That lousy young lump of garbage, being self-employed, had all the time in the world to go looking. He had a mean streak, as well as a nasty temper.

So off in a hurry went Dodgy Dan to lose himself in the crowds that always swarmed into Petticoat Lane's market on Sundays. While there he thought some honest endeavour might earn him a bob or two, or even a quid or two, to add to the savings that were going to take him to Blackpool and far away from Curly Harris. Honest endeavour meant hard-working concentration on what might come a bloke's way, such as an open handbag asking to be dipped or something on the edge of a stall asking to be nicked.

Of all things, his hard-working eyes spotted a wallet on the ground just beside the feet of a customer buying something at a stall. Talk about honest endeavour paying off, talk about a case of finders keepers. Life was suddenly on his side, and about time. Corblimey, in the wallet were four pound notes, a ten-bob note and a driving licence, along with some postage stamps and a letter. He put the stamps and letter back in the wallet, returned to the spot where he'd found it, and, amid the various bodies around the stall, he let it drop to the ground. That, he reckoned, was a bit of a good turn. Well, if its owner searched for it in the right place, he'd find it and get his stamps and letter back. Dodgy Dan couldn't think fairer.

As for the driving licence, if a bloke knew the right kind of contact, he could always sell it, and Dodgy Dan did know one. Sam Sloppergaas, who'd originated somewhere in Armenia, had a pad in Liverpool Street. He gave Dodgy Dan five bob for the licence.

Backtracking down south to Peckham, the hairy old tramp spent a very happy night in a shelter for the homeless at a cost of one and six, and on Monday treated himself to a shave, a haircut, a noteworthy lunch of superior fish and chips, and a high-class supper of eggs, bacon, sausages and baked beans, with two cups of tea and bread and butter on the side.

All that set him up very nicely for Tuesday's gambit. He made his way across the water again, went to the LNWR station and picked up the old case containing his belongings at the left luggage office. Then he bought a ticket to Blackpool. A single.

Curly Harris, meanwhile, having got wind of Dodgy Dan's present whereabouts, was combing Hackney and Whitechapel. He was still fixed in his intention to do the bugger a real bit of no good for indirectly depriving him of a cushy nest with Elvira Figgins. Mind, he was on another cushy number at the house in Streatham owned by an old lady, except that the silly old cow was always trying to talk to him about her sailor husband who'd never come back from a voyage to South America. And once she had him by the earhole, she didn't know how to let go.

One thing for certain was that his altered appearance was helping to keep him safely out of the arms of the bleedin' law. He reckoned he could stick around in London until he'd squared accounts with Dodgy Dan before transferring himself to Brighton or Bournemouth. There were easy pickings in both those places, as long as he didn't upset the local mafia.

He was asking around in Hackney that afternoon, at a time when Dodgy Dan was on the way to Blackpool, having paid for his train seat.

Other passengers kept their distance.

Mrs Cassie Brown informed Mr Freddy Brown that evening that she'd thought about his suggestion to move, and had now decided not to, but to stay in Walworth. Walworth was where they'd both been born, where they'd spent their happiest days, and where Freddy was going to be the executive manager of Sammy's new project, a proper department store. They couldn't go and live in the country, far away from it.

'Well, Purley, say, isn't in the country,' said Freddy.

'Freddy, of course it is,' said Cassie, 'I remember Boots's mother once saying so. In fact, she said it was as good as in foreign parts.'

Freddy didn't argue. If his Cassie wanted to stay where she'd been born, then why not? Come to that, her old dad, the Gaffer, wasn't keen on being uprooted.

'Fair enough, Cassie,' he said, 'here we've been born, and here we'll stay. We'll just have the house redecorated. What say?'

'Lovely,' said Cassie.

Chapter Twenty-eight

'Hello?'

'Yes?' said Boots. It was Wednesday evening and he had answered the phone, leaving Polly, James and Gemma to guard the Monopoly board. They were all involved in the game while waiting for a Jimmy Edwards comedy show to light up the television.

'Good evening, is that Mr Adams?'

'It is.'

'Hello, Mr Adams, I'm Perry Peters, the Saturday assistant at your firm's Walworth store.'

'What can I do for you, Perry?'

'Could you ask Gemma if I could have a word with her?'

'That won't strain my muscles – hold on a moment.' Boots took himself into the living room. 'Gemma, your new friend's on the phone and would like to talk to you.'

'Oh, Charlie, you mean?' Gemma surprised herself by how quickly she stood up.

'I think he's Perry, not Charlie,' smiled Boots.

'Yes, righty-oh, Daddy,' said Gemma blithely, and went into the hall and picked up the phone. 'Hello?'

'Hello, Gemma, I couldn't resist your invitation to phone you,' said Peregrine.

Gemma actually fluttered a bit. Well, his voice carried warm little vibrations into her ear. A phone line did have an effect on some voices. It kind of muffled or even strangled some, and you had to ask the caller to speak up. It added music to others, like her dad's baritone, and it was doing something to Charlie's younger baritone as he made known his wish to have a chat with her. She found herself drawing mental pictures of his healthy physique. Very stirring.

'What?' she said.

'Sorry, I thought you were with me,' said Peregrine, 'you aren't going away before our chat has hardly started, are you, Gemma?'

The vibrations recurred. Gemma went swoony.

'Pardon?' she said faintly.

'Gemma?'

'What day is it?'

'Wednesday.'

'Wednesday?'

'Yes, is there a problem with that?'

'No. Would you talk to me, please?'

'About tennis on Sunday?'

'Yes. You will be there, Charlie, won't you?'

'You bet I will. What about Jane?'

'Jane?'

'Yes, is her ankle better?'

'Oh, that Jane.'

'Are you OK, Gemma? You sound a little short of breath.'

'I'm fine. Look, about Jane.'

'Yes, what about her?'

'Charlie, two's company and three's a crowd, don't you know that?'

'Oh, right, Gemma, just you and me on Sunday, then, as before?'

'Oh, yes!' said Gemma.

It had happened. The radiant young divinity of the Elysian Fields and the modern equivalent of Achilles, disguised as a store assistant, were gone on each other.

In his office at twelve twenty the next morning, Boots was looking forward to a light lunch and a coffee in the canteen. Something took his mind back to yesterday evening and to Gemma returning to the fold after a fairly prolonged phone conversation with the young man she called Charlie. There was a distinctly dizzy look in her eyes, and on the resumption of the game of Monopoly, all her usual verve went haywire. James asked what was up with her. What? she said. You're not concentrating, he said. What? she said. Darling, said Polly, don't keep saying what. What? she said. And James said the phone call had done something to her.

Boots smiled at his recollections. He took a phone call himself then. The switchboard girl was on the line.

'Yes?'

'Mr Adams, a Mr Palmer wants to speak to you.'

'Palmer?'

'Yes, Mr Adams.'

'The name rings a bell somewhere, I'm sure– OK, Jill, put him through.' The connection was made. 'Hello?'

'Oh, good morning, Mr Adams, George Palmer here. Sorry to disturb you, but I thought you might like to know that our one-time barman, Joe Reynolds, is here in the saloon bar. He's almost fully recovered and is taking the opportunity to say goodbye to all his regulars. That very nasty incident prevented him doing so before, as you personally will clearly remember. I thought I'd let you know in case you'd like to pop over and see him.'

'Well, I'm obliged,' said Boots, having recalled that George Palmer was one of the two brothers who owned the pub, a free house. 'Yes, I will pop over and see my old friend.'

'Any drinks for regulars, Mr Adams, are on the house.'

'Mine's an old ale.'

The beer would come straight from the barrel.

Ten minutes later Boots, after letting Rosie

and Rachel know where he was going, went across to the pub. In the well-favoured comfort of the saloon bar he found Joe going the rounds, shaking hands with all those patrons who had been his personal customers for many years, and saying good morning to everyone else. As soon as he noted the arrival of Boots he came across.

'Hello there, Mr Adams.'

'Good to see you, Joe,' said Boots, noting his grey-haired old friend had lost a little weight and a little colour, but was still his agreeable self. He shook hands with him. 'Everything right with you now?'

'Fine,' said Joe, 'fine. I'm convalescing at home, with my old lady seeing to my comforts. I felt well enough this morning to come and say hello to all you gents. You sit down, Mr Adams, and let me bring you what you ordered from Mr George, an old ale. That right?'

'Right enough, Joe, but should you be dashing about?' ventured Boots.

'I'm not doing no dashing, Mr Adams,' grinned Joe, 'I'm just doing myself the pleasure of serving some of my old customers. I won't be wearing my feet out, so you just hold on for a couple of ticks.'

Off he went, and by no means a wounded figure. He was quite firm on his feet. Boots sat down at a table to join a couple of customers whom he knew by sight, exchanging some friendly words with them. The saloon bar was still a favourite watering hole for busy businessmen of Camberwell. The new barman was attending to the usual kind of orders for food and drink. Yes, thought Boots, same old ritual, and may it never change in this new world of constant change. James and Gemma are going with the trends, but I rather fancy Polly and I are being left behind without letting it bother us.

Curly Harris was silently laughing himself sick. Not one of this lot recognized him, not even that lippy old sod of a barman or that tidy-looking bloke who'd just arrived, the bloke who'd had the bleedin' nerve to chase after him. After another failure to track down Dodgy Dan, what a lark to come back here and challenge the whole sniffy-nosed outfit to recognize him. It just showed what a first-class haircut, a gent's superior raincoat, a bowler hat, a pair of specs and a bit of spit-in-your-eye could do for a feller who'd had the bad luck to be landed with lousy parents. He could have put himself out of the way in the public bar, but there was nothing to relish in that.

Casually, he took off the bowler, placed it on the table, helped himself to a swig of light ale, and looked around, a slight grin on his face as he challenged recognition.

Boots, receiving his glass of beer from Joe, thanked him.

'On the house, Mr Adams,' said Joe.

'Well, it's that kind of pub and always has been,' smiled Boots. 'It's genuine, is it, old lad, that your chest is fully repaired?'

'It looks a bit like a map of the Thames at Putney,' said Joe, 'but I can wear me flannel vests again once my old lady has warmed them up. Well, best of luck to you, Mr Adams, and me compliments to Mrs Adams. Been a pleasure serving you your wants for more than a few years.'

'The pleasure's been mutual, Joe,' said Boots. 'Regards to your missus and enjoy your retirement.'

'I will,' said Joe, and made his way back to the bar and a stool to take the weight off his feet. Halfway there, he caught a glance from a young man wearing a good-quality rain-coat and horn-rimmed glasses. He didn't know him, but gave him a friendly nod.

Curly Harris silently laughed himself sick again, then ordered another light ale from the new barman.

Boots sat musing while he enjoyed his drink. He'd go back to the offices when he'd finished it, and have lunch in the canteen. He glanced around. Quite a few faces were familiar. George Palmer had probably made several phone calls to old customers. Joe would be missed. The whole world was subject to evolution, to natural progress and development, but he supposed many people, including himself, would like some things to stay as they were.

Absently, he took in the look of trouser legs emerging from a raincoat, together with a pair of grimy, crêpe-soled suede shoes. His glance became fixed.

Then, casually, he came to his feet.

'Chief Inspector Walters?'

'Hope this is an important call, Mr Adams, I was halfway through my lunch when told you wanted to speak to me.'

'Yes, it's important. I'm ringing from the owners' office at the Horse and Groom pub to tell you your man is here, and I don't think he'll be going yet. He's just been served with a new glass of beer.'

Chief Inspector Walters alerted.

'You're talking about Curly Harris?'

'I am. He's obviously had a handsome haircut and treated himself to some spectacles and a good-looking raincoat, but he's wearing the same dirty grey crêpe-soled shoes as on the day he knifed Joe. Come and get him, Chief Inspector, and if you'll permit me to say so, don't hang about, even if he has only just started his new glass of beer.'

'You're sure it's Harris? Only a lot of young men wear crêpe-soled suede shoes these days.'

'I know. But there's a brown stain on one

shoe that settled it for me. Come and get him, Inspector.'

The police arrived in force outside the pub just a few minutes later, but only Chief Inspector Walters, in plain clothes, entered the saloon bar. Seeing Boots, he approached. At this point Boots was occupying an upholstered wall seat, a favourite relaxing spot of his. He shifted to make room, and Walters sat down beside him. Boots ordered a beer for him, and the new barman brought it. Boots then began a quiet conversation with his apparent friend. Amid the general hum of the saloon, he suggested the chief inspector should take a casual look around and observe the young man in raincoat and spectacles, who was seated at a table on which his bowler hat rested.

'He was a hairy hound on the day in question, but he's had a very trim cut since. Note his filthy shoes.'

'Not uncommon among loutish types these days,' murmured Walters. 'You're really sure it's our GBH suspect?'

'I'm sure. By reason of the suede shoes and the brown stain on the left one. He's an ugly piece of work, but daring, and I'd say he's laughing at everyone here for not recognizing him. At Joe particularly, I fancy, and me probably.'

'Noted, Mr Adams,' said Walters. They were pursuing the conversation in whispers, while taking no apparent notice of the suspect. 'You'll identify him for us?'

'I'll identify him by reason of his footwear, and if he has that knife with him, I'll identify that too. So, I'm sure, will other customers who were here then and are here now.'

'Right, shan't be more than a few ticks, Mr Adams,' said the chief inspector. Rising, he wandered out. He returned only seconds later in company with a detective sergeant and a detective constable. All three men were chatting, with Walters apparently leading the way to the table on which his partly consumed beer was waiting for him.

Perhaps Curly Harris sensed something was up, perhaps he had taken suspicious note of Boots's chat with a newcomer, or perhaps he simply smelt the arrival of the plod. In any event, he downed what was left of his ale, put on his bowler hat, came to his feet and walked as casually as he could towards the door, his right hand in his raincoat pocket.

Much to his spitting, foul-mouthed disgust, the three plain-clothes men jumped him. Under the startled eyes of customers, as well as the new barman and Joe himself, he was thrown to the floor and spreadeagled face down. He had no chance to use his knife, or even draw it, and consequently one or two lady customers blanched at his language. Handcuffed, he was hauled to his feet and the knife found on his person, whereupon he was placed under arrest on suspicion of having committed grievous bodily harm on these very premises.

He didn't take kindly to that.

'What're you talking about, you bleedin' wallies?' he exploded. 'You out of your tiny minds? You got the wrong man, can't yer see that?'

'I think we might have the right knife,' said Chief Inspector Walters, and he held it up for everyone to see. Stunned customers eyed it silently. Its sharp, pointed blade glinted, its bone handle shone. To Boots it looked as evil as its livid-eyed owner. 'Does anyone recognize this?' asked the chief inspector.

'I do.' Several men spoke up in unison.

'And so do I,' said Joe calmly and quietly.

'You lippy old sod, I'll settle you for good next time I see yer,' hissed the prisoner, which threat was officially noted. He was turning the Queen's English into indescribable jargon that smoked a bit as the police led him away. The saloon bar was left buzzing, with ex-barman Joe receiving everyone's good wishes in respect of Curly Harris's come-uppance.

'Eh?' said Sammy a little later.

'It's a fact, Sammy, the police nailed him right on the spot where he nearly ended Joe's retirement before the old lad had actually started it,' said Boots. He described

394

events in detail, all of which kept Sammy's ears wide open, and he finished by suggesting the new-look Curly Harris had come back to the pub out of sheer bravado. Certainly, no-one had recognized him, and Boots himself only did so when his attention was caught by the grimy suede shoes. 'Yes, he changed his look, Sammy, but didn't bother about his filthy footwear.'

'Well, good on you for noticing, Boots,' said Sammy, 'hope he gets Dartmoor for life. But might I say it gives me a pain to note that that kind of sloppy footwear is taking over the feet of too many young people. They'll be wearing carpet slippers next. And listen, old mate, watch out when Chinese Lady finds out from the local paper that when the evil geezer did a runner you went after him. She'll read you her own kind of riot act, and it'll be a mile long. Anyway, what now, Boots?'

'Well, first I want to ring Polly,' said Boots, 'then down to the canteen for a slice of the chef's veal and ham pie with a salad, if there's any left.'

'Good luck, I had sauté potatoes with mine,' said Sammy.

Polly received the news with a natural amount of relief and pleasure, relief that a dangerous hooligan had been taken off the streets, and pleasure that it would almost certainly be for a long time.

'Well done, old sport,' she said.

'Fluke,' said Boots.

'Fluke my eye,' said Polly.

'I'd have been out of the picture if George Palmer hadn't invited me over,' said Boots.

'Wise old George, then,' said Polly, 'he must have acted on sound instinct. Boots dear man, you've made my day by phoning to tell me the louse is now under lock and key.'

'Always a pleasure, Polly, to deliver good news to you.'

'Did I ever tell you that one day the dream of my life came true?'

'Which day was that?'

'The day you married me. So long, old soldier, see you.'

Speaking of dreams, Boots dreamt that night of peace and quiet, and Sammy dreamt of the converted store turning into the Self-ridges of Walworth and ruining the vast Elephant and Castle shopping complex by draining it of customers. In his dream, the profit and loss account looked like a work of art in a gold frame.

Marjorie Alsop dreamt of a very pleasant Brixton GP, a bachelor, to whom she had been introduced by Lulu and who, as a Labour Party supporter, had invited her to compare notes with him.

In Blackpool, Dodgy Dan was sleeping

rough because no landlady of any boarding house would let him get one foot inside her door on account of a certainty that he had fleas, all of which would be looking for new pastures. So Dodgy Dan, hurt to the quick, naturally dreamt of the delights of dear old Bermondsey.

James dreamt he was playing rugby for England, with Cathy cheering him on. She was dressed all in white fur and looking like an Eskimo princess. Her Aunt Marie lay awake thinking of the Sunday tea at which she would meet James's parents and re-enter social life as a woman no longer haunted by what might be lying in wait for her.

Gemma dreamt of Perseus riding Pegasus to the rescue of Andromeda, who was being forced to play tennis with a dragon using balls of fire. Perseus looked like Charlie, Andromeda looked like herself, and the dragon looked like nothing on earth.

Peregrine dreamt of saucy street kids following him about all over Camberwell and yelling, 'Who's a Charlie, then?'

Felicity dreamt of visiting Harrods and buying new baby clothes. Well, she had an appointment with her gynaecologist in the offing.

Chinese Lady dreamt that Lizzy had run off with a gentleman burglar, which was more of a nightmare than a dream. It woke her up, and what a blessed relief that was, because she knew immediately that it wasn't true.

Chief Inspector Walters dreamt of being promoted to giddy heights on account of bringing in Curly Harris, real name now known to be Frank Camfrey, son of entirely respectable Lewisham parents.

Polly dreamt not at all. She slept the sleep of a woman content with life, even though the sighs of old age could be faintly heard in the distance.

The publishers hope that this book has given you enjoyable reading. Large Print Books are especially designed to be as easy to see and hold as possible. If you wish a complete list of our books please ask at your local library or write directly to:

Magna Large Print Books
Magna House, Long Preston,
Skipton, North Yorkshire.
BD23 4ND

This Large Print Book, for people
who cannot read normal print,
is published under the auspices of

THE ULVERSCROFT FOUNDATION

... we hope you have enjoyed this book.
Please think for a moment about those
who have worse eyesight than you ...
and are unable to even read or enjoy
Large Print without great difficulty.

You can help them by sending a
donation, large or small, to:

**The Ulverscroft Foundation,
1, The Green, Bradgate Road,
Anstey, Leicestershire, LE7 7FU,
England.**
or request a copy of our brochure for
more details.

The Foundation will use all donations
to assist those people who are visually
impaired and need special attention
with medical research, diagnosis
and treatment.

Thank you very much for your help.